AD BRITANNIA II

First Century Roman Britannia

With episodes in *Mauretania, Germania, Hispania, Gallia,* and *Italia*
Book Two—AD 52 to 63

Image: "Western Roman Empire" courtesy of Wikipedia File "Roman Empire"

This Historical Novel by

Colonel Donald A. Walbrecht, Ph.D.

Order this book online at www.trafford.com
or email orders@trafford.com

Most Trafford titles are also available at major online book retailers.

Print information available on the last page.

ISBN: 978-1-4907-8383-3 (sc)
ISBN: 978-1-4907-8387-1 (e)

Trafford rev. 09/12/2017

 www.trafford.com

North America & international
toll-free: 1 888 232 4444 (USA & Canada)
fax: 812 355 4082

DEDICATION

Dedicated to the Memories of My Maternal Grandparents
ANTONE AND MARYANN BRAGA
19th Century Idaho Pioneers

CONTENTS

AUTHOR'S NOTE

In AD 60 and 61, a Celtic queen called *Boudica* led a rebellion of her ancient Britannic tribe, resulting in three cities being destroyed, thousands of her enemies slaughtered, and a hundred-thousand of her own followers killed in a mighty battle against the occupying Roman forces. The earliest record of this woman appears in the writings of two ancient historians, whose accounts vary, leaving modern readers with a mythic image of that woman. Primary-source records of her anti-Roman revenge are limited to *Tacitus* and *Dio Cassius* works.

Tacitus was about five years old when the revolt took place, and wrote about it about 37 years later. His works, *The Agricola* and *The Annals of Imperial Rome* are considered the most reliable sources about Boudica and her tribe's revolt. His first work is a biography of his father-in-law, *Agricola*, who served on the staff of Britannia's military governor during the revolt. It places Tacitus close to the revolt period (written in AD 97-98). Although it's considered a good description of Britannia, it mentions none of the major Roman towns. Fortunately, he was concise with details. *Dio Cassius'* added some details, having spent ten years researching the work of other historians for his history. Although born more than a hundred years after the revolt, Dio's account is *conditionally accepted* because "other sources are thought to have existed from which he could have borrowed."

Although the Celts wrote nothing known about Boudica, archeological digs have yielded dateable debris from three destroyed cities along her rampaging pathway across southeast Britannia. Most secondary-source writings seem to be layered upon the foundations set by Tacitus and Dio. Dozens of academic interpretations have followed in attempts to authenticate Boudica. Despite the lack new historical support, most historians agree that a revolt did take place in the mid-first century in which three cities were destroyed. Still, its heroic leader remains clouded in mystery with interpretive portrayals in books and movies based on myth, legend, and fiction. Hence, she remains an enigma despite my efforts to learn more about her. Perhaps a best condensed view of her and her revenge can be found in Nic Field's and Peter Dennis' *Boudicca's Rebellion AD 60-61, The Britons Rise Up Against Rome*. Osprey Publishing, Ltd. 2011.

PREFACE

Britannia

Britannia was the Roman name of the distant region inhabited by Celtic Britons. That Latinized variation derives from the Greek name *"Prettaniai"* of the far "white-cliffs island, *Albion*," where Bronze-Age *Prettani* tribesmen lived. The first writer to record that name was the Greek explorer *Pytheas*, who (in the 4th century BC) called those northwestern islands *Prettanike*. Three centuries later, *Diodorus Siculus* called all of them *Pretannia*, which Roman mariners called *Insulae Britannicae* that included *Albion* (England), *Hibernia* (Erie), and *Thule* (Orkney). Later, *Albion* became Roman Britannia, which yielded similar versions of that Latin name to most modern languages. (See appendices for descriptions of Britannia, Germania, Mauretania, and Hispania).

Roman vessels and maritime commerce

Early Phoenician exploration led to large-scale oceanic commerce during the 3rd-century BC. After Rome won the 2nd Punic War in 201 BC, it began building big fleets of fast warships propelled by banks of oarsmen. In the next century (as Rome grew toward a million people) Roman merchants began moving products over long distances on slower vessels to ensure regular deliveries of food to the world's biggest city. Merchant-captains employed a widening variety of transport ships for many uses as hundreds of products were exchanged across the entire length of the Mediterranean Sea. Various food-carrying vessels had capacities ranging from 70-to-150 tons and 1,200-to-3,000 *amphorae*. Some higher-capacity ships held up to 400-tons, but one called the *Syracusia* could carry the greatest tonnages, but couldn't enter most ports. Sea transports moved heavy products across long distances (without prohibitive costs) with advantages over slow-and-dangerous land carriers. With a favorable wind, a transport ship could travel 90 miles in a day. Six-day trips were common from Egypt to Rome, and seven days across the western Mediterranean from *Cadiz, Spain* to Rome's *Port of Ostia*. Some voyages could be much longer, depending on weather and sea currents.

Rome at the center of Mediterranean trade

Grain was the foundation of Rome's food supply. Under Emperor Augustus, Egypt sent 140,000 tons of grain a year. Fifty years later (during Emperor Nero's reign) 420,000 tons of grain had to reach Rome each year. The June arrival of Alexandria's grain fleet was an event of great importance. Merchant ships (escorted by warships) would release the overgrown city's populace from hunger. In addition, wine, olive oil, and sauces were needed in most Roman kitchens. Iron, copper and lead ingots were transported from Spain and Britain. Rare animals and marble came from Africa and Asia Minor, granite from Egypt, and spices and silk from the Far East. Perishable products came in *amphora* jars made of baked clay. Oil and wine jars were discarded in enormous numbers in Rome (a 35-meter-high hill on the right bank of the Tiber River held millions of amphorae fragments). Nearby Gallia also supplied Rome with increasing volumes of wine starting in the 1st century. Africa furnished oil, fish, and wine. Because of Rome's increasing demands, Mediterranean merchants delivered grain and wine from Crete, Rhodes, Chios, and Asia Minor. As Rome became evermore dependent on imports, trade was stimulated across the empire.

Ports of Ostia and Pozzuoli

Increasing tonnages of grain reached Rome every year by a fleet of 1,200 vessels carrying from 150 to 350 tons each. Since transport was suspended during four winter months, only five big grain ships arrived each "navigable day." *Amphorae* ships arrived each day from *Baetica* (Spain) carrying up to 3,000 200-lb clay jars. Seven more arrived every week from other European and African ports carrying wine and fish products. The *naves lapidariae* transported marble and stone blocks; others carried wild animals for circuses; hundreds of small craft served local commerce. Since all kinds of merchandise were needed in

Rome, a special port was needed at coastal *Ostia* to receive big ships. Because merchant ships exceeding a 3000-*amphora* capacity could not travel up the Tiber, their captains had to anchor at sea where bulk cargoes were moved to vessels that shuttled goods to the new port. These operations were slow and dangerous because the coastline was low and sandy. At the end of the Republic, when Rome began its sudden growth, food supplies often fell dangerously low, forcing dangerous winter trips to replenish reserves. To alleviate winter famines, Emperor Claudius had the port at *Ostia* constructed in AD 42.

Pozzuoli (at Naples) served as the emergency port for large grain fleets from Sardinia, Sicily, and Alexandria with 90 smaller vessels journeying back and forth from *Pozzuoli* to *Ostia*. In AD 39 Emperor Caligula's "bridge of boats" between *Baia* and *Pozzuoli* used 400 requisitioned vessels that were often immobilized by weather. When the fleet could not restock Rome, terrible famines occurred during three winters. The *Pozzuoli-Ostia* trip took two days, but loading and unloading added three days to deliveries up the Tiber.

Equites

Equites constituted the lower half of Rome's aristocratic classes, ranking below patricians as members of the equestrian order. During Rome's Kingdom and Republic, its cavalry came from wealthy patricians who provided 300 horses for a legion's six cavalry centuries. Around 400 BC, 12 additional cavalry centuries were added. A hundred years later, Rome doubled its annual levy to four legions (1,200 horses). The cavalry then began recruiting 1st class commoners outside of the basic 18 centuries. In the Second Punic War, all 1st class commoners were required to serve as cavalrymen, but their numbers declined after 200 BC as only equites could serve as senior officers. As more legions were added, fewer equites were available for cavalry service. After 88 BC, they no longer served in the cavalry, but remained obligated to leadership service through the first half of the 500-year Imperial period.

Equites membership was defined by property ownership with rank passed from father to son; however, high Roman officials (censors) could remove members who couldn't sustain property-value requirements. In the 1st century BC, Roman Senators and their offspring became an unofficial elite, but laws limited their ability to engage in commerce, allowing lower equites to dominate mining, shipping and manufacturing. Under Augustus, the senatorial elite gained *ordo senatorius* status with even higher wealth thresholds, gaining superior rank and privileges. During the early Empire, equites filled the top administrative positions and senior military posts with a clear division between jobs reserved for senators and sub-senatorial equites. The career structure was broadly similar with both filling junior administrative posts followed by a decade of military service as a senior officer or administrator in the provinces. Senators and equites formed a split-level elite of 10,000 members who monopolized political, military, and economic power positions in the expanding empire that eventually grew to 50 million inhabitants.

Review-Preview

Ad Britannia Part I ended in AD 52 as 29-year-old *Ivano Valburga* (a mid-ranking cavalry officer) prepared to leave Rome on an oceanic voyage to *Germania* with his 26-year-old wife *Aurelia* and their young sons (*Marco* and *Vespan*). Also traveling to Germania was 30-year-old *Marcus Cornelius Lentulus (Aquilus)* with his 18-year old bride *Sabina Valentia*. Near the end of their trip, Ivano planned to divert to *Britannia* to visit his brother *Milo* before continuing to *Colonia Claudia Ara Agrippinensium* (Cologne) where he'd serve as *Praefectus Cohortis* of *Colonia's* 120-man cavalry squadron. *Marcus* would also serve as *Tribunus Cohortis* (commanding a 600-man legionary detachment) pending orders to command *Legio II's* 5,000-man force at *Mogontiacum* (Mainz) that his father had commanded 16 years earlier.

The Cast

Main Characters:

    Ivo (Ivano) Valburga––Chatti-Roman Cavalry Officer

    Aurelia––Ivo's Wife (Marcus' Sister) Mother of Marco and Vespan

    Marcus Gnaeus Cornelius Lentulus (Aquilus)––Legionary Officer

    Sabina Valentia––Marcus' Wife (Daughter of Consul *Maximus Carpentius*)
        Mother of twin sets and an adopted daughter)

    Maximus Honorious Carpentius––Consul-Senator and *Villa Sciarra* Owner

    Senator Aquilus––Patron of Marcus and Ivo; *Villa Antigua* Owner

    Milo Valburga––Chatti Roman Engineer (Ivo's Brother)

    Spur––Centurion Spurius Matius Cogitatus (Senior Legionary Engineer)

    Sabatini––Hosidius Mallius Sabatinus (Malevolent *Tribune Laticlavus*)

Antón—Antón Silviera—Lusitanian Cavalry Tactician (Ivo's Equerry)

Vibi—Vibius Volci Tuccianus (Etrurian Storyteller and Scribe)

Geron—King Geronimus Valburga of the Chattti Tribe (Ivo's Uncle)

Ansgar—Chatti War Chief (Ivo's hostile cousin)

Secondary Characters:

Acacia— Milo's Wife (Mother of Odalric, Clodvech, and Karloman)

Fulko—Geron's murdered son (Ivo's cousin)

Swanhilde—Expiring Chatti Queen (Ivo's Great Aunt)

Aldo, Lanzo, Vulfgang, and *Hartwig* (Ivo's other militant cousins)

Luki—Lucius Aemilius Lepidus (Sabatini's business associate)

Captain Val—Lucius Valerianus Hispanicus (Captain–Former Admiral)

Capitáno Gil—Eanes Pacheco Gilhardo (Captain of Golden Eye)

Important Romans:

Claudius—Tiberius Claudius Caesar Augustus Germanicus (4th Emperor)

Nero—Lucius Domintius Ahenobarus (5th Emperor)

Octavia (Daughter of Claudius—Wife of Nero);

Claudia Acte (Nero's Courtesan)

Agrippina Minor—Empress of Rome (Claudius' Wife—Mother of Nero)

Vespasianus—Former legate at Mogontiacum (Future Emperor)

Suetonius—Governor Suetonius Paulinus of Britannia

Veranius—Quintus Veranius (Short-term Governor of Britannia)

Catus—Procurator *Catus Decianus* in Londinium

Turp—Governor *Petronius Turpilianus* of Britannia

Scap—Governor *Ostorius Scapula* of Britannia

Aulus—Governor *Aulus Didus Gallus* of Britannia

Gordo—Governor of *Tarraconensis* (Hispania)

Pompeius—Governor *Pompeus Paulinus* of Germania Inferior

Bibaculus—Antonius Camillus Bibaculus (Nero's Inspector General)

Senior Officers:

Poenius—Praefectus Castrorum Poenius Potumius (Legio II Acting Commander)

Caesius—Legatus Quintus Caelius Rufus (Commander of Legio IX at Lindum)

Cerialus—Legatus Petillius Cerialus (Next Commander Legio IX at Lindum)

Franco—Legatus Calidius Galerius Franco (Commander at Legio, Hispania)

Carantus—Legatus Amulius Virous Carantus (Commander at *Noviomagus*)

Crito—Numerus Gratus Crito

Marvelo—Legatus Decius Stentius Marvelos (Commander in North Hispania)

Rufus—Procurator-Commandant *Rufus Calpurnicus* of *Mauretania*

Lupo––*Tribunus Decius Fenicus Lupis* (Political spy at *Colonia*)

Macro––*Tribunus Macrianus* sent to replace Ivo at *Venta Icenorum*

Flavi––*Flavius Quintilius* (Roman nobleman friend who settled in Gallia)

Barbartus––*Primus Pilus Amulius Fenius Barbartus* with Ivo in Britannia

Ponditius––*Primus Pilus Ponditius Callus* at *Lindum*

Kings and Queens:

Esurpatus––*King Prasatagus* of the *Iceni* Tribe (also known as *Esparato*)

Boudica––*Queen* of the *Iceni* Tribe

Cartimandua––*Queen of the Briganti* Tribe

Vellocatus––Prince Consort of the *Briganti* Tribe

Venitius––Former co-ruler of the *Briganti* Tribe

Vibilius––King of the *Marcomanni* Tribe

Mauretanians:

Zodi Mazak––Atlas Mountain Guide

Kel Tamacheq––Nomad Chieftan

Amghar––The Old Slow One

Azi––*Zodi's* devious brother

Rhoati––Fezzian Woman

Others:

Stane and Mundus Flooren––Dutch Dog Handlers

Solon Dorotheos––Greek Philosopher/Teacher

Publitor/Marcipor––Esquiline Villa Housekeeper

Trupo––Rescued Galician child

Many legionaries, Auxiliaries and Tribal Members

CHAPTER 1

DEPARTING ROME

On June 26th AD 52, Marcus and I waited (with families and retinues) at Rome's port of *Ostia* for the arrival of a senior Roman official with whom we'd be traveling to *Britannia* on a specially outfitted *trireme* with luxurious cabins for *patrician-class* travelers. Two supporting *biremes* were loaded with our personal aides, accompanying legionaries, and our horses. As mid-ranking officers on this trip, Marcus and I were each allowed three personal aides to accompany us to *Germania*. Mine were *Antón Silviera* (my Lusitanian cavalry tactician), *Vibius Volci Tuccianus* (my Etrurian scribe and historian), and *Munius Batavicus* (an imperial-palace guard, who would be my second-in-command). In addition, *Aurelia* brought two faithful *matronae* to care for our young sons, *Marco*, and *Vespan* (ages three and one). My brother-in-law, Marcus, had three junior officers selected by Emperor Claudius to be sub-commanders and one *matrona* to serve his bride, Sabina. Both Marcus and I had brought our Lusitani horses to serve as status symbols of our new commands.

At my last palace visit, I'd learned *Emperor Claudius* was troubled with his latest wife, *Agrippina Minor*, who'd been maneuvering to ensure *Lucius Domitius Ahenobarbus* (her son Nero) could become Claudius' successor. She was increasingly hostile toward many senators, including *Senator Publius Horatius Aquilus* (Marcus' and Aurelia's adoptive father and my adoptive uncle). Meanwhile, *Hosidius Mallius Sabatinus* (the *Tribune Laticlavus* called *Sabatini* who'd murdered my cousin *Fulko*) had fled and was said to be hiding among the fierce *Picti* tribesmen in far *Caledonia*, where he was reportedly organizing a tribal revolt against Rome's presence in the

Midlands and organizing a full-scale revolt among Roman client tribes in Britannia's South.

An Unexpected Change

While we awaited the senior official, an arrogant tribune told us, "General *Aulus Didius Gallus* (who'd replaced the late *Ostorius Scapula* as Governor of Roman Britannia) is hurrying to begin his important military command." Because of the governor's seniority, the tribune ordered, "You shall relinquish your cabins and remove your families from this ship!" The aide also claimed our horses ordering, "Find another ship for your travel!"

Since the governor and his retinue departed *Ostia* before we located another ship, we weren't able to leave until well after the special trireme and its two supporting biremes were gone. Because no fast ships were available, *Marcus* and *Lupercus* raced around the dock-front, seeking opportunist captains (with light *liburnia* or *hemiolia*-class vessels adopted for fast movements). On Marcus' return, he told me he'd found a former naval *nauarchus* (previous holder of high naval rank) who'd double his earnings by delivering us to the port of *Gades* in *Hispania* in a week (or all the way to *Britannia* if no naval transports would be found).

Because Marcus had offered a newly minted silver *denarius* to each of the ship's money-hungry crewmembers, and because the full moon would illuminate our night passage across the *Mare Nostrum*, our prospective *trierarchus* promised Marcus, "I'll pass that showy *trireme* whose junior captain'll be resting his fat ass and his overpaid *remigi* (rowers)." I then told Aurelia, "We're fortunate to have six *milites classiari* (former marines) with us who've volunteered to earn extra *denari* that Marcus paid the captain to hire his old ship and its Graecian rowers."

Within an hour, an unpainted shallow-draft *hemiolia-style* ship glided smoothly up to our empty dock where our marines and a score of the crewmen loaded our baggage and raised two leather tents on the deck (one for the captain, Marcus and me; the other for our aides). To our surprise, the captain relinquished his small cabin to Aurelia and Sabina, and the two *matronae* with Marco and Vespan.

At Sea

An hour past noon on the Ides of May, Captain Lucius Valerianus Hispanicus asked Marcus, "Be ye ready ta depart, me honored Tribunus Cohortis?" To which Marcus replied, "Onward to Hispania, our gallant Praefectus Classis del Mare Nostrum (Admiral of the Mediterranean Sea). Take us safely beyond the Herculean Pillars and far on the vast Oceanus Atlanticus to our distant Britannic and Germanic destinations."

Within an hour (propelled by 60 hardy oarsmen), we'd lost sight of Etruria's and Latium's coastlines. While observing the smooth surface of the quiet *Mare Tyrrhenum* and its lack of seabirds, I noticed the boat was pointed more sunward than I'd have expected on this part the *Mare Internum*. When I questioned the captain why the sun's position was almost directly over the boat's prow, he smiled saying,

> Good observation, Sir Ivano! You've noted my *nautum* (helmsman) is carrying a strong drift correction to prevent the coastal current from carrying us off course. My first target is *Bucchi di Bunifaziu*, a narrow strait between Corsica and Sardina, notorious for troubling shoals. After we pass, we'll rest and feast at Sardina's port of *Turris Lybissonis* (Porto Tores).

He then looked at me more closely, asking, "Did you once serve in the Imperial Palace? Perhaps I saw you there two years ago when I visited my uncle who'd associated with Julio-Claudian family members." When I told him of my service in the Germani Custodes (Palace Guards), he continued,

> I remember you now, Sir. We met in the Emperor's library from where you escorted me to the golden atrium where I met Uncle Decimus Valerius Asiaticus, whom you may remember for roles in palace intrigues. Picture me then, as Admiral Lucius Valerianus Hispanicus—a uniformed staff officer of Rome's naval forces.

He then told of his naval service and his uncle's ties to the Valerius family, telling this tale:

Uncle *Decimus Valerius Asiaticus* came from *Gallia Narbonensis* where my great-grandfather gained Roman citizenship from Governor *Gaius Valerius Flaccus* (of Transalpine Gallia) from whom he inherited the name Valerius. Forty years ago he visited *Antonia Minor* (mother of future Emperor Claudius), and married *Lollia Saturnina* (sister of Caligula's 3rd wife). The beautiful Saturnina was Emperor Tiberius' and Claudius Drusus' cousin. Uncle Val's career zoomed, serving as suffect consul and became Caligula's friend until the Emperor divorced *Lollia Paulina* and took *Saturnina* as a mistress. When Caligula rejected her, Uncle Val instigated an assassination plot. When the Praetorians killed Caligula, Val joined Claudius in his Britannia campaign. As tax collector, Val gained great wealth and acquired the Grand Pleasure Gardens—Rome's most magnificent property. In AD 47, *Senator Publius Suillius Rufus filed* adultery charges (involving Empress Valeria Messalina) against Uncle Val in a plot to seize the Gardens. Although no threat to Claudius, the Emperor condemned Val, forcing suicide. Claudius deplored Uncle Val and confiscated all his properties except one in Gallia that had been promised to me. Instead, a freed slave got those properties in *Colonia Claudia Augusta Lugdunum* (Lyon) leaving me landless.

As we plodded onward, Captain Val suggested, "You might wish to sleep; there's little else to do or see out here on the *Mare Tyrrhenum*." Fortunately, we'd begun our long sea voyage after the storm season with the ocean shinning like a polished metal mirror. Soon the rhythmic dip of oars induced dreamless sleep into us for hours. When I awoke, the moon was past zenith and all but Marcus and Antón were asleep. The two had been talking with the ship's navigator schooled by Greek astronomers who could accurately estimate night hours by the rotation of *Ursa Major*. He pointed to the dipper-shaped cluster of stars that swept around a dim square of tiny stars called *Ursa Minorus* that navigators use to steer their craft accurately on cloudless nights.

As the dawn began to hide all but the *Morning Star* (revered as the goddess *Venus*), Captain *Val* ordered, "Rest on your oars my *Remigi*." He told us, "My lads are lowborn Greeks who'll earn Roman citizenship and gain land grants in Rome's newer provinces after serving 26 years."

By noon we reached the *Bucchi di Bunifaziu* straits between *Sardina* and *Corsica* where our passage was smooth. During that transit, we saw scattered debris of ships whose captains had risked the narrow crossing in stormy conditions. We echoed the crews' cheers as we slid into a vast bay, on which our *nautum* aimed straightway toward a distant peninsula where the townspeople of *Turris Lybissonis* awaited passing ships to feed hundreds of hungry crewmen. At this remote site, our widely-traveled captain led us to a seaside-feeding tent, saying,

> *Phoenician* settlers came here 3,000 years ago. Two millennia later, the Romans captured this place during the 2nd Punic War where our legionaries were fed on their way to end Carthaginian attempts to conquer Rome. Because of its support role, *Turris* became the 2nd largest town on Sardinia. Julius Caesar came here 100 years ago during his Gallic Wars, establishing a Roman colony. Because of plentiful fish and hungry travelers, these cooks are the best! My *Remigi* surely agree; look at 'em eat!

After a first-rate meal of *bouillabaisse* and wine, the crew swam and took a well-earned nap. We then headed toward the *Baleares Islands* where our hardy captain told me, "We'll overnight at *Maó-Mahón* on *Insula Minor.*" On our way there, we talked about piracy, noting we were unsuitably armed to deter brigands. First to comment was Vibi who'd remembered his grandfather's tales about pirates. He began,

> Prior to Rome's occupation, *Iberian* and *Graecian* tribes settled the *Baleares. Majorca* had been a *Sardinian* and *Gallian* pirate base. *Consul Quintus Caecilius Metellus* conquered these islands 175 tears ago, earning the cognomen *Balearicus* for bringing them under Roman control. Earlier, pirates came here to escape Roman campaigns in Transalpine Gallia and Sardinia. Since the *Baleares* were the last western hiding place for pirates, Roman marines came here to pacify Gallia and Sardinia, still under pirate control.

Because Captain Val had been an admiral before being fired by Emperor Caligula, he knew a lot about the thousand-year history of *Mare Interum* piracy, telling us other stories about ancient pirates:

> The most famous of old-time pirates were the *Illyriani* and *Tyrrheniani* sea-raiders who operated fast fleets from *Cilicia* (south Turkey). They'd

5

scourged the *Mare Adriaticus* and swept westward, supporting the vast Persian and Roman slave trade. For centuries, the Egyptians clashed with these *Anatolian Sea Peoples*, calling them, *"The worst of our Nine-Bow enemies."* Others included *Habiru Hebrews* and *Tjekers* from Crete, and 12 ancient *Lukkai* and *Sherdeni* pirate companies. After the *Great Alexander* died 300 years ago, pirate raids exploded from *Cilicia* and *Southern Anatolia*, causing great devastation. Their *Lembis* surged from coastal inlets attacking and vanishing. These fast oar-ships carried 50 warriors. Philip employed these swift boats in his *1ˢᵗ Macedonian War* (215-204 BC). Over 200 years ago, the Romans tried to end piracy by taking *Illyria* as a province. Despite great efforts, the threat continued along the *Anatolian* coast. The Romans had never sent a force against pirates because they'd provided Rome with thousands of slaves for laborers, making profit on both ends.

Marcus noted, "Our mentor, *Senator Aquilus,* still receives captives each year to replace his dead slaves." Captain Val added a humorous tale about young Julius Caesar who'd been captured by *Cilciani* pirates:

They'd captured 25-year-old *Julius* 127 years ago and held him for 38 days on *Pharmacusa Island* between Crete and Anatolia. His captors demanded a 20-talent gold ransom, but Caesar bragged, "I'm worth more." After a 50-talent payment, the arrogant young officer sailed back to *Miletus* where he found his captors and crucified most of them.

Captain Val continued about Rome's efforts to end piracy across the *Mare Interum*, announcing,

When pirates set *Ostia* afire and kidnapped two prominent senators, the Senate outlawed piracy and blocked the profitable slave trade. Rome's *Lex Gabinia* laws named pirates *"communes hostes gentium"* (enemies) granting Pompey unprecedented treasury access to build a huge naval fleet for raiding pirate strongholds across the entire *Mare* and into cities on *Cilicia, Crete, Illyria,* and *Delos*. After killing thousands, Pompey implemented his "Edict of Clemency," pardoning those who'd move to honest courses of life. This changed piracy to privateering, causing Emperor Augustus to exclaim, "People can prosper by peaceful trading; those who remain barbaric are undeserving of my benefits."

As Captain Val promised, we glided into *Maó-Mahón* harbor on *Minorca* where we enjoyed colonial hospitality with Sabina commenting, "This beautiful island is a fine place to escape overcrowded Rome." Val replied,

> You'll like *Majorca* even more. We shall stop there on our way to *Ceuta* and *Tingis* where Marcus served. We'll then race on to *Gades* (Cadiz), the most ancient city on western *Hispania* from where we'll strike north past *Lusitania, Tarraconensis* and *Gallic Lugdunensis* before reaching Britannia.

As we docked on *Majorca,* our well-informed captain told us,

> *Quintus Caecilius Metellus* led forces to capture this wondrous island 175 years ago. His legionaries landed right here on these beautiful beaches and guarded them against pirates who attacked *Pollentia.* Now *Olea, vino* and *sal* (Olives, wine and salt) support the economy. Marcus knows the value of Balearic soldiers for their slingshot accuracy. You may know *Pollentia* is favored in Rome because of its special fabrics for the finest togas.

CHAPTER 2

TINGIS

On the 4ᵗʰ day of our trip, we stopped at *Carthago Nova* on the southeast tip of *Hispania* for another big seafood meal and where Vibi and Val told us of this city's history. As before, Vibi began,

> This city lies on top of an ancient *Iberian* settlement called *Mastia*. *Hasdrubal Barca* captured it 277 years ago and named it *Qart-Hadasat* (the base of *Hannibal Barca's* trans-alpine operations against Rome). The new Punic city had the best harbor in the western *Mare Internum* with rich silver and lead mines nearby, and abundant salt pans for curing fish. It also had *esparto-grass* farms that furnished rope. After a siege, *General Scipio* captured it 261 years ago, making it a Roman city named *Urbs Iulia Nova Carthago*.

Since Captain Val had passed through here often, he led us on a tour, pointing out the main attractions. Moving to a vantage point, he noted,

> *Carthago Nova* is bounded by the *Almarjal Lagoon* with tall hills around its bay guarded by *Escombreras Island* (named after huge mackerel schools along the warm coast). The *Aesculapius Temple* crowns its highest hill and the *Arx Hasdrubalis* stands on *Kronos Mountain* where *Hasdrubal Barca* surrendered to *Scipio*. Roman walls connect the hills that surround 30,000 people whose earnings come from its busy harbor, a thriving market, exports of esparto grass and salt-fish. Its mines produce tons

of silver, enriching the empire, financing powerful legions, and paying for our fastest warships.

After a big mackerel feast and drinking too much of Cartago Nova's sweet wines, we embarked on a coastal sweep toward the *Pillars of Hercules* where Marcus wanted to visit *Septem* (Ceuta), an important Mauretanian trade and military waypoint for ancient cultures, beginning with Phoenicians who'd called it *Abyla*. He said, "The Greeks called it 'One *Pillar*'––the tallest of seven hills called *Septem Fratres* (Seven Brothers), now the name of Rome's *Castellum ad Septem Fratres* fort." Approaching the port, Captain Val told us,

> When I arrived 20 years ago, I learned a small Berber settlement had existed here when Phoenician ships arrived over 2,000 years ago. During the Punic Wars, Hannibal used this port, but we made it more important during Augustus' rule, when colonists took over trade opportunities. The economy surged, fueled by fish-salting factories here. I've transported thousands of *amphorae* to faraway customers. *Septem* is growing even richer now as Hispanic provincials arrive to enjoy full Roman citizenship rights.

Marcus commented, "When I came here three years ago, I spent six months learning local languages and controlling migrations to and from Hispania." Captain Val then told us why ships needed to stop here before transiting the narrow *Pillars of Hercules* seaway,

> *Mauretania* and *Hispania* are separated by eight miles at the strait's narrowest point. This narrow waterway links the *Mare Internus* with the *Oceanus Atlanticus* fed by counter-flowing currents that create wave patterns amplified by tidal interactions. As ocean water flows inward, its saltier waters sink as the less-saline *Mare Internus* waters rise. Consequently, we often encounter turbulence where the crossing tides meet. When large oceanic flows enter the strait, and high *Atlanticus* tides relax; internal waves give us surprisingly rough rides.

As we entered *Septem's* harbor, Marcus told of his Mauretanian years and moves from city to city, beginning at this port.

Septem sits on a narrow isthmus that connects *Mount Hecho* to the mainland. That 700-foot-high hill is the *Southern Hurculean Pillar.* Its top held a fort from where Carthaginians and Graecians protected their ivory, gold, and slave trade. While here, I dealt with piracy along Mauretania's coast down the *Mare Atlanticus* as far south as *Lixus.* Some pirates remain, but most of their *Lembi* ships have been confiscated or destroyed.

Onward to Tingis

At Septem's headquarters, we enjoyed a good rest and the best mackerel and *garum* dinner we'd eaten so far. Mid-morning, we rejoined Captain Val for an expected rough passage through the strait. He told me,

> We'll arrive at Tingis late today, but I'll warn you of excessive pitching and rolling as we pass through the roughest waves. We'll be in no danger, but this old ship will groan and bend, and will take on water. Therefore, I'll beach it short of our destination to drain the hull, inspect for leaks, and add sealant. I may need an extra day at Tingis to strengthen it before we head north into the stormier *Mare Atlanticus.*

Since Aurelia had traveled through here after leaving Germania 12 years ago, she minimized the dangers announcing, "I'll be on deck with Marco through the worst part. Because Sabina's an expert horse rider, she'll join me, but one *matrona* must remain below with Vespan."

Midway we struck turbulence that raised whoops from the *regemi,* but soon the waves grew surprising high, silencing the boldest seamen. As Captain Val had warned, his ship groaned and rolled, but the *Nautus* kept the bow aimed straight into the waves, which gave us the appearance of plunging down into the sea then reversing to exaggerated lofts. After dozens of gallops through shocking waves, they suddenly calmed, as soaked crewmen and passengers shouted praises to Neptune. Captain Val then ordered, "Turn to the strand where we've beached before."

On touching the gravely shore, he ordered, "every man boost the ship to drain tons of water from the hull." That effort exposed new leaks that might have ended our trip before we'd reached *Hispania.*

While ashore on this northern tip of *Mauretania*, we were greeted by light-skinned *Fezmen* who'd often welcomed nautical arrivals to sell dates, raisins, flat breads, and fresh water to captains for their hard-pressed crewmen. Because the ship needed repairs, we spent the night ashore where two competing Fez clans sold us other goods, and where Marco and Vespan danced around the campfire with *Fezitos,* as Antón called them. While camped, Marcus told us of *Tinginita*––the western province of Mauretania:

> *Phoenici* sailors visited this coastal peninsula 2,000 years ago. Much later, Hispanic merchants reached *Mogador Island,* their southernmost trading station. This place became ours 20 years ago when Caligula added trading links with *Sala* and *Volubilis.* Twelve years ago, Claudius split Mauretania where I served my *aedelship* in *Tingis* without venturing into the Atlas Mountains held by Barbaric tribes. Land travel was difficult, but we lengthened our roads to serve legionary forts and watchtowers being built by our soldiers. While here, I learned this land stretches to incredible distances over the Atlas Mountains and beyond the great sand ocean.

Responding to Marcus' telling of the great land to our south, I told of Claudius' mention of a *Herodotean* scroll claiming, "*Pharaoh Neco* sent an expedition around the continent." His sailors claimed, "We sailed 2½ years, returning through the Pillars of Hercules."

> Claudius told me he'd read that scroll three times, adding, "Herodotus told exaggerated tales, but details made the report seem truthful." The sailors testified, "We saw the sun stand on our right as we sailed west past the bottom of that great land. Those sailors knew they were heading west with the sun coming up behind them each morning and setting ahead each evening." Claudius argued, "Many details made me believe the voyage really took place. I'm convinced a distant passage exists far below to make the sun look so different at those southern places." *Pharaoh Neco* had said, "My sailors sailed far below the great sand ocean, passing the bottom of Egypt's farthest land." Two and a half years seems a proper duration for such a voyage. Perhaps the Greek philosophers are correct who said, "Our world is round!"

Even Captain Val remained silent as each person in our group struggled to comprehend the magnitude of what I'd just told them and of new marvels that might lie beyond our expanding Roman world.

The next morning, we watched the crew apply another layer of tar to the ship's leaks, allowing it to harden into afternoon when Val's *regemi* picked up the water-free *lembi* and carried it into strait's calm waters. That evening we approached *Tingis* where Marcus had spent most of his years in Mauretania. Before docking, Marcus told Aurelia and Sabina,

> My first visit will be a courtesy call to the *Procurator-Augusti* where I'll introduce Ivo. While we're at the *principia*, you can visit the market place to see some strong-faced tribesmen who're profiting from trade arrangements we made during Emperor Claudius' reign. Vibi, Antón, and some retirees shall accompany you with our *Molossus* dog to protect all of you. Later I'll show you around Tingis while Captain Val is adding ship repairs for our northward journey to *Gades* (Cadiz).

Marcus then led me to the headquarters where we were announced as the Germania-bound cavalry officers who'd been expected two days earlier on the "Golden-Eye" bireme that had passed through with the future Governor of Britannia. After introductions to *Commandant Rufus Calpurnicus*, four long-serving legionaries arrived to welcome Marcus who told of their road projects reaching toward southern coastal cities.

We'd just been served strong coffee and slices of date bread when a junior officer stepped in announcing, "Sir, there's a disturbance at the gate where some travelers are shouting for your visitors to come with great haste; it seems a child has disappeared."

Knowing my children were the only little ones with us, I rushed to where I found Aurelia sobbing inconsolably, unable to tell me of the disappearance of Marco. While embracing her and moving her into the gatehouse, Marcus and the commandant arrived to hear Vibi's and Sabina's reports of the kidnapping, saying, "Antón and our legionaries are scouring the market place with my *Mollosus* to sniff out likely paths." As Marcus and I rushed to find Antón, the commandant ordered an assemblage of all nearby troops, and called for a meeting with tribal leaders in and around the city. When I located Antón, he told me,

We lost Marco in a densely crowded area near the camel enclosure at the waterside end of the market. We'd been distracted by a display of gold nuggets from the great mountains south of here. Since your dog lost Marco's scent in the camel enclosure, we fear Marco's been rushed away before any of us were aware of his disappearance. It's possible he's hidden on a boat in the adjacent harbor, but the troops are searching the dispersing merchants who appear to be cooperating.

When we returned to the *Principia*, Aurelia asked desperately, "Have you found little Marco?" When I grimaced, "Not yet, My Dearest," tears flooded her eyes again as she moaned, "Who might've taken him, and why?" Sabrina whispered to Marcus,

Since you've spent two years out here, you must know about these wretched tribal practices. Who'd take a tiny white-skinned lad and where'd they take him? How much ransom will it take to buy him back? You know I can get money from father, if that'll help.

Marcus answered, "Sabina dearest, I have no answers; Ivo and I shall ask the commandant for legionary help to expand the search." At that meeting, one Berber chieftain bragged to the *Primus Pilus*. "Your officer will never find his boy! He's already moving toward the far mountains to grow up as a tribal warrior." Later that evening, Marcus and I made plans that might cost us our commands in Germania:

First, we agreed to pursue Marco's faint trail wherever it might lead.
Second, we agreed to send the family members back to *Tusculum*.
Third, I ordered Vibi to accompany them and return with money.
Fourth, we asked Antón to sail on to *Bracara* to acquire new horses.
Fifth, Marcus ordered his deputy onward to tell of our urgent mission.
Sixth, I ordered Munius Lupercus to tell Emperor Claudius we'd reach our commands in October, "unless reassigned."

Meanwhile, a staff officer reported,

Scenting dogs have begun following three separate trails. One led to the docks where it disappeared among fishing boats still being searched. Another headed south along the Roman road, but faded too quickly to be favored. A third has crossed the other trails and is heading east toward the *Rif Mountains*. Each trail is being followed, Sir!

Since I knew nothing of the nearby mountains, Marcus explained,

> The *Rifs* are part of the *Transmarean* extension of the *Baetic* Mountains in Hispania across the *Fretum Gaditanum* (Strait of Gibraltar). They're not part of the vast Atlas Ranges to the south that have been inhabited by Berbers since prehistoric times. Although the *Rifs* are nearby, we've never subdued the piratic *Riffians* who speak a *Tarifit* dialect there.

We then joined the widening search, but found it might take weeks to find Marco. We told Aurelia and Sabina, "Since we'll be gone a month, we're sending you home!" Both disagreed sharply––with headstrong Sabina shouting, "We'll not leave until we know you've found Marco! We'll stay with the commandant's wife or move on to *Gades* where father's friends will welcome us in their *Hispanic latifundi*".

With most demands seemingly settled (including Sabina's to remain in Mauretania), we made a dozen support arrangements with Commandant *Calpurnicus* who'd agreed to help us "in every possible way." First, he offered a century of legionary troops to fight any opposition, which we declined because of increased dangers to Marco. Instead, we accepted the support of six non-uniformed retirees and six desert-specialized cavalrymen who'd send signals back to the fort through dozens of prepositioned infantrymen. The commandant also offered his own sniffer dogs he claimed, "are best for long-range tracking," adding,

> My *Laconi* and *Vertragi* hounds are the best sniffers. The swiftest pair came from top lines that equestrian Romans use for *canis venaticus* (hunting) while your *Molossos* was herd-trained for *canis pastoralis* (guarding). Yours is a great breed, but lacks endurance for long pursuits.

To avoid argument, I commented obliquely,

> When I was a palace guard, I read that Cato wrote, "No farm is safe without well-trained guardians." Varro wrote, "Dogs wear nail-studded *Melia* because wolves rarely attack dogs wearing spiked collars.

I also keep black *Molossi* to terrify thieves." I therefore told him, "I'd
be honored to borrow your *Laconi* for speed, endurance, and scenting,
but I'll take my *Molossus* for his strength and courage."

He replied,

> Excellent choice Ivo! I'll send *Castor* and *Pollux*, and will add *Apollo*, my
> faithful *Vertragus*, who races beside me on full-gallop horseback hunts.
> I'll also provide you with strong mountain horses, legionary supplies,
> and a fat pouch of newly minted gold *Aureri* and silver *denari* borrowed
> from my treasury as incentive for Marco's ransom.

During the afternoon, the authoritative *Primus pilus* assembled 40
troops (including dog handlers) and provided hardy horses along with
equipment and supplies for our journey. Meanwhile, the commandant's
young wife, *Scaptia Hosidius Flavia,* hosted a tea to reassure our tearful
ladies, adding, "You'll have our fullest support throughout this crisis."
We kissed our wives goodbye, saluted the commandant, and rode
eastward along newly surveyed paths that split at *Tetouan* with one
track paralleling the coast on which we headed south toward *Quezzane*
where we crossed the western hills. As we rode deeper into the *Rif,* we
restrained the dogs for fear of losing them to the Berbers. Whenever
the *Laconi* seemed to be tracking well, we faced hostile tribesmen who
delayed our movement. Meanwhile, fast-moving Berbers gained added
advantages as tribesmen dispersed scent packets, creating promising
leads to distract our dogs. When I asked Marcus why these tribesmen
would kidnap a Roman child, he replied,

> For ransom, Ivo! Despite Emperor Claudius' efforts to stop raiding
> and pillaging, it continued, forcing us to keep a large garrison of
> auxiliaries with ties to these desert brigands. To make matters worse,
> the Rif Mountains had been left to the Moors who often capture rich
> Romans for ransom—a practice we continue to face here.

As we moved on, we came to a deep canyon containing a well-traveled
cross-trail that wound southward. Marcus told our dog handlers to follow
a false lead; meanwhile. we climbed onto a high overlook from where we
saw six gray horses moving far ahead into a broad valley that led toward

the distant *Sebu River* where a Moorish settlement was known. Marcus mirror-signaled the others, telling them to send a runner back to *Tingis* to report, *"We're moving south toward the Sebu."* When the others joined us, we hurried to close the gap with the fast-moving kidnappers. At the *Sebu*, we were dismayed to find more tribal helpers scattering scent trails to confuse our excited *Laconi*. Finally, under the watch of thousands, we moved slowly upriver where we eventually met three cavalry scouts, who reported,

> When your messenger reached Tingis, the commandant dispatched us to the mouth of the *Sebu*. We moved 10 leagues upstream to *Thamusida* where we offloaded our equipment and sped northeast across the *Wadis Bet* and *Rdem* to *Volubilis* and onward to *Tocolocidis* where we established a marching camp. From there, we three headed forward to intercept you on the upper *Sebu*. You're to build signal fires so they can find us before we reach the *Mid-Atlas Range*.

Senior among the advancing troops was the *Primus Pilus* who sent this note:

> We found a Moor in *Tingis* who'd grown up beyond the Middle Atlas Range who told me, "I can guide you to places no Roman has seen and onto high mountain meadows where our clans gather each summer to feed their flocks." He'll be most valuable in our search.

As instructed, we set hilltop fires that led the legionaries to our riverside camp where we met our mountain guide called *Zodi Mazak* who told me, *"You will travel far following son's captors."* He also told us,

> *We'll follow the Asif n Shu Wasif River into Middle Atlas Range where it's called Guigou or Asif n Gigu. Its tributaries flow from mountains to water the fertile Aquae Dacicas region. Have you been to Middle Atlas Mountains?*

Marcus replied, "I traveled to *Volubilis* two years ago and saw that impressive city far inland. Because of the region's fertile farmlands, the city grew rapidly under our rule with many people moving within its encircling wall." *Zodi* countered, *"None of you know the Middle Range!"* Hearing no response, he said, *"I shall take you there if you pay well——be prepared for hardships."*

CHAPTER 3

ATLAS MOUNTAINS

As we ascended a troublesome ridge, Zodi, told us, *"Every spring for thousand years, Barbaricae nomads trek from homes to cool pastures in Grand Atlas Mountains."* He then looked at me, saying, *"There's where they take son. I ask again, Have you thousand silver denari for ransom?"*

The next morning, we mounted fresh horses the troops had provided and headed toward an elevated village called *Azrou,* 50 leagues south of the last village we'd passed. This friendly *Barbar* town in the cedar-forested hills was called *"the rock"* that sat on a broad lava field. From there we rode toward the *Middle Atlas Mountains,* moving along the upper *Asif n Isaffen* "river of rivers" (also called "the Mother of Springtime") until we found a pass into a valley by the *Grand Atlas Mountains.* There we met stoic Barbars who sold us three grumpy camels for a difficult trek to remote pastures where Zodi told me in a surly tone, *"Your Marco is beyond reach of rich Romans."*

After struggling an hour on the beastly camels, we returned to our desert-adapted horses with my over-tired *Molossos* and the dejected *Laconi* trailing behind. To my surprise, Zodi commented, *"Those Laconi are best searching hounds with sharp nose and keen eye. I've heard these two before, bellowing dog songs."* He added, *"Your fat dog will die in rugged mountains ahead."*

Much farther, we met a band of nomads sheltering from the noonday sun. Three dark-skinned *Irgazen* recognized their distant clansman, *Zodi Mazak,* and led us to a leathery elder they called *"Kel Tamacheq"* who welcomed us in poor Latin, explaining, *"We come from great sand ocean where no grazing remains and go to summer pastures where good grass grows."*

Aside Marcus told me, "I know little of these nomads." Pointing to the mountains, the chief added, *"Up there we join others where clans live peacefully under blue sky."* Marcus then translated Kel's stern warning, "It's a long uphill trek through remote canyons, eating cheese, dates, olives, and almonds and drinking bad tea. Your horses will die on rocky slopes. You must ride camels!"

The next morning, I watched Kel's men pack their camels thinking, *Baby camels look too pure to become such ugly beasts.* Marcus saw my puzzled expression, adding, "Camels are troublesome wretches, but these nomads know how to handle them." That very morning, the men left without us, leading their camels to the next campsite without stopping. The women moved far behind, allowing their goats and sheep to graze along the way. The oldest man named *Amghar* ("*The Slow One*") shouted, *"I've trekked up here 30 years, but grandfather gave me his house in a miserable camel-shit village. My woman liked it, but I got fat and lazy. I'll get strong again as I walk my hills."* As we rode away, he bragged, *"Even if you give me 1,000 denari, I rot in that dirty village. Give me one camel and ten sheep and I'll stay here 'til I die."*

Each day we slogged along dry trails from where I saw the women far behind, leading the goats up barren ridges where they nibbled about. At midday, Marcus and I stopped to eat dates and looked back for old *Amghar* far below on the hill we'd just crossed. *Kel* walked up pointing, *"Slow One is shading by big rock."* Much farther back I could see the dust of our Roman escorts moving slowly to keep a proper distance from our *Barbaricae irgazen* who were setting up their next night's camp. Two hours later *Amghar* staggered into camp announcing, *"I must sleep; give tea and dates."* When the flocks were an hour away, Marcus and I climbed a ridge and opened a jug of raisin wine, with him musing, "I'm glad these *Barbars* are friendly."

At dinner, Marcus asked Kel, "How will you spend the money we will pay?" He smiled, *"I buy tea and sugar. If we find son-boy and paid more, I buy young camels."* Old *Amghar* added, *"I buy young wife to walk with me in mountains."* Kel's wife walked up grumbling, *"I don't like men laying down all afternoon."*

Curiosity aroused, I asked Kel, "Why don't your boys herd the flocks?" In response he asked, *"Do Roman men do women work?"* One smug teenager mocked, *"Herding is for 12-year-old sister."*

The next day, *Kel* left me with his wife saying, *"Control goats up that slope."* Despite my best effort, the flock scattered, leaving me bewildered as the women laughed and moved to get the goats back together. After two hours,

Kel's wife commanded, *"Move sheep, Roman man!"* After ten leagues of tiring work, I stopped to eat olives and dates, allowing the goats to scatter.

While I dozed in the sunshine, her full-breasted 16-year-old daughter laid close pretending to massage my tired legs. Although the mother smiled, she showed no concern as the girl's hands moved up my legs. As exciting as it was, I thought of Aurelia and moved away to the girl's disappointment. Soon after, the mother frowned at my rejection of her daughter's warming gestures. When I showed her a symbol of my marriage, she pointed to my white skin and blond hair, and arched her hands above her belly, indicating a desired pregnancy for her daughter.

The next day, I rejoined the trailing legionaries and ask the *Primus Pilus*, "Why do these women want white-skinned babies?" He smiled,

> Sir, many Moors in *Tingis* are of mixed blood and have positions in Romanized society. The men don't like it, but women seek blond men as partners for their blossoming daughters. Have you been approached, Sir?

I asked, "Will you send two blond lads to satisfy their youthful desires?"

Into Higher Mountains

As we gained elevation, the nights grew cold with ice on snowmelt streamlets each morning. I'd slept poorly until Kel gave me a woolsack and a knitted scarf. Thereafter, I slept well and noticed they'd slept in thick robes, leaving one man to guard against jackals that moved closer to the flocks after midnight. After my herding experience, I was happy to join the men to loaf in the afternoon. On the 4th day with the clan, we reached a high pass where a cold wind blew down upon us. From there I could see snow on the highest peaks, causing *Kel* to announce,

> *My clan's summer paradise is below tall ones. I've made this long climb every summer after wintering where life is dull. Like many men I know, some went to cities, giving away their freedom. They no longer see blue sky, bright mountains, shining stars, and cool rains. How could they live without such beauty?*

19

The next day, we led our horses along sheer cliffs, climbing higher as storm clouds swept around us as Kel's camels moved across clean white snowfields. When Marcus and I stumbled into camp, *Amghar* approached whispering, *"Very tired; give dates."* Later he moaned, *"This is last trek!"*

Amid rain and snow showers, Marcus expressed increasing doubts about finding Marco in this rocky wilderness. Before today, everything had been arid, offering no reason for him to be up here. Marcus sighed, "This Berber paradise is nothing like our Alps. I believe we're the first Romans to come here." The next morning, we led our hungry horses down a shale slope behind the camels into a long canyon from where we saw a broad green valley and distant tribal camps. I marveled at the wondrous blue-sky, framing rugged mountains where one high peak called *Jbel Azourki* stood out from the others, to which *Kel* pointed proudly proclaiming,

> *It is special to us! After you leave, I shall climb with other chiefs to slaughter a goat for our protection. We'll stay four months, then move down to desert to welcome winter rains. For 3,000 years, our people lived this way; I hope it can continue.*

That afternoon, Marcus and I walked in the warm sunshine, waiting for *Zodi* to lead us among the clans eager to find Marco. To divert my worries, Marcus commented,

> I asked *Kel* what was so special about this place; he told me, *"It's where tribes meet each year and where boy is cared for by childless woman."* Tomorrow we find Marco; perhaps speaking one hundred Tamasheq words.

Among the Clans

That evening *Zodi* returned from four nearby camps to tell me, "No chief knows of a white child among meadow-camp women. Other clans have not arrived; therefore, more days will complete their moves. Meanwhile, we search nearby valleys."

Feeling dejected, I told Marcus, "This journey may be fruitless!" I asked, "What can we do to make these people more cooperative?" He answered, "Stay confident, Ivo! Force will push Marco's captors deeper into this wilderness." I then asked, "Should we loose the hounds to find a scent trail?" He replied, "It's too soon to have these special dogs running free; we might lose them. Instead, let's be friendly with everyone and let it be known that 100 silver *denari* will go to anyone leading us to Marco."

As we met each arriving clan chief and told of our lives and families, we seemed accepted among the people, even though one hostile young *argaz* spitefully called us *Rich Roman Slavers!* Fortunately, I was able to teach their bored youngsters Roman childrens' games, which made me a favorite playmate. In addition, my sun-bleached hair was the focus of many dark-eyed *tarbats* who wanted to touch it. After being accepted by settled and late-arriving clans, we found no one who knew of Marco. The chiefs allowed small groups of soldiers to visit their campsites until two young troopers abused their welcome and were told to leave. Meanwhile, Marcus and I continued our careful diplomacy, but after another fruitless week he told me, "I'm leaving tomorrow with the *Pilus* and half of his troops. You can stay on, but your chances of finding Marco are dimming. If you agree, I'll go back to Rome to ask Emperor Claudius for a legion to punish these nomads." I answered,

> Not yet Marcus. I shall stay on. Old *Amghar* told me of secret mountain hideouts where he'd spent summers 30 years ago—places where he and his cousins hid after raiding other clans. Let's visit him; I'll give him a camel if he'll tell me where their hideouts are located.

Amghar's Confession

That afternoon we found the old one willing to tell of what the *Irgazen* called *"Amghar's glory days"*—when he and nine fellow *raiders* (led by Zodi's father, *Hami*) were champions of the young *tarbats*. His tales seemed overstated, but we listened with renewed interest because he'd previously avoided telling of his disdain for *Hami* and his *Mazak* clan. When I mentioned I was going to sell the camels I'd purchased in *Azrou*, he brightened saying, *"I want two, but have no money. It is said you pay 100 denari to find little one. Perhaps I help."*

With expectations suddenly elevated, I blurted, "Can you tell me where he's being held?" To which he mumbled, *"Do you trust Zodi?"* Marcus and I looked at each other, reflecting on our weeks with him and the frequent delays he'd caused, which may've allowed the runners to stay ahead of us. I also noted he'd shown no respect for our soldiers and had often asked of my ability to pay a greater ransom. *Amghar* then fell silent again, perhaps realizing he'd endangered himself by revealing tribal secrets. Nonetheless, he continued, speaking thoughtfully in his *Amazigh* Atlas-Mountain dialect,

> *Long ago, Hami and I argued over split of stolen horses and tarbati, causing him to move to Tingis where he raised Zodi and Azi. When he boasted of new wealth, I knew he lied. My people knew little of Hami's evil past.*

We then pressed *Amghar* to tell us where Marco could be found and if *Azi* might be holding him. Again, the old *argaz* didn't answer, knowing he'd face danger by telling of *Zodi's* involvement. I repeated, "I'll give you two camels as a reward." That announcement brightened the old one, who said,

> *I know of hillside canyon cave-holes in big mountains where we hid after raids. No one found us because few knew of far holes. If you be most careful, I lead you to nearest one tomorrow. You must carry silver for boy's safety.*

We left early the next morning climbing southward out of the valley then down a long trail behind two tall peaks into a dry canyon where few people had passed, except for three desert-edge clans that had moved to their high Atlas pastures. Late that day, we arrived at *Amghar's* least likely cave, hidden high in a difficult rocky *uden* (hill face) that showed no sign of recent habitation. We continued west toward another cave he called, *"My favorite hideout where I spent one summer with a lovable tamghart* (mature woman)."

Bargaining

As we climbed toward that cave's entrance, we were told in sharp *Tarifit*, *"Turn away! You shall not enter!"* Suspecting the presence of *Azi*, the old one shouted confidently, *"Dear nephew Azi, it is old Uncle Amghar. I've brought father of boy who will pay for release. May we continue to your shelter to drink special tea from Tingis?"*

A hesitant reply followed, *"Only if you come without weapons and after I see no soldiers following you. Tell me Uncle Amgi, is brother Zodi with you?"* To which the old man shouted, *"Not now my nephew! Perhaps you may talk without brother. My new friend brings silver."* Immediately *Azi* asked, *"How much?"* To which *Amghar* spread one hand showing his thumb and four fingers indicating five *timidi* (500 *denari*). *Azi* shouted back,

> *Tell rich Romans get more silver. You can tell father one, My long-barren Tamghart wishes to keep golden-haired child whom I shall train to be my tizzitish* (brave) *anti-Roman warrior. When older, he can slay father-man and many Mauretani Romans.*

Because we'd made little progress, we withdrew to boil some tea and consider our tactics. Seeing us resting from our difficult ride, *Azi* shouted down, *"Uncle Amgi, I wish to see silver. I send Rhoati down with boy's sandals. She will count denari and bring back one timidi (100). If she sees 500, we can talk."*

Agreed, we watched *Rhoati* descend to greet *Amghar* as a respected elder. We offered her strong tea before I asked of Marco's health. She replied, *"Little Gold-Boy is strong, but stiff from long ride with him holding me. He calls me Tante Rhommi"* (Hispano-Riffian for aunt).

We then showed her 700 newly minted Claudian *denari*, which she counted twice before shouting to *Azi*, *"seven timidi"* (700), who made no reply. Meanwhile, she touched my sun-bleached hair and suddenly cried in muffled moans, realizing she might lose the child to whom she'd become bonded over the previous weeks.

Aside, *Amghar* consoled her, saying something calming. He then told Marcus, *"We might complete agreement if you pay one agim and two timidi (1,200) denari."* I also learned our clever old trader had told *Rhoati*, *"Father-man will buy you another light-skinned child in slave market at Tingis."* That promise brought a smile to her saddened face.

She then climbed back to the cave entrance, from where a strident argument echoed down to us. An hour later, *Azi* exited the cave holding Marco upside-down by his ankles, brandishing a curved *Nimcha* (a *saif*-like scimitar), indicating he'd rejected our offer. He then dropped the crying boy on his head, waved the *Nimcha*, shouting, *"two agim denari,"* thrusting a hand overhead, opening and closing it four times to indicate 20 *timidi* (2,000 denari).

At that point, Marcus whispered, "I'm carrying the 50 gold *aurei* Senator *Publius Horatius Aquilus* gave me at the wedding." Since one *aureus* is worth 25 *denari*, that handful of coins would provide us a bargaining value of 1,250 *denari*. Before I could ask him for its use, he barked, "Take Sabina's gold to end this standoff!" Marcus then told *Amghar*, "Recall *Rhoati* and tell her to bring *Marco* down with a good horse. He then told me, "I'll pay *Azi* 1,500 *denari* to end this oppressive haggling."

Rhoati descended again where I handed her a single *aureus* to carry up to *Azi*. As soon as she reached him, we could see he was excited with the gold coin and bit it to test its malleability. Soon after, *Azi* and *Rhoati* began descending with *Marco* to a mid-point where we met to conclude our transaction. Even then, *Azi* attempted further bargaining before he'd allow *Rhoati* to remove a wrap from Marco's bruised head, while still demanding another hundred *denari* before he'd expose the full face of Marco—to which I agreed. To my great relief, *Azi* told *Rhoati* to hand *Marco* to me, which she did reluctantly. Marco was unsure to release Rhoati, but soon clutched me tightly while glowering hurtfully at *Azi*, whom he clearly feared. As we prepared to depart, *Azi* said, *"Sorry, no horse! We ran them too hard coming here; you must find fresh ones among clans."*

As we mounted the ill-behaving camels I'd given to Amghar, *Rhoati* asked, *"What of promised slave child before you leave Tingis?"* I replied, "That promise will be honored!" When we return to the city, I shall accompany you to the big market to make a selection."

Return

After thanking *Amghar* and *Kel Tamacheq's* clan, we rejoined the soldiers at their marching camp from where (with fresh Mauretanian horses) we struck toward *Volubilis* and on to *Thamusida* and *Tocolocidis*. After three hard-days ride to the legionaries' *Mare Atlanticus* port, we boarded an awaiting bireme to end our long trans-Mauretanian journey back at *Tingis*. As we entered the harbor, word spread that a ship was arriving from the south containing the forty legionaries who'd sailed a month before in support of the rescue mission that had generated wide interest, including that of Emperor Claudius in Rome.

Marcus was first to see Sabina and Aurelia (in glistening white robes) standing on the farthest point of the dock, looking earnestly to see if we'd returned with Marco. When they saw me holding him high, a cry arose from Aurelia followed by cheers from a hundred Roman friends, and repeated horn blasts that echoed from legionary *cornicen trumpeti*. As soon as we debarked, Aurelia grabbed Marco from me babbling tearfully, "We'll never lose you again, my dear boy." She then kissed me repeatedly through my sun-bleached beard, saying, "I thought I'd lost you both. It's been a terrible month without you——not knowing if I'd ever see either of you again."

CHAPTER 4

GADES

After a few private hours with Aurelia, we joined Sabina and Marcus at the *principia* where *Rufus Calpurnicus* and his wife, *Scaptia Hosidius Flavia*, honored us with a Roman feast where bewildered little Marco was the center of attention for an hour. We then enjoyed the finest Hispanic cuisine and wine, during which both Marcus and I recounted the travails of our month-long search for Marco, spoke of the high-Atlas marvels, and thanked the commandant and our legionary friends for their support on our mission.

The next day we wrote commendatory reports to the emperor and letters of thanks to those who'd supported us. We also signaled senior officials we'd be hurrying to Germania to fulfill our command duties. We then arranged oceanic passage to Cadiz where the special trireme waited to take us to Britannia. To Aurelia's surprise, our friend, Captain Val, had just returned to Tingis and had rushed to offer his services.

The day before we planned to leave, I received a hand-delivered note from a *Fezzian* called *Aduzi Mazak* asking, "Will you honor your promise to cousin *Rhoati?* If so, meet us at the busy slave market today."

I answered, "I shall be there!" When I asked Marcus to borrow some gold coins, Sabina insisted, "I shall join you; I've never been to a slave sale." Although Marcus rejected her demand, she pled, "I must see how slavers treat captive children who are sold like sheep and goats."

On schedule, we met *Rhoati, Aduzi,* and *Hami* who led us among 16 stalls of naked children wearing slate placards telling age, weight, and source. Many were dark skinned, underfed, ill, and lowest priced. Others were Nilotic, almond skinned, healthier, and mid-priced. Fewer were Graecic, Turkic, and Pontic, somewhat older and slightly educated, and higher priced. Finally, we saw ten light-skinned Britons and red-blond *Gallaecians* who brought top prices in Tinginita's slave market. Suddenly, *Rhoati* exclaimed in Fezzi-Hispano *tarafit*, *"El,"* pointing at a blond four-year-old, similar to Marco, priced at 400 *denari*. In response, the seller insisted, *"Sister-tarbat must go with little-man––only 300 more denari."* Rhoati looked away, muttering, *"No tarbati."* Upon seeing the skinny three-year-old in distress, Sabina suddenly shouted, "I'll buy her," and paid 12 *aurei* before Marcus could stop her.

After she'd paid the full price without bargaining, *Hami,* tried to sell *Rhoati's* purchase to Marcus for 1,000 denari, but she disappeared with the boy before that offer could be discussed. As we walked toward the fort, I jibed Marcus, "Welcome to fatherhood, old friend; I'll be proud to serve as the little one's uncle; what will you call her?" He answered, "Ask Sabina; she's in charge, as you can see!"

That evening at a farewell dinner, the commandant asked, "Sabina, what will you name your new daughter?" Caught ill-prepared to speak, she looked to *Flavia* sitting beside her, announcing, "She shall be *Flavia* if our marvelous hostess agrees." To which the lady responded, "Yes, Dear Sabina; I'm proud to share my name with this fortunate child who has gained honorable parents and will soon be the sister of a sibling of one whom Aurelia and I learned about today." The news of Sabina's pregnancy brought forth a resounding cheer and a question of her future child's name. Marcus responded, "He or she shall honor our parents."

Northbound at Last

The next morning, we boarded Captain Val's fully renovated *Lembi* and moved away to the blasts of the ceremonial *cornicines* who'd trumpeted our return from the Atlas Mountains. As we departed *Tingis*, we saluted Commandant *Rufus* and waved to many friends we'd found there. While paralleling the shoreline, I saw a tearful *Tamghart* holding the hand of a small boy who waved as we glided past, causing little *Flavia* to wave and shout at her brother *Trupo* until he passed from sight.

Happy to see us again, Captain Val told us of his *Mare Atlanticus* travels during the past month, and how he'd delivered Antón to *Portus*

Calle (Oporto) at the mouth of the *Durius* River (Douro) from where he'd proceeded on to *Bracara Augusta* (Braga) for horse buying. Val said, "On that trip, I delivered hundreds of *amphorae* of *garum* and Hispanic wines, and tons of dried mackerel to legionary forts in Britannia." Val was fascinated with our Atlas-Mountain tale and soon became *Marco* and *Flavia's* favorite storyteller whom she called *Tio Porcus* because of his rotundity and bounding sense of humor.

Nearing sundown, we sailed along the Iberian shoreline before the sun dipped behind the sea's crimson waters. In the summer twilight, we approached *Gades* (Cadiz), about which Captain Val told us,

> *Tyrenian Phoenicians* founded this ancient city a thousand years ago for access to this area's mineral wealth, making it a battleground for control of the western *Mare*. With *Phoenici* decline, the status of ancient *Gadir* shifted. Six centuries ago, the *Carthagi* captured the city and made it part of their growing empire. During the 2nd Punic War, *Hamilcar Barca* had made it his base to plunder Iberia for its resources. As with *Carthago Nova*, the city was captured by *Scipio Africanus'* legions. After the war, the city prospered by serving as a major naval base and shipbuilding center. Since the city had supported Caesar against Pompey, he granted it municipal status and named it *Gades*, whose colony became known as *Urba Iulia Gaditana*.

When we docked, Marcus dispatched a note to Sabina's father's senatorial friend, requesting an overnight visit. Soon after, we were led to the grandest tile-and-stucco villa where we met the wealthiest landowners in the region. They'd heard of the kidnapping and were surprised to learn that *Consul Maximus Carpentius'* daughter, *Sabina*, had married *Marcus Gnaeus Cornelius Lentulus* and that I was Marcus' brother-in-law.

At dinner, a neighboring grandee's haughty wife spoiled the pleasant atmosphere by asking Sabina, "Why would a pretty lady like you, purchase a dirty little *Galliciani* slave girl to become an adopted daughter of an equestrian Roman family?" In response, Sabina returned the insult by demeaning the arrogant one's *Turdetani* heritage, which annoyed others at the table. Fortunately, our *Cilbicnsi* host and his *Tartessi* and *Celtici* neighbors cooled tribal conflicts by the host's timely introduction of costumed musicians who performed colorful regional dances.

We'd planned to leave early to soften Sabina's rage, but our host implored us to remain two more days until the special legionary trireme could be loaded with products from the neighboring farms to be carried forward to our Britannic and Germanic legions, perhaps to ease the concerns of our six-week-late arrival, and redeem their own standing with Sabina's father, who'd certainly hear of his daughter's insult. In addition, our gregarious captain had become popular among members of this Hispanic society, with *Consul Maximus* later writing to Marcus,

> We shall petition the senate to restore the former rank of admiral to our new friend *Valerius*, despite the emperor's detestation of Val's uncle *Decimus Valerius Asiaticus*, who'd owned and lost Rome's spectacular Pleasure Gardens. Perhaps Emperor Claudius will accept our praise of this gentlemanly naval officer who wishes to settle among those in *Gadir* and serve in protecting our port city.

Farther North

As we boarded the *Golden Eye,* its *Capitán Eanes Casae* apologized for deserting us at *Ostia* six weeks ago when Britannia's new Governor, *Aulus Didius Gallus,* displaced us from the high-status trireme for our trip to Germania. *Capitán Casae* also carried a note from the governor that read, "Thank you for the horses for which I shall arrange payment—visit me when you pass through Britannia." The captain warned me,

> You'll never recover those fine horses. Be on your best behavior when you visit the governor, he's a treacherous senior official who's ruined the careers of rising young officers. I was happy to be rid of him and his haughty aides when we arrived at *Camulodunum.*

From *Gadir,* we camped one night on the *Sacrum Promontory* beyond *Lagobriga.* We then continued north to *Olisippo* (Lisbon) where we followed a similar routine before striking further north along the western Iberian coast to the *Munda River.* The next leg took us to *Portus Cale* (Oporto) at the *Durius River* mouth because *Capitán Gil* wanted to visit his father who'd retired there after his 25 years as a Roman engineer and to buy 50 big *amphorae* of a dark-red *Durian* wine. While there, *Capitán*

Casae's father told us of his *Lusitani* and *Gallaeci* provinces, of tribes here before the Roman invasion 300 years ago, and of two centuries of romanization. He also told us, "I was raised in northern *Lusitania* and southern *Gallaecia* where I later built baths, temples, bridges, roads, theaters, and country villae." He continued, "We had to adopt the Roman trinomial naming system, so my son became *Eanes Pacheco Gilhardo*––Eanes (son of João) *Pacheco* (from Pacheca) *Gilhardo* (gallant)." While moving on to *Lambriaca*, our captain told us,

> Romanization began here during the 2nd Punic War when legions conquered *Lusitania* to preclude Hasdrubal's access to our copper, tin, gold, and silver. Rome then exploited our silver mines at *Aljusitrel* (Vipasca) and *Mértola* (Sâo Domingo) in a mineral belt that reached to *Hispalis* (Seville). North Lusitania was difficult to conquer due to resistance led by *Viriatus* who waged relentless guerrilla war against successive Roman generals. Rome's conquest was completed after its legions defeated our *Cantabri, Asturi* and *Gallaeci* tribes in the *Cantabrian Wars.* The Romans developed our farms, cultivated vines and cereals at *Alentejo,* and expanded our fishing fleets along the *Algarve, Póvoa de Varzim, Matosinhos,* and *Olisppo* coasts from where *garum* jars are now being exported across the empire.

When he mentioned *garum*, Sabina asked, "Many coastal cities are exporting that tasty sauce. How can they sell so much of this luxury?" *Capitan Gil* answered,

> We call that fermented fish sauce *Liquamen,* a condiment used in many Roman cuisines, similar to older ones used by the *Graecians.* Our word *garum* came from their word *garos*––a fish from which it's made. Some call it the ancestor of *Colatura di Alici* anchovy sauce.

Shifting to money and transportation, our captain concluded,

> Roman coinage and father's roads, bridges, and aqueducts aided all of our business transactions. Naval and commercial shipping brought mobility and increased interactions across the entire Roman world. Soldiers from distant provinces have served in our towns; miners came to our metal-rich areas; slaves built grand marble structures in *Olisipo,*

Bracara Augusta, Aeminium, and *Pax Julia,* leaving impressive Roman legacies to all of us. Army Latin became our language, and soldiers brought *Mithrasic* and *Christianic* mystery religions to *Lusitania.*

On the mention of his *Christiani* followers, I ask if he'd known *Antón Silviera,* a battle-injured *Lusitani* cavalryman, who'd come from a village near *Bracara.* He denied knowing him, but recognized the family gens known for horsemanship. He'd also told of *Christiani* cells in the *Bracara* region, sponsored by retiree soldiers who'd served in *Judaea.* Since the secretive sect had been rejected in Rome, Capitán Gil turned the discussion to *Mithras* and was pleased to learn that Marcus and I were both initiates, which led to added religious discussions on the trip.

CHAPTER 5

ONWARD

The next leg of our journey took us near *Lambriaca* at the mouth of the *Ulla River* where we camped near *Cileni* and *Prestamrchi* tribesmen who visited dozens of crewmen who'd been born here. Capitán Gil explained,

> When I first became commander of this ship, most *regemi* were *Graeci,*
> *Dalmati, Dardani,* and *Macedoni* lads who came with the ship. Steadily
> over the years, some retired, some quit, and some died. I've replaced
> most with Iberians who wanted to earn Roman coins and see much of
> the enriched Roman world. Hence, you'll hear a variety of pre-Celtic
> dialects spoken here from 30 different tribes that inhabit this region.

The next day we rounded the northwestern *Callaeci* region where we went ashore by *Brigantium* to camp on the *Lapatia Corus Trileucum Promontory.* There, Gil ordered his trireme boosted ashore with the help of local tribesmen to drain all leakage, while explaining two paths ahead.

> I can choose between hugging Hispania's northern coast and Gallia's
> west coast (assisted by the Biscayan current beyond *Condivicnum*) and float
> on to the *Gesocrivate Gabaeum Promontorium* (Brest)––taking eight days.
> Or we can strike directly across the landless *Mare Cantabricum* against
> a steady southbound current to the *Armoricaine* lands 500 miles away,
> before proceeding to Britannia. That trip will require four hard days
> and nights, but is risky without rest camps, facing changeable weather
> conditions.

I asked Capitán Gil, "Have you made the direct crossing before, and how many people will fit in your rescue boats?" He answered,

I've made the straight trip five times and the coastal one more than 20, all safely. Once we had heavy leakage, but father had given me a *Graecian* pump that saved us. He later installed two, which relieved all inflows. My two rescue boats will carry all of you and my senior crewmen, but my *regemi* are at risk and they know it. When I choose the open-water course, I double their pay or find substitutes (for higher pay). Over the years, many ships have never reached their destinations, but this ship is the very best with a hardwood hull for equestrian transport. Unless Marcus chooses otherwise, I shall aim straight to *Gesocrivate* where we'll rest two days.

After discussions with Aurelia and Sabina (both eager to press rapidly onward), I told Capitán Gil, "We'll go as you've decided." He then asked if any crewman wanted a substitute. Only five chose to remain in *Gallaecia* without pay until the ship returned. When the *Golden Eye* was refloated, we headed north into summer twilight where the oncoming night was illuminated by a thousand stars. I watched as our *nautum* aimed the ship toward familiar stars he called "the flank of *Ursae Minoris* that didn't move like other stars." As clouds formed, Gil ordered, "Rest on your oars lads; sleep 'til sunrise." The nautum, *Pánfilo Cão*, told us,

You must see my navigation charts and my *astrolabi* that I use to sight asterisms. They both help me calculate north and south latitudes by measuring the sun's noon height above the southern horizon. East and west positions are unreliable because we know little about the exact times of star positions. Nevertheless, we skilled *Nautii* can do clever tricks that take us to our distant destinations.

We made our passage across the *Mare Cantabricum's* expanse with two rowers manning the pumps. Although we enjoyed a warm breeze that filled our sail (helping to counter strong southbound sea currents), we made steady progress in summer weather with our sun-blond boys running around the deck. Because of the sun's intensity, the crewmen wore broad-brimmed shades, which we adopted to avoid sunburns. To divert endless boredom, the crew sang tribal chants and bawdy rowing tunes, while

Vibi filled hours with oft-retold stories. Our captain told us of his trips to many ports and of all classes of people he'd known. Some subjects that filled our afternoons and evenings were religion and slavery. Capitán Gil spoke of mystery religious cults, beginning,

> *Mithraic* mysteries have been opened to slaves and freedmen. Since the cult values submission to authority and promotion through an earned ladder, many slaves are kept in harmony with Roman Society and posc no threat with Mithraic membership. Graecian *Stoics* teach, "All men are manifestations of the same universal spirit, and are equal." They hold, "Being enslaved doesn't impede one from practicing self-mastery." These cults oppose ill treatment of slaves, but accept slavery in Roman society.

We'd been surrounded by slaves all our lives; however, the subject aroused responses from each of us, realizing that our structured society depended heavily on slave labor to support it. Nevertheless, we were surprised when Sabina (better educated than most Roman women and raised among thousands of slaves) spoke out sharply, saying,

> I've read the *Christiani* advocate for pay and fair treatment of slaves, like my father does at our Tusculum *latfundium*. Although their pay is low, all are cared for and well fed. Father and Senator Aquilus have always advised their slaves to obey so they can lawfully obtain freedom.

Many such practices were discussed during our days afloat with Sabina telling of her father's *manumissio* ceremonies,

> He held public ceremonies before a judge, touching his most faithful slaves with a decorated staff saying, "You are free to live your lives!" He gave them a small bag of denari and a *Pileus* cap as a symbol of manumission. He'd free some for good deeds, out of friendship, or when one purchased another. Our educated ones were paid to teach the brightest children on our farm. Because the *manumissio* practice was expanding, the emperor limited the numbers we could free.

Our conversations turned to Latin writers, revealing that Capitán Gil was well read. Since I'd met some famous intellectuals in the Claudian library, I was able to impress our group with my knowledge of the works of *Horace, Livy, Ovid, Petronius, Tibullus,* and *Virgil.* To my surprise, our captain fetched tubes containing copies of Virgil's *Aeneid* and Rufus' *Stoic Philosophy* that influenced *Epictetus* and other important Stoics.

As a result, I asked Capitán Gil if he'd allow my aide, *Vibi,* to read some scrolls to our group in need of entertainment. Since most were written in High Latin, Capitán Gil asked if Vibi had a stentorian voice sufficient to be heard by his rowers. Because Vibi's grandfather had trained the lad in oratorical skills, my aide filled our hours with dramatic and thoughtful readings that often floated o'er the heads of Gil's rowers hindered by native dialects. My group was pleased when Gil told us,

I've a dozen more scrolls Vibi can read all the way to Britannia if his voice holds out and if *Oceanus* remains steady for a week. I wouldn't like my scrolls damaged by sea sprays. Tomorrow he can read Petronius' *Satyricon* followed by Ovid's *Metamorphoseon* and his *Ars amatoria.* Further on he can read Livy's and Paterculus' histories.

CHAPTER 6

OCEANUS

As we approached the *Gabaeium Promontory* (Brest), Marcus asked about naval commands at sea. Capitán Gil answered,

> Each ship is commanded by a political-appointee *trierarchus* who often rises to command a squadron of ten or more ships. Some rise higher to become *nacharchus princips* commanding several squadrons. Those *magistrati* or *promagistrati*, who command a fleet, are of consular or praetorian rank. Such *praefecti* have little knowledge of naval matters.

Regarding his position, Gil admitted, "I cannot rise further because I'm a *provinciali* (a tribesman with earned Roman citizenship), holding auxiliary rank and status." He added,

> I earned my position as *capitáno* where I lead an *optio*, a *beneficiarus*, four *principales*, and six *immunes*, equal to army auxiliaries. My officers include a helmsman (*celeusta*), navigator (*natum*), master of rowers (*gubernator*), political officer (*pentacontarchos*), lookout (*proreta*), and doctor (*medicus*). My *remigi* are freeborn non-citizens (*peregrini*) recruited from Hispanic tribes. Since they serve as *centuriae*, they sign on as marines, rowers, or craftsmen, called *milites* (soldiers). They are *Classiari*, subordinated below legionaries and auxiliaries. Emperor Claudius finally gave rowers privileges, enabling them to earn citizenship after 26 years and a cash payment at retirement.

When Marcus asked, "Is your ship unique?" Capitán Gil answered,

Our merchant navy uses sail-driven *navis onerariae* (*burden-carriers*) and lighter *liburniae* and *hemioliae* ships adopted as scouts and light transports. Since *the Battle of Actium,* the fighting navy's main task has been policing our waterways and rivers, suppressing piracy, escorting grain shipments, and supporting expeditions, for which lighter ships are better. After Augustus reorganized his fleet 60 years ago, we've used *triremes* and *liburnia* in the provincial fleets, and 30-oar *navis actuaria* with shallow-draft keels for coastal and fluvial operations. Even *actuariae* have been replaced by *navis lusoriae* for patrolling the river frontiers. Two Praetorian fleets also serve as the emperor's reserve for patrol and transport duties, while seven lesser fleets and two legionary squadrons control our coasts, rivers, and harbors.

He then said, "Sorry Marcus, I've not yet told you of the uniqueness of my ship." He continued,

I've enjoyed my naval carrier, rising to serve as *Legio XXII's* commanding centurion of boats on the *Rhenus* and *Moenus* Rivers. One terrible day in October 37, my ship was assigned to move wives and children down river to board a trireme to carry them to Rome. A raid was sprung upon us ten leagues below *Mogontiacum* by hundreds of *Chatti* warriors. In their destruction of our rivercraft, all my passengers and most of our marines and rowers were slaughtered or drowned in the Rhenus. The few crewmen who survived were transferred to remote assignments while our legion's commander was later executed for unrelated causes. His successor reduced my punishment, but transferred me to undesirable duties, where I slowly redeemed my rank to command slow *navis onerariae* (*burden carrier*) ships. Two years ago, I finally regained the privilege to transport equestrian-class passengers on this *'Golden-Eye'* trireme.

Stunned by his tale, Marcus and I remained silent, wondering if we should reveal our own life-altering part of the captain's revelation. In the awkward silence, Sabina made an innocent remark that broke the spell, asking, "That story sounds familiar! Aurelia, didn't you tell me of a similar experience in that river?" I finally chose to defuse the tension, realizing my grandfather's punitive raid had harshly affected Capitán Gil's career, and still haunted Aurelia's dreams of trying to reach her drowning mother.

I then asked him, "How well do you remember *Gnaeus Cornelius Lentulus Gaeticulus, Hosidius Mallius Sabatinus,* and *Spurius Matius Cogitatus* at Mogontiacum?" To which he answered,

> Yes, I'd met them, but they were above my status. The first was *Legio XXII's* legate who'd fired me and the other naval officers. The second was *Sabatini,* the one some people called the *"Malevolent Tribune Laticlavus,"* rumored to have caused the raid, and one of the few who'd survived. The last was *Spur,* the legion's senior engineer, who used many captives on building his great bridge and other projects.

I then shocked him by introducing Marcus and Aurelia using their full Roman names,

> Sir, May I introduce to you my wife and my brother-in-law, *Aurelia Cornelius Lentulus* and *Marcus Gnaeus Cornelius Lentulus,* the daughter and son of *Gnaeus Cornelius Lentulus Gaeticulus,* your former commander at *Mogontiacum.* I am *Ivano Valburga,* the grandson of Odalric Valburga (our clan's leader) who'd planned and executed the raid to kill *Sabatini* for murdering one of his grandsons——my ten-year-old cousin, Fulko.

Capitán Gil paled, reflecting on what I'd told him. Chokingly he said,

> I didn't know any of these people had lived beyond that tragic October morning. Since many bodies were never found, I heard, "Only *Tribune Sabatini,* and me, and some marines had been rescued." How did Marcus and Aurelia survive their swim in that frigid river?

I responded,

> I was fishing downstream from the attack with my young cousins. From our positions, I saw three Roman children (clinging to bundles) whom we pulled ashore and warmed by our fire. *Grossfater Odalric* hurried us away to our tribal-king's hideout deep in Germania's winter forests where we lived for two years. *Ur-Onkle Cladovech* and

Tante Swanhilda—my tribe's king and queen––adopted 12-year-old Aureila as a granddaughter, but eventually we traded the adolescent Romans for enslaved Chattimen held as laborers at *Mogontiacum*. From that arrangement, Legate Vespasianus sent Marcus and me to Rome to become Roman cavalry officers. Now, 15 years later, you are transporting Marcus and me to our new commands in Germania.

Our gallant Hispano-Roman *Trierarchus,* whom we both addressed as *Capitáno Eanes Pacheco Gilhardo,* saluted us as he solemnly withdrew to his cabin saying in *Hispano-Latin, "Siempre Amigos"* that Marcus and I echoed, *"Immer Freunde"* (forever friends).

CHAPTER 7

SPUR AND MILO

As we rounded Gallia's northwest *Gabaeium Promontory* and entered Britannia's *Sinus Oestrymnicus* below *Isca Dumnoniorum*, we enjoyed a strong sea current that added eight knots toward our night stop at *Portus Magnus* behind *Vectis* (the Isle of Wight). While there, I told of my crossing of Southern Britannia in the summer of AD 43 with Vespasian in his conquest of the southwestern tribes.

Early the next morning, we struck eastward beneath the tall white cliffs past *Anderida* (Pevensey) and *Portus Lemnanis* (Lynne) where we encountered strong head currents as we approached *Portus Dubris* (Dover). Although we were less than 60 leagues from *Camulodunum*, we overnighted at *Dubris* to arrive at the colony in the early afternoon. As we approached the dock, a crowd formed, with Capitán Gil saying, "It's not usual to see such gatherings when my ship arrives, because we often bring important visitors." The excitement diminished when no one of significance was recognized. Nevertheless, a *Trinovanti* official and two legionary retirees greeted us and led us to the *principia* where we entered guest quarters and received invitations to dine with members of our former cavalry units.

The first person we encountered was *Centurion Spurius Matius Cogitatus*, (Marcus' old friend, Spur) who'd been the senior engineer in Germania, and had come to Britannia to supervise Rome's many building projects needed after the invasion nine years ago. On recognizing us, he invited us to his villa where his concubine and four of

40

his five sons and one small daughter all lived near the unfinished *Temple of Claudius* in this vigorous colonial city.

My first question involved *Milo*, who'd arrived during the invasion to build docks, roads, and bridges, and had found a concubine who'd produced two sons. I asked Spur, "Where might I find *Brother Milo* who's been building military roads somewhere north of *Londinium*?" He replied,

> He's upcountry. You may know, military roads have been our top engineering priority in Britannia for advancing the conquest, but tribal resistance has slowed us. Although he leads survey teams, inspects highways, and conducts road-opening ceremonies, he comes home four days each month to be with his family. I believe he's now beyond *Lactodurum* (Towcester) along *Watling Street*. I'll send word for him to meet us at the *Icknield's* crossing of *Ermine Way*. If you can stay long enough to make such a meeting possible, I'll dispatch a rider up there tonight.

I agreed, saying, "While your rider is outbound, I'd like to meet your family and Milo's. I'd also like for Aurelia and Sabina to spend some time with both families, and have arrangements readied for our departure when we return." Early the next morning, Spur and his second son, *Valerianus*, led us on a two-day ride to that rendezvous point, during which we retold old stories and I recounted my month-long mountain search for three-year-old Marco. Spur then told us,

> You may remember, Milo designed the Claudian Temple you've seen half-built near my villa. His proposal was chosen by the emperor and would've been completed by now, but we've faced many delays in getting special marbles here to finish our project. We'll need at least 20 more shiploads of that special stone from Gallia. On our ride, we'll cross *Iceni* territory that's unfriendly. You may've heard our legion fought a battle four years ago against their clans on the western edge of the Fens. As a result, we're not friendly with tribesmen ruled by *Prasatagus*, who's been their king for much of this century. His fiery young wife, *Queen Boudica*, often speaks against us, even though he's a client king of Rome. I'll send a rider to announce our transit of his land.

The returned rider reported, "The *Iceni* king said, 'You must visit me before you leave Britannia'." When we arrived at our meeting point with Milo above *Durocobrivae* (Dunstable), we waited two hours in the twilight for the arrival of the deeply tanned and blond-haired engineer with his retinue of six legionaries. There beside Milo's recently paved roadway, Spur and his retirees set up camp and roasted a score of grouse and purchased three big *amphorae* of locally brewed mead for the reunion.

On seeing Milo after many years, I remarked, "You look like *Opa Odalric* with your sun-bleached hair." He responded, *"Du siehst als wie ein reicher romanischer Equestrian, mein langen verlorener Bruder"* (You look like a rich Roman equestrian, my long-lost brother). After handshakes all around, and the passing around of two borrowed *steins*, the evening afterglow was filled with lively songs and rowdy stories 'til the summer stars faded into morning when local *Catuvellauni* tribesfolk served us a hearty breakfast of eel and buttered coarse-grain loaves, for which I paid four new Claudian *denari*.

I'd told Milo of our families and our command assignments in Germania, to which he bragged, "I shall bring my clan there soon to see you and sweet little Aurelia again. Is she still as beautiful as when we saved her from the cold river?" "Evermoreso," I replied, "You must see her and our two bright-eyed boys—both shining images of her."

As we all mounted our horses to depart, I shouted, *"Bis später, mein Bruder; Bitte bringe unseren alten Fruend Spur mit."* (Until later my brother; please bring our old friend Spur with you.)"

On our return to *Camulodunum*, we rode along the old *Icknield Way* around the south edge of the reed-bound Fens past *Grantchester* and *Icklingham* to an *Iceni* fortress near the ancient *Peddar Way* where we met *King Prasatagus* and his tribal guards. There, Spur introduced us as cavalary commanders visiting the Chatti-Roman engineer-roadbuilder with a *Trinovanti* wife who many *Iceni* tribesmen already knew.

On recognizing my Germanic dialect, the king asked directly, *"Sind Sie auch Chatti, mein neuer germanisher Freund?"* (Are you also Chattian, my new German friend?). He continued, *"Meine Urgrossvaetern kommen alle aus Germania. Nächstes Jahr werde ich zurück zu ihrem in Britannia mit uns zu besuchen, Herr Ivano."* (My great-grandfathers all came from Germany. You must come to visit us the next time you come to Britain). I replied, *"Danke*

Sehr, König Prasatagus, Nächtstes Jahr werde ich zu ihrem königreich kommen."
(Thank you King Prasatagus; next year I shall come back to your kingdom).

We then headed 30 leagues south to *Camulodunum* where Capitán Gil and our families waited for our transit across the *Oceanus Germanicus* to the mouth of the *Rhenus Fluss* where a river ship with 30 oarsmen awaited us for a 90-league upriver trip to *Vetera Castra* and the final winding passage past the *Rura Fluss* to our ultimate destination—the vigorous colony of *Agrippina* where we'd live for the next two years. After all of our delaying difficulties, Sabina exclaimed sharply to me,

So, this is our new home! I expected high mountains and beautiful valleys filled with happy people. Perhaps some *Sigambri* ale will soften the pain of our seven-week trip. I hope the next five months of my pregnancy goes smoothly with Marcus campaigning somewhere beyond the fortification line. I also hope your warrior cousins will behave themselves until my child is born and we can go back to those warm and wonderful *Baleares* islands we liked so well.

CHAPTER 8

REPORTING

Immediately after debarking, Marcus and I ran to the *principia* where we reported our arrival and waited to be introduced to the commandant, *Decius Blandus Asprenus*, to explain our late arrival. Fortunately, he was upstream at *Mogonitacum* and would not be returning until two days later, which gave us time to settle into an annex by the *principia*. In the commandant's absence, his *Tribune Laticlavus* and staff members welcomed us. We also learned Antón Silviera had arrived three days earlier with 14 semi-trained cavalry recruits (riding their own mounts) and leading 16 top-grade *Lusitani* horses.

Most important was easing Aurelia and Sabina into colonial and military societies, and finding playmates for our children, including Sabina's adopted daughter who avoided Roman children who were unable to understand her mixed Mauretani-Iberian dialect. To our gratification, everyone seemed pleasant, including scores of retired legionaries and their tribal wives. Fortunately, Aurelia was fluent in Chatti-Celtic languages because of her years with *Onkle Ludvig* and *Tante Swanhilde* that allowed her to speak with most *Germanic Frauen*, making her immediately popular in the colony where she found multilingual friends for the children.

When word reached Mogontiacum we'd arrived, both *Commandant Blandus* and *Legio XXII's* legate returned to conduct changes-of-command ceremonies. Fortunately, the legate had served as a junior officer under Marcus's father and told tales about Marcus and his pretty little sister, and of their godfather, Spur, defusing remarks from the odd commandant. That evening we attended a farewell dinner for our predecessors who spoke sadly about leaving those they'd led for 3½ years.

The next day we watched a full-dress parade in their honor, after which we met many soldiers while enjoying a "bull-roast" served with barrels of ale. As the day ended, Antón asked if it would be appropriate to offer the senior commanders two of the top horses he'd driven from *Lusitania*. I consulted Marcus, after which I announced, "My aide, Antón Silviera has a presentation for our leaders." At that point, Antón rode in on a tall black horse, leading a pearl-white one, announcing in a stentorian voice,

> As fighting men on horseback, we've long served in the shadow of the infantry. As tokens from us who've galloped headlong into battle, we wish to welcome our leaders to our brotherhood of *Equitandi*. Stand up, proud cavalrymen as we present our commanders these fine Iberian stallions. Join me in saluting our distinguished *Equinus-Mounted Knights of Battle!*"

Quieted by Antón's elevated delivery, the spirited legate considered which horse to choose and how to respond to Antón's remarks. In silence, every man's drink descended until the legate raised his hand to the silky mane of the black he called "*Midnight*." He then vaulted onto its back and jumped to a standing position on its broad muscular hips where he echoed Antón's sentiment before springing lightly to the ground and bowing to his adoring crowd who boomed another round of salutatory cheers.

All attention then turned to *Commandant Blandus*, who'd never been a warrior and was totally unprepared for a classy oratorical response, and no match for the legate's showy instincts. Among battle-hardened veterans, he felt foolish, but managed to thank Antón as the legate raised his cup in a return salute to the troopers. As the legate handed *Midnight*'s reigns to a stableman, I saw *Blandus* glance spitefully at me for embarrassing him. I suddenly realized I'd poisoned a professional relationship with one who could damage my career. It was also clear that my troopers were concerned because few came near the little administrator, nor looked him in the eye.

The next morning, Marcus and I departed on our first intelligence-gathering mission into tribelands with a half-century of troopers to open discussions with King Geron of my own clan, and other tribal kings with hopes of opening new client-king provinces behind the existing *Rhenus-Fluss Limes* so our legions could reach peacefully into *Germania Magna*.

Contact

Operating from *Colonia*, we moved east on an ancient trackway north of the *Taunus Mountains* toward my own clan's home site where I'd lived when I was young. When we arrived, I found remains of a deserted village that brought back memories of youthful play and hard training, followed by hours of practical schooling enforced by *Opa Odalric*. Later that day, Marcus dispatched an eight-man *Contubernia* north and east with plans to regroup at a central point halfway back from their most distant searches.

When back with us, one team reported having been shadowed near three river valleys of the west-flowing *Rura* (Ruhr), the east-flowing *Adrana Fork* of the *Visurgis* (Vistula), and the northwest tip of the *Laugana* (Lahn). We returned the following day where we found a fortified *Oppidium* occupied by dispersed *Sigambri* and *Chatti* clans. I also learned of other Chatti clans northeast beyond the eastern forks of the *Visurgis*. We finally came upon an old Chatti woman called *Rhodala* who informed me, "*King Clodovech* died two years ago and his son *Geronimus* was now the tribe's king." She also told me, "The new king lives with his mother, *Queen Swanhilde*, at the *Oppidium* where the *Oba* tribe lived before it moved to the riverside *Oppidium Ubiorum* that the Romans now call *Claudia Ara Agrippinensium*."

She then said to me, "Although you're a Roman soldier, you must be *Chatti*; your dialect is too good for an outlander. Tell me young man, who was your grandfather?" I answered, "*Mein Grossfater war Odalric Valburga; Mein Fater war Ivannes, und der alte König Clodovech war mein Urgrossonkel Ludwig.*" She exclaimed, "*Mein Gott, du muss Ivano sein!*" (My God, you must be Ivano!) After a discourse about good times, and her membership in a neighboring clan, she said,

> You must visit *King Geronimus* and Queen-Mother *Swanhilde*. The fort is only five leagues ahead. The queen-lady is gravely ill and may die soon. I'm certain she'll welcome you home, Sir Ivano; however, I've heard

your cousins talk badly of you. Perhaps you should leave your soldiers
here and allow me lead you to the fort.

I agreed and boosted her onto a spare horse, which she handled well.
Meanwhile, I ordered the troops to wait our return and rode directly to
the fort. There she led me to the *King's* great-hall, followed by Marcus
and Antón. At the king's heavy door, she charged in without knocking,
causing him to ask, "What brings you here, *Rhodala*, and who's that
troublesome lad you've drug in for royal judgment?" Before she could
answer, he recognized me, shouting, "Look who's finally come home! It's
good to see you looking so strong and sun-browned *Ivo*. Where've you
been, and where's *Milo*? He then looked at Marcus, asking, "Who's this
familiar-looking Roman?"

After we answered his first questions, he asked about our suntans,
which led to the telling of my Mauretanian search for Marco, and my
marriage to Aurelia. He then demanded, "Before you tell me everything,
you must visit *Queen Swanhilde* to tell her of *Aurelia* and your children.
You must call me *King Geron* when with our people or simply *Gero* when
unaccompanied."

We then proceeded to her room, where (on seeing us) she shouted,
"Come in my pretty lads and tell me of my golden girl." When I told
her, "Aurelia and my two sons (and Marcus' beautiful bride) were only 40
leagues away," she exclaimed, "Bring them to me as soon as possible.
Otherwise, I may not live long enough to hold them." We talked for an
hour before *King Geron* said, "She must rest." Finally, he asked, "What is
the purpose of your visit, Ivo?" I answered, "To propose Client status
for you to lead a big Germano-Roman Province to enrich many of your
men through cross-empire trade arrangements." Politely he replied, "If I
consented, Ivo, your embittered cousins would seek to depose me. Some
are expecting another Roman thrust into our lands. *Ansgar* will surely
incite more anti-Roman hatred when he learns you're here."

He then asked, "Have you captured or killed *Tribune Sabatini*, as you'd
promised, who murdered my son *Fulko*?" I attempted to explain my
efforts to find *Sabatini* in the *Combrogian-Cymru* lands known as *Cymruia*
(later called *Cambria—Wales*) or in *Queen Cartimandura's Brigantian Midlands*,
but he'd fled far north to hide among the "hard-foot" *Pictavi* tribesmen in
Caledonia. I also told King Geron, "If I'm sent to Britannia, I shall pursue
Sabatini. Meanwhile, I've been ordered to arrange a peace treaty with you

and as many *Germanic* tribes as I might be able to influence. *King Geron* answered,

> It's time for you to leave, Ivo. Nevertheless, you're welcome to bring your families here for a visit with our queen as soon as I can arrange it. I'll dispatch a messenger to confirm a date. Tell your leaders that further fighting won't bring surrenders, but will cost too many lives on both sides of your *Limes* border your Roman engineers are starting to establish too deep on my side of the *Rhein.*

We then rejoined our troops and headed back to *Colonia* where I reported, "There's resistance from the new Chatti king whom I've known from childhood." Since we'd carried that unwanted news back to our officials, I realized I'd earn no praise from the hostile commandant who frowned darkly at me, saying, "Tomorrow you shall report your failure to the governor and later to *Mogontiacum's* legate."

CHAPTER 9

TROUBLES

When Marcus and I reported my lack of success in the meeting with my tribe's king, the governor showed no surprise, saying, "Little change has taken place in this troubled region other than increased migration into *Germania Inferior* during my time here." After our discussion, the commandant apparently told the governor, "I question Ivo's loyalty to Rome." The next day I learned my command position would be withheld, and that I'd serve in "undetermined duties, pending a review of my loyalties." When the legate at Mogontiacun was informed, he responded,

> A petty feud arose from an event where your administrative commandant bungled an oratorical opportunity in front of hundreds of his troops and blamed his cavalry commander for not forewarning him of the surprise presentation of a special horse and not preparing scripted remarks for the occasion.

As I was preparing to move 90 leagues upstream, a message arrived from *King Geron*, saying,

> I've ordered my people to respect your entry into our territory to honor *Queen Swanhilde*. Carry this note of passage to remain if funerary ceremonies become likely. Beware of threats from your cousins who've been displaying their tall *Suebenknotten*. In honor of our queen, I've ordered all to remain civil. Please hurry——her time is short!

Before we left, Marcus learned the governor had favored the legate's view and had reversed the commandant's recommendation, suggesting instead, "It's time to send *Blandus* back to Rome and elevate Marcus to the commandant position at *Colonia*, taking effect three weeks from now.

The Funeral

We journeyed to King Geron's distant *oppidum* in September, arriving during twilight to find *Tante Swanhilde* alert, but wasted, and surrounded by her many descendants anticipating her imminent death. As King Geron escorted us to her bedside, a low murmur arose from my cousins, but their remarks were constrained by an elevated hand of their king. As Aurelia stepped forward, the queen brightened, saying, "At last you're with me again, my Golden One." After a tearful embrace, Aurelia introduced Sabina and each child (including Sabina's adopted one), all who seemed bewildered by the weak hugs and the gloomy sight of the "old one" whom little Marco called, *"Oma Geistus"* (Grandma Ghosty).

As we each held the queen's fleeting attention, the others kept a respectful silence until we were escorted into the great timber hall where *Ansgar* made threatening remarks, calling us "dirty Romans." It was difficult to restrain myself, but Marcus calmed the drink-embolden cousins by speaking of our days under *Odalric*'s training when he'd called us, *"my future warriors,"* allowing Ansgar to brag of his athletic superiority. Later that night (as we sat at the king's long table raising steins to our queen and former king), one of her attendants entered the hall to whisper to King Geron of *Queen Swanhilde's passing.*

That night she was shrouded in her finest linens and brought to the hall in a splendid carved oak coffin for tomorrow's ceremony. That morning (with hundreds attending), six grandsons carried her body to the nearby burial ground where each descendant placed a single bloom on her casket as her bearers lowered it beside former *King Clodovech*. A special feast followed with kegs of *Dunkelbraun Bier.* To avoid an unpleasant scene, I told Marcus,

> Gather our families while I get the horses. We must leave before strong drink ruins this day. If we remain, incivility will arise (fueled by harsh invective). I'll ask *King Geron* to meet us in front so we can bid

him a respectful farewell. Tell Sabina and Aurelia we'll stop halfway at a Chatti farmhouse to bed the children for the night.

Back at *Claudia Ara Agrippinensium*

To my great surprise, I was told I was not being sent to Mogontiacum as previously ordered; but assigned to replace *Blandus*. Because of the governor's decision, Sabina and Aurelia would become leaders in our Romano-tribal society. In addition, our children would learn tribal dialects from daily contacts with Germanic and Celtic playmates. Aurelia became a tribal favorite because she spoke Chatti and Cherusci dialects almost fluently. She was also called *Das Lorelei Mädchen* who'd risen from the Rhein *"um Ihr goldenes Haar im Abendsonnenschein zu kaemmen"* (to comb her golden hair in the evening sunshine). Wherever she went in the city, children followed her singing *ein Märchen aus alten Zeiten* (a tale from old times).

Soon word spread among the *Ubi* tribesfolk of Aurelia's power to charm the children as the enchanting *Rheinmädchen* who'd survived the disastrous October 37 AD raid, thereby inheriting the mythical *Lorelei's* riverine powers to charm all whom she met. Therefore, she became more of a diplomat than me and received endless invitations to dine with all levels of *Colonia's* society. Meanwhile, Marco and Vespan enjoyed their own celebrity and became increasingly active as winter passed into the Ides of March of AD 53 when Marco turned four and Vespan two.

At the same time, Sabina's pregnancy was normal with an expected delivery in May. Although she could've returned to Rome, she chose to birth her first child in *Colonia*, saying, "We have top-quality midwives here; Aurelia's *matronae* can instruct me during the final days. The fetus must surely be a boy—it kicks so much."

Ten days later (on April 5th, after nine hours of labor), Sabina delivered two blue-eyed girls, one who'd been given a boy's name. When Marcus arrived, he asked, "Where's my boy?" To which Aurelia said,

> Sabina's resting. Meanwhile, your daughters await female names. You may see them when e'er you wish. Perhaps Brother, you should suggest their grandmothers' names when you speak to Sabina. Since

our mother is dead and Sabina's still lives, ours should precede. Meanwhile, we've called one *Marcia*, a feminized version of Marcus.

Marcus answered, "Good choice, Aurelia! Take me to Sabina, I shall tell her to name the children after our mothers. We'll use *Marcella* first (from which you've derived Marcia). Sabina's mother's name, *Helena,* will follow, from the Trojan beauty whose face launched a thousand ships."

He then led little *Flavia* to see the tiny newborns, who Marcus held like fragile ornaments. He then passed one to Flavia, who spoke sadly in *Galego, "I want faraway brother Trupo."* Just then, Sabina awoke saying, "Perhaps a boy next time, Dear Marcus! What names have you chosen for our *bambine?*" He replied, "They shall be *Marcella* and *Helena,* inheriting their grandmother's beauty. You know Ivo and I will be afield through this summer, but I'll return whenever possible. Take good care of *Marcella, Helena,* and *Flavia.*"

Antón's Lusitani Troopers and Horses

Three months before, when searching for Marco in Mauritania, I'd sent Antón north to *Oporto* to buy replacement horses for ours that *Aulus Didius Gallus* had confiscated at Ostia. Not surprisingly, that powerful proconsul, who was now Governor-General of Britannia, had promised to pay for our elegant animals, but no money had arrived. Marcus forwarded another bill (acknowledged by a staff tribune), but no payment was made because he called the horses "army property."

One afternoon Antón introduced his 16 *Lusitani* recruits who'd come to *Colonia* riding their own good warhorses. They'd also driven 12 mixed-breed workhorses, and five stately *Lusitanis* that Antón had kept as replacements for those the Britannic governor now rides.

We welcomed those skilled young riders into my unit, feeding and quartering them with Hispanic bowmen in a new barrack we'd completed. At dinner Antón told me of his brother's difficulties of finding and buying these rare horses and of problems driving them across Iberia and Gallia to prevent thievery by horse-hungry tribesmen. His brother, *Joãozinho* (Litte John) who'd come to Germania, was eager to tell us of his monotheistic religion that he said, "Is now reaching the farthest corners of Iberia."

After *João*'s inspired religious lecture, I inspected Antón's herd, from which I chose a mature dabbled grey (surely related to those in Britannia). Marcus chose a nearly identical one, while Antón kept the black one his brother had ridden from *Lusitania*, leaving me with two pretty black colts for Marco and Vespan to ride when older.

Antón told me he'd learned of this special breed that had come from a single white Persian stud found high in the Atlas Mountains. He added,

I met a *Salamantican* grandee on a remote *Sierra de Gata latifundium* in *Estremadura* who breeds these intelligent horses with uphill stamina beyond any he'd known. He told me, "Since you've brought me gold coins, I shall reserve some of the best young ones for you." He then called one, saying, "This colt was born black, but will turn white or grey as it matures." He then touched its brow, saying proudly, "Someday my expanding *de Gata* lineage will be known as the finest horses anywhere."

CHAPTER 10

GERMANIA

Until now, my troopers had performed only guard duties. Since frequent threats had risen from my cousins (who'd become war chiefs), I was ordered to make contact with less warlike kings to deter conflict, or tell them "they'd feel the wrath of Rome's mighty legions." This trip began with another dash into Chatti territory to negotiate with Geron and his chiefs about expanding trade. For security, I took 36 Germanic auxiliaries——most of whom camped a league behind in case of trouble. When I arrived at Geron's *oppidum*, 14 neighboring clan chiefs greeted me coolly, backed by hard-faced guards. Although some chiefs listened closely when talk turned to profit, the overall conclusion held with one saying, "We value our freedom too much to be ruled by Rome!" I then explained,

> The *Suebi* and *Agri Decumati* tribes to the south and the *Usipeti* and *Gugerni* to the far north are already participating in our client-society experiment and are becoming rich. Many of their young men are now serving in our army and are living in distant cities across the Empire. Speak with any of my Germanic auxiliaries camped behind us.

Despite talks with my troops, King Geron reported, "Most chiefs dislike your proposals." To avoid unpleasantness, I told him of Roman threats and asked him to delay any response. We got approval to continue across the *Visurgis River* into the *Hereynian Forest* to visit other tribes that had dispersed to avoid reprisals. When we met another tribal king, I was welcomed because Geron had sent a rider who told of my regal heritage and of eased relationships with other *transrhenic* leaders. At one fortress, an old warrior-chief (who'd fought at Teutoberg 44 years ago) told us of Roman brutality and slaughter, pronouncing, "Sir Ivano, we can never be at peace with Rome. There are thousands of tribesmen in a dozen tribes east of here whom you'll never defeat. Tell your greedy rulers to stay west of our river. Where go you now, Odalric's Chatti-Romano Prince?" In response, I insisted, "I'm no prince, only a cavalryman!" To which he answered,

> You are a grandson of *Odalric*, under whom I served in the greatest battle ever fought on our Germanic homelands. If you be anything like *Odalric*, my brave young peacemaker, you are indeed a Chattian prince and will someday fight in another great battle! So, *Prince Ivano*, I'm honored to be meeting with you. Please convey my words to *King Geron* that I can call ten thousand men to arms, should he need them.

In answer to his question about where I was headed next, I told him,

> Since you've convinced me I won't win converts among our clans, I shall lead my Germanic auxiliaries to visit *Sigambri* and *Bructeri* tribes and their outlying clansmen who may be ready to enjoy empire client privileges. If they're unwilling, the legions may invade again.

He replied, "Don't waste your troops, Chatti Ivano! We'll be waiting! You're unlikely to find friendship among those tribes." As we moved onward to visit more clans, I told our men,

> The *Sigambri* are a battered old tribe of warriors who've lived many years between the *Lippe* and *Sieg* Rivers. They're bordered to the east by *Marsi*, to the west by *Gallic Celts*, to the north by the *Usipeti*, and by the south by *Tencteri*. Despite current unfriendliness, they've supplied auxiliaries to our armies after the *anti-Drususian* campaigns fifty years ago.

When we arrived, the oldest chief didn't greet me. Instead, he sent his Latin-speaking son who insisted, "You Romans aren't welcome here; please explain why a Chatti prince is now a Roman officer." I replied,

"I come in friendship to explain advantages of clientships with Rome." To which he smirked, adding, "I've been to Rome and heard it all before, I've explained it to my elders, but they hold bitter memories." He continued,

> A century ago, Caesar crossed the Rhein, burning villages for 18 days. Our people were on the east bank with the *Eburoni* tribe between the *Sieg* and *Wupper Flüsse*. Two years later, 200 of our warriors defeated *Quintus Tullius Cicero* at *Atuatuca* where he was leading seven cohorts of *Legio XIV*. Caesar re-invaded our territory and left 12 cohorts on our side of the river to remind us of his strength, which stopped us from raiding into Gaillia.

I added, "After Augustus established his *Pax Romana*, many *Barbarian* Tribes became *foederati* (brother tribes), settling in the Empire. The *Sigambri* subchief shouted, "Hold, my Roman friend, I've much to say about your *Augustus*."

> That bloody tryant treated us poorly. After subduing the *Vindelici* tribe many years ago, he sent *Drusus Germanicus* who defeated us and our allies. In turn, we crushed one of his legions, invaded *Gallia*, and plundered Romanized territories. His cavalry rushed to the rescue with another disastrous outcome for his legionaries whom we destroyed in ambush. We also defeated *Marco Lollius* and captured his legionary eagle. *Augustus* came to extend Rome's burdens, but *Suebi*, *Cherusci* and *Sigambi* tribesmen surrounded *Druso's* army in a dense forest where we were winning until the battle favored his legionaries, who captured and sold some clans in their vast slave market.

We then discussed aftereffects of the Teutoberg disaster where three legions had been annihilated, which led *Tiberius* and *Germanicus* to carry out bloody campaigns to avenge the insult. After drinking many beers, we became friends, but I made no progress toward linking the *Sigambri* to the Empire. I departed agreeing to recruit more of his youth as auxiliary cavalrymen. As I was leaving, an old chief spoke remorsefully,

> We once occupied all of the lands between the *Rhein* and *Weser* Rivers. We remained the most reluctant tribe to join Rome, even after

being severely beaten during *Tiberius'* brutal campaigns. Because our neighbors were deported to *Gallia,* my people refused to move, causing thousands to become slaves or accept death. We still harbor deep resentments toward Rome even though one of my auxiliary cohorts participated in *Consul Gaius Sabino's* war against the *Thraci.*

As we mounted our horses, I thanked the chief's son for his big steins of his good *Sigambric* beer. He replied, I'm likely to become the next chief of this shattered tribe; that responsibility will depend upon an election by our clan chiefs. If I win, I shall speak with you again, *Chatti Ivano.* Despite our new friendship, our *Sigambri* warriors shall remain independent."

CHAPTER 11

AD 53 AND 54

In November, we returned from our diplomatic sortie among the Germanic tribes to prepare for Europa's hard winter already upon us. After a warm welcome from our wives and children, we immediately plunged into preparations for winter. While we'd been gone, most of our population had spent the entire autumn harvesting bumper crops of spelt and building rainproof granaries for added food storage. Meanwhile, the women had dried all kinds of food items to help sustain our soldiers, town-folk, and farm animals over the next five months. Controlling winter food supplies brought Marcus and me to become *Uberagrimeisters* (farm overmasters) from our experience at the Tusculum *latifundium*.

During the long winter, we discussed new farming methods to be added in Germania. In talks with local leaders, Marcus told them,

> Thousands of captives do most of Rome's farm-and-orchard work. That practice is expanding across the Empire as many thousands more arrive to do our hardest fieldwork. Captives plow tillable fields in the fall and spring using iron-tipped plows to break the sod and enrich the soil with manure. We still harvest grain by hand, but a Roman engineer invented a reaping machine that makes harvesting faster on large fields. Since these *vallus* machines are new in Germania, *spelt* is still beaten by women to separate grain from chaff. Men in Italia pull a *tribulum* sled over big grain fields to remove seed-heads from dry stalks. That combing device speeds seed separation. We'll import a score of those *Punic Carts* to make winnowing quicker and less labor-intensive.

Roman farmers dry seeds on warm *hypocaust* floors and store grains in rat-proof granaries. Soon we'll be milling, screening, and sifting flour for baking rich loaves of bread.

Marcus also told our *Villicae*:

> Next year, you'll need to produce more grain to feed our growing population. Since much of our food comes from warmer climates, we must produce more here or stop the inflow of eastern people. We'll establish more orchards on the sunny riverside slopes. Like Rome's food production, we must expand ours on the big estates owned by *Colonia's* wealthy equestrians. You, my *Unteragrimeisters*, shall supervise our food-crop programs on these estates where new captives will work. Over 90 percent of our food-producing people will become a huge field army of skilled farm workers who must work or starve. Meanwhile, we must build more shelters so our new workers can survive the winter.

Family Time

Despite our attention to our food-storage and distribution problems, both Marcus and I spent many winter hours with our wives and children who'd remained healthy during these coldest times. Aurelia and Sabina were the prettiest women here, while Marco, Vespan, Flavia, Marcella, and Helena were our joys whenever we told stories and could see them grow into attentive personalities. Our children enjoyed the advantage of having two Grecian teachers, who'd been among the Athenian elite before recent uprisings. The youngsters were fortunate to have multilingual playmates from Belgic and Germanic families and loved our storyteller, *Vibi*, who was always ready to entertain all who eagerly awaited his folk tales.

Although we counted Rome's years from 753 BC, each year was named for two consuls who held office each year. Hence, AUC *806* (AD 53) became the year of *Decimus Junius Silanus Torquatus* and *Quintus Haterius Antoninus*. In addition, we learned of an imperial decree that gave financial jurisdiction to procurators, strengthening Emperor Claudius' power over the Senate. We also heard that 16-year-old *Nero* had married the emperor's daughter (Claudia Octavia) and that *Claudius* had foolishly accepted *Nero* as his successor (instead of his son *Britannicus*), foreshadowing a future ruler that few citizens could favor.

As the summer of AUC 807 (AD 54) approached, I attempted another round of diplomatic appeals, offering ten tribal chiefs added economic advantages. Most refused. Marcus had moved upstream to Mogontiacum to become Legate of *Legio XXII* and I became *praefectus castrorum* and acting *tribune laticlavus*, commanding *Colonia's* vexillations.

Another Assassination

Emperor Claudius had married *Agrippina the Younger* in AD 49, becoming the stepfather of Nero. Now (in AD 54) Nero became emperor after his great-uncle/stepfather Emperor Claudius was poisoned by the power-hungry Agrippina. Therefore, *"bumbling Claudius"* (as he was sometimes called) was succeeded by his *"even more bumbling"* teenage stepson (*Nero Claudius Caesar Augustus Germanicus*) who most citizens believed, "hadn't been involved in the Emperor's death." News of the assassination reached us five days later, announcing, "Nero didn't instigate the murder, but likely knew of his mother's plan. After Claudius' death, Nero insulted Claudius' memory, charging him with cruelty and calling his decrees, "the works of a madman."

From my time in the Guards, I knew that *Agrippina, Seneca,* and *Burrus* had dominated young Nero. A power struggle arose among those ambitious advisers with Agrippina trying to dispose of *Seneca* who'd been providing Nero the advice he wanted to hear. At the same time, Nero's friends told him to beware of his scheming mother. We soon heard,

> Young Emperor *Nero* was dissatisfied with his wife. Because of his affair with slave-girl *Claudia Acte*, he resisted his mother's attempt to intervene. He'd met *Acte* when he was 16 and continued a passionate affair during his marriage. As mistress, she learned *Agrippina* exercised erotic powers over her son. Fearing for her safety, *Acte* warned Nero, "There'll be repercussions if your incest becomes public." Because her relationship had reduced *Agrippina's* influence, *Nero* rejected his mother's control.

As my Claudian favorites were being displaced, Marcus told me, "It's a good time to be far from Rome, especially during Nero's disposal of those loyal to Claudius that will soon reach appointees like us in the provinces." That belief was reinforced by orders to all recent appointees, "Retain your current positions until further notice," delaying Marcus' assumption of legionary command at Mogontiacum and leaving me in temporary command at *Colonia*—not a bad consideration while Nero's actions were affecting many across his troubled empire.

In Nero's first year, violence erupted in *Judaea* from an ordinance restricting Jewish rights. Rome's garrison had sided with the Jews, causing armed men to hold the port of *Caesarea Maritima*. *Governor Antonius Felix* ordered an attack, foreshadowing years of trouble in that province. In Britannia, *King Venutius* had revolted against his ex-wife (the Brigantian Queen) *Cartimandua* (now a Roman ally), causing *Governor Aulus Didius Gallus* to send *Caesius Nasica's Legio IX* to defeat *Venutius'* Brigantian rebels.

A New Governor at Colonia Agrippina

After affairs settled following the Claudian assassination, Nero's appointees began arriving with *Pompeius Paulinus* assigned to govern *Germania Inferior* from *Colonia*. Since I'd been serving as commandant there, Aurelia and I greeted the new governor and his wife. My first impression was *"another weak equestrian,"* who regretted being posted far from Rome. I'd also learned he'd never been a soldier and looked with distain on combat officers. At our welcoming dinner, our new governor bragged,

> I've served as Rome's *Prefect of Provisions*—the highest official charged with distributing the limited grain supply throughout the City. In times of scarcity, I rationed all provisions. In my second year, *tax-collector greed* made the emperor repeal indirect taxes to win the hearts of his people. Many senators worked to halt his beneficence, pointing out, "the empire will dissolve if revenues are diminished." To solve that problem, I devised an accounting system of income and disbursements. My restraint on tax collectors was unpopular with my rich friends, so the emperor gave me judicial precedence against

the collectors. Thereafter, grain ships weren't taxed making food movements less costly.

I soon found the new governor understood many tribal problems, but was eager to let me deal with the tribes, especially if they'd remain peaceful. He'd been here one week when I told him,

Up to now, everything's been quiet here. To keep our soldiers busy, we've completed an embankment project begun 63 years ago to confine rising waters of the Rhein. Our troops also finished a canal that linked the Moselle and the Arar Rivers to the Rhone so we could float cargoes from the Moselle and Rhein to the *Mare Atlanticus*. As a result, movements have been hastened from Germania to the *Mare Internum*.

CHAPTER 12

AD 55

With Nero's attention focused on his own problems and those in eastern provinces, we enjoyed a peaceful period in *Germania*. Because of Senator *Aquilus'* influence, the Senate confirmed both Marcus and me in our current positions. To our surprise, those assignments were approved by Emperor Nero who'd accepted only ten others, setting in motion command changes of legates and subordinate commanders, forcing early retirements of nine highly qualified officers and a score of tribunes. Despite many changes, our year remained quiet, allowing us to concentrate on food production, trade, tribal matters, security, and enjoying life with our wives and children.

Marco (age 6) was the commander of his playmates and Vespan (age 4) was speaking three fractured languages. Meanwhile, Sabina had written that Flavia (age 6½) and Marcella and Helena (both age 2) were thriving, but pretty little Flavia was haunted by memories of her lost brother somewhere in far away Mauretania. As a result, Aurelia said, "I want to visit Sabina this summer while our people are busy with farming matters."

At the end of June, we boarded a red-and-grey 20-oared actuaria-class executive transport called *"Falko Pullus"* (grey falcon) and headed upriver past the west-bank settlements of *Bonna* (Bonn) and *Rigomagus* (Remagen), and to *Confluentes* (Koblenz) where we spent the night. The next morning, we sped past *Boudobriga* (Boppard) and slowly by the site where I'd rescued Aurelia and Marcus from the Rhein 17 years ago. Later, we passed *Bingium* (Bingen) before arriving at *Mogontiacum* where we were greeted by Sabina and her children (plus senior staff officers and their wives). We soon learned Marcus was away on an inspection tour up the *Moenus River* (the Main) visiting scores of legionaries posted at border forts guarding river crossings vulnerable to penetrations along the eastern edge of *Germania Superior.* When he returned, we enjoyed a reunion where Marcus told of his need for a stronger border between *Germania Superior* and *Germania Magna,*

> Since Emperor Augustus' death, we've accepted the *Rhenus* and *Danuvius Rivers* (Rhein and Danube) as frontier's boundaries. Beyond these rivers we've tried to secure a vast plain along the southern fords to the Black Forest. Your downstream section, where the Rhein is deep and broad, has been a key boundary for 40 years. However, my upstream part called the *Agri Decumates* is different because my narrow rivers are easily crossed. My frontier is too long to enclose the huge territory I'm asked to control.

Late that afternoon he continued,

> Roman officials are calling for a longer *"Limes Germanicus Grenze"* (border) to separate the unsubdued tribes from *Germania Inferior, Germania Superior,* and *Raetia.* When complete, it should stretch from the North Sea, breaking east here and running south through forests and rivers to *Castra Regina* (Regensburg) on the *Danuvius.* The major rivers had afforded natural protection from incursions into our territory; however, the weakest part is my gap from here to *Castra Regina.*

At dinner, he added,

> Roman engineers want to extend the *Limes Germanicus* across the Taunus Mountains to the *Moenus* (Main) then east to that river's "knee" and south to *Virolunum* (Württemberg). Its full length will be 350 miles and include 60 forts and hundreds of watchtowers. The weakest part will be my gap to the *Danuvius.* These 200 miles between the rivers permit large groups to move west; hence, forts are needed along roads, at fords, and on hilltops. I'll be gone when it's done, but now my troops are scattered along this dismal line, shivering in half-built camps and cold towers.

Marcus then told me,

> *Spur* wrote that *Milo* will lead survey teams across the north edge of my
> region to mark a roadway paralleling the future fortification line. I've been
> ordered to provide protection and logistic support during his mapping
> effort. Perhaps you and Aurelia could host his family this summer.

The following Monday, Aurelia and I, with our rowdy boys, boarded
a sleek riverboat for a fast downstream run to *Colonia*. Although it was
difficult for the captain to slow his boat past the steep granite cliff,
the rowers stroked to hold a position where I recounted the tale of my
tribe's AD 37 raid, on which Aurelia, Marcus, and their mother (and other
Roman family members) had been traveling. After I told how we'd saved
Aurelia and Marcus, little Marco asked, "Where's *Oma* now?"

Embarrassed by Marco's inquiry, I told him, "Your grandmother was
lost in the river." I turned to comfort Aurelia from the memory of her
loss on the very spot where I'd saved her from the frigid river. Although
my telling had backfired, it had reinforced my love for Aurelia, realizing
how fortunate we'd been for 17 years. We then sat close, holding the boys
as we sped downstream, pointing out occasional *Hirsh* and *Roe Deer* (at the
river's edge) that fled as we passed.

Soon we were home where I read a note from Milo telling of his
upcoming duties and proposing a family visit as soon as possible. He was
also asking for details on hostile tribes in his survey region and seeking
assistance from retired legionaries who spoke regional dialects, or from
Romanized Germanic auxiliaries serving in our legions.

The Survey Team

Ten days later, Milo arrived at *Colonia* with his family and 62-year-old
Spur, showing orders from Rome that obligated us to provide security,
logistical support, and surveyors from our own squadrons. Since Milo
was the project's leader, he'd command 21 surveyors (7 from Britannia and
14 whom Marcus and I would provide). In addition, Marcus would provide
80 guards, while I'd provide cooks, camp tenders, and medical personnel,
as well as boats and rowers from the *Classis Germanica* (the Rhein Naval
squadron) based at Colonia's port.

After a round of business, Milo and Acacia settled into guest quarters with their boys, accompanied by Spur and his wife. That evening we hosted a dinner attended by staff officers and retirees who'd served with Spur and Milo in Britannia. At that event, we learned Milo's Claudian temple project had fallen far behind schedule after Nero became emperor. Nevertheless, Milo's engineers (with tribal labor) had completed almost two hundred miles of high-standard military roads in southern Britannia, despite occasional outbreaks of tribal resistance against Rome's northward expansion. After a round of toasts, Spur told of his recent trip to Rome and of the marvelous marble buildings he'd seen after being away for 30 years. Milo followed, thanking us and saying,

> I welcome this opportunity to revisit my homeland. Although Brother Ivo rarely mentions it, I helped rescue Aurelia and Marcus from the river 17 years ago. That event led to my education in Rome and brought me back to my homelands where I'm obligated to protect *Roman Germania* from my tribesmen and neighbors who are breaking into Rome's peaceful empire.

As the event ended, Milo added,

> Tomorrow we shall begin our three-part survey. Ivo, your *Colonia*-based engineers will survey the first segment over the Taunus Mountains to the *Main River*. We'll gather support and protection from Marcus at *Mogontiacum*, where Spur's team will work along the *Main* through *Mittenburg* and beyond the *Necker* toward *Vicus Aurelius*. Finally, I'll lead my team into the southern segment along the *Limes Transdanubianus* line to Rome's Raetian fortress at *Castra Regina*. I want to reassemble all three teams back here at *Colonia* about six weeks from now. To all of you, be safe and accurate in your work!

The next morning, we sent Milo and my personnel upstream to *Legio XXII's* headquarters where Marcus met them. At the same time, I launched my team toward the Taunus Mountains on a segment we hoped to map with little resistance because of appeals to my Chatti cousins, asking them, "Please don't interfere with my survey team that will pass through *"Opa Oldaric's Forests."*

CHAPTER 13

SURVEY

We soon received reports from Marcus and Milo as their teams moved without interference. When Milo's first report came in, I briefed the governor about the tribes with whom his team had been dealing. I began,

> Sir, as you may already know, the *Hermunduri* formerly occupied the upper Elbe River system. When Governor *Domitius* ruled the *Danubian* districts, he intercepted that tribe's scouts who were seeking a new home north of the Danube. They're now mixing with the *Irminones (Hermioni)* who claim to be loyal to Rome. Hence, we expect favorable dealings with both tribes.

Milo's next report told of the largest tribe, about which I told the governor,

> The *Marcomanni* (Suebic-confederation co-leaders) live north of the *Danube* where they're called *frontier men*. They'd settled near the *Main* 60 years ago where Drusus defeated five tribes (including *my Chatti* people). When Drusus pushed the *Marcomanni* into *Boihaemum, King Marbod* established a powerful kingdom Augustus called, *"a serious threat to Rome."* After more tribal mergers, *Vibilius* became king with whom Milo is currently dealing.

Soon after, Marcus reported,

The Suebs control many subordinate tribes in *Germania Magna*. The confederation uses the name *Suebi* instead of *Germani* when identifying itself. South Germania was Celtic, but the *Helvetii, Boii,* and *Tectosagi Celts* left the *Hercynian Forest* and joined the *Suebic* confederation.

I continued,

Some Celts live north of the Danube, allowing the *Marcomanni* to hold the *Boihaemum* area. The Suebic king united six tribes and moved against our frontier. As the *Hermunduri* entered Raetia, they forced other tribes to move. The *Quadi* entered the *Luna Forest,* the *Adrabaecampi* occupied the *Gambreta Forest,* and the *Varisti* settled north in the *Sudetes Mountains.*

At that point, the governor responded, telling me,

That bully Caesar forced many tribes from their homes, pushing them into the *Bacenis Forest* where the *Marcomanni* dominated from the Elbe to the Rhein. Although the *Langobardi* and *Hermunduri* now live past the Elbe, you'll find other eastern clans crowding our border. Augustus planned to incorporate Germania as one big province he called *Germania Magna,* but he was frustrated when *Arminius* forced his legions back to the Rhein. Later, our legions began expeditions to fortify our holdings, operating bases at *Castra Vetera* and *Mogontiacum* from where the legions radiated.

When the governor finished, I read Marcus' mid-segment report,

My team has dealt with tribal leaders speaking *Gallic* and *Pannonic* dialects. We've met *Lugi-Buri* leaders in the *Askibourgi Hills* near *Sidoni* and *Cotini; I've also met Visburgi* tribes in the *Hercyian Forest.* We'll soon meet with *Didounoi* and *Burgundi* leaders beyond the Oder.

Governor Pompeius continued,

Claudius wanted a strong border to hold back thrusts into our vulnerable provinces. If we don't slow them, we'll face unrelenting pressures on our border. Your legionaries will face a million wanderers who want to grab our expanded food production. We need to recruit more friendly border tribes to cushion what will become a strongly fortified *Limes*.

The next time I met Governor Pompeius, he was even more agitated after receiving letters from Nero's staff. I briefed him on Spur's moves in the middle region, mentioning that no report had come from Milo's team. Causing him to shout, "Can't your dumb-ass brother write a simple progress report?" I responded, "Since no contact has been made, Marcus has dispatched two legionary centuries to search for the team." On hearing that news, the governor fell silent, then mused,

> When powerful Suevi warrior kings moved down the Rhein's east bank a century ago, they stopped at the Main. Later members of that alliance slaughtered scores of our centurions. To counter their cruelty, Drusus marched into that middle region to subdue 12 tribes, but didn't conquer them. The Marcomanni king confederated four more tribes and appeared peaceful, but their current war-making potential worries me.

Pompeius fell silent when a staff tribune asked, "What shall we do, Sir?" In a delayed response, the governor blurted,

> Mount a century of your best riders and join *Legio XXII's* infantry on a march into the Danubian lands north of *Raetia*. Send a dispatch to the garrison commander at *Argentoratum* (Strassburg) of our move. I'll write the Raetian governor at *Augusta Vindelicorum* (Augsburg) telling of Milo's missing team and ask for support should resistance arise.

Our Attempted Rescue Mission

I led 80 mounted bowmen to *Mogontiacum* in September, finding Marcus had already led 160 legionaries to *Noviumagus* (Speyer) where they'd built a marching camp at *Vicus Aurelius* (Öhringen). Since we were behind, we crossed the *Mogontiacum Bridge* and followed the Necker on a two-day move toward *Iciniacum* (Theilenhofen) that served as part of Rome's boundary. We met Marcus there and proceeded together to the end of Milo's survey markers near *Osterburken*'s wooden observation tower.

In talks with Raetian soldiers, I learned Milo's team had crossed the *Jagst* and *Kocher* tributaries of the *Necker* from where they'd trekked into the *Agri decumantes* wing above Roman *Raetia* moving toward *Opia, Losodica,* and *Bricana* (Oberdorf, Munningen, and Weidennurg). As we followed Milo's trail, we met friendly *Naristi* tribesmen and Roman soldiers from *Augusta Vindelicum* who told us, "The team headed east, following the *Alcmona River* to the Danube at *Alkimoennis* (Kelheim) short of *Castra Regina*." After we'd traveled six days, we found more survey markers at the ford of a north-flowing tributary of the *Regnitz* where we entered the forests of *Hermunduri, Fosi, Semnoni, Langobardi,* and *Warni* tribes. We then followed Milo's tracks that led toward a tribal center at the *Regnitz-Pegnitz* confluence.

When we arrived, we faced scores of armed warriors who outnumbered us ten times with some wearing Roman armor and brandishing Milo's guards' *scuta* (shields) and *gladii* (short swords). Since Marcus and I agreed we faced unwinnable odds, we parlayed to avoid bloodshed, which might have led to warfare that might take years to resolve. Therefore, I rode with Marcus and Antón on our showy *Lusitani* horses toward a white-bearded elder, who wore a *Suebenknott*, looking much like my grandfather *Odalric*.

As we approached with *Antón* riding his black Lusitani mare, all eyes were on our horses rather than us. I dismounted in front of the one I assumed to be *King Vibilius*, remaining silent until he spoke. He looked me over, saying, *Bist du der Bruder der Chatti Mann, wer unser Markomanni Land misst? Warum kommst du mit so vielem Soldaten um uns zu besuchen?* (Are you the brother of the Chatti man who measures our land. Why do you come with many soldiers to visit us).

I addressed him formally (presenting the Governor's greeting) before asking of my soldiers' welfare, to which he answered, *"Mit den Soldaten und Ihrem inetlligenten Bruder ist alles gut."* (All is good with the soldiers and your smart brother). As he eased his warriors, he spoke, *"Ich sehe dass du mir ein gutes Pferd gebraht hast. Vielen Dank für das schwartze dass ihr hispanicsher Mann reitet."* (I see you've brought me a good horse. Thank you for the black one your Hispanian rides). As Antón slowly yielded his horse, I saw his "stone-faced look of regret" as he handed his horse's reigns to the King's nearest aide.

On my signal, Marcus dismounted. To the surprise of *King Vibilius*, the Roman legate spoke in a polished Chatti-Germanic dialect. Later, when we entered the King's oppidum, Milo came forward with his team and most of his supporting force, telling me, "Two soldiers drowned in a river and three auxiliaries found lovers here and have chosen to remain as *Markomanni*."

We remained two nights, discussing land claims, food-production, and how population growth had increased competition for *Germania's* lands, pushing weaker tribes into marginal areas. I told him of our desire to restrain the confederation's westward push, to which he replied,

Tell your masters I shall remain peaceful, but I have five million hungry tribesmen behind me who wish to push westward. Many have seen the enjoyments of your Equites. My warriors have tasted your foods and wines and want more. When they drink, they talk of taking Rhein valleys and your villas. After I'm dead, our young may come against Rome again.

I then explained a Roman view, telling him,

King Vibilius. Rome's expansion is based on similar needs. We too have five-million hungry people in our empire with a million in Rome. We depend on workers in many provinces to grow tons of grain and transport large shipments of meat and fish to sustain lives in our cities. Bread is in great demand during winter when grain comes only from Egypt. We need more workers to support our growing population.

Marcus added,

You must recognize Rome's legions can destroy any army you may mount. Despite our strength, we wish to remain peaceful and help finish this survey across your part of *Germania Magna* and extend the tranquil time our emperor calls the *Augustan Pax Romanorum*.

The king leveled his focus on Marcus whispering,

You Romans have poor memories. Less than 50 years ago, *Hermann der Cherusker* destroyed three of your emperor's best legions. I was not part of the confederation back then that included your *Chattimen*, but

I'll wager Ivano's clansmen were there at Teutoberg; *nicht wahr?* (Is that not true?).

I answered, *"Mein Grossvater* led Chatti clans in that memorable battle. He told me, "It was the fiercest warfare our tribe had ever seen." Marcus admitted, "I've heard much about *Die Schlacht im Teutoberger Wald*—the worst Roman defeat since *Hannibal Barca* killed 55,000 Roman soldiers at *Cannae* 271 years ago." That evening, the king hosted a ceremonial dinner where we agreed to hold further discussions, but no permission was granted for Milo to continue marking a border or build towers on what *King Vibilius* called *"Mein Markomannen Land."* As we mounted to depart, he told us,

> Tell your governor, "As long as I live, we'll block Germanic migrations into your *Agri decumantes* region." You can tell your emperor, "After I'm gone, Rome will need more *Foederati* tribes inside your proposed *Grenze* to withstand even greater migrations." I'll agree to work with you who understand our needs. You'll be welcome here for further discussions.

CHAPTER 14

COLONIA

We departed King Vibilius' *oppidium* heading west on a four-day march
to the Necker and on to *Lopodunum* where we loaded our infantrymen
and survey equipment on rivercraft to *Mogontiacum*. Meanwhile, Marcus,
Milo, Antón, and I rode on Roman roads west of the Rhein through
Borbetomagus, Altiaensum, Bingium, and *Boudobriga* (Worms, Alzey, Bingen,
and Boppard), and home to *Colonia* where we reported arrangements made
with *King Vibilius* to restrain migrations, and of our failure to complete
Milo's border survey. Unfortunately, Governor Paulinus was in no mood
to tell Emperor Nero of our failure and shouted,

> Both of you are relieved of your commands. I'm transferring Milo here
> to direct my wall-building effort, my aqueduct project for channeling
> clear water into Colonia, my two special shrines dedicated to Mars and
> Mithras, and my headquarters to control all my army units along the
> Rhein.

Marcus tried to appeal our dismissal saying,

> We've made important progress and introduced the idea of hiring
> *foederoti* tribes to cushion against big migrations. Why not let Emperor
> Nero judge the value of our dealings with King Vibilius and of our
> reach to other chiefs? This fortified-border project may be premature,
> but you could claim your own *Pax Neronum* that will enrich this

city and help build your own new engineering works in peaceful Germania.

The governor remained quiet, digesting what Marcus had explained, then commented to disguise his aroused personal-profit motive (that Marcus had implied). Governor Pompeius softened his tone, saying, "I'm not convinced you can succeed against our enemies. Therefore, I want you to write a report telling Nero of my dealings with important kings and how we should delay *Limes* construction to sustain *"My Pax Neronum."* As we left the *praetorium,* Marcus said, "I was hoping to serve as *Legio XXII's legatus* so I could enter the senate as a heroic officer and live at Tusculum where Sabina and I could raise the children in style and comfort."

I told him, "Be patient my friend; you've planted the seed of an idea that may save us from Pompeius' wrath. Our salvation will depend on our report's content, which must favor the pompous bastard." After more discussion, I mentioned *"a light of greed"* I'd seen shining in the governor's eyes at the prospect of great wealth. Marcus denied introducing a greed motive, but he agreed Pompeius had suddenly tempered his vituperative remarks after hearing what he desired——a way to gain favor in Rome.

Two days later we finished the report that spoke in "glowing terms" of the governor's idea of sponsoring friendly near-border tribes as guardians inside the border in place of legionaries——thereby avoiding the cost of 200 miles of fortifications and saving the lives of hundreds of our infantrymen. I told Marcus, the winning slogan had come from *Pompeius'* own words: *"Europa's Pax Neronum."*

When Emperor Nero praised the governor for delaying fortifications, Pompeius shouted, "Disregard your firings; go spend a week with your families and your hot-headed cousins." Since all appeared to have turned out well, I sent a messenger to *King Geron,* requesting another visit to propose peace talks with cousins *Ansgar, Aldo, Lanzo, Vulfgang,* and *Hartwig,* and for Milo to visit uncles *Edmar* and *Anzo.* Gero responded promptly, inviting us to come before late-autumn weather made it too difficult for us to bring our wives and children. I returned a message immediately, announcing, "We shall arrive within four days."

Beyond the Taunus Mountains

In late October, I instructed Antón to position a dozen horses far up the *Logona* (the Lahn). Two days later we met Marcus and his family at *Confluentes* (Koblentz) where we rode an oared craft up the Lahn to where Antón waited with our well-fed horses. From there, we moved leisurely toward the site of the clan's village near the source of the *Adrana* tributary of *Visurgis* that flowed north to the *Mare Germanicum*.

As we approached, *Cousin Aldo* greeted us with his two smiling, toe-headed sons who offered us a big bag of *Brötchen und Würstchen* (hard rolls and sausages) and a big earthen jar of *Bier*. After a warm welcome, he led us to the great hall where King Geron had assembled clanmembers who sang an old *Folkslied*, then turned their attention to Milo, his Britonic *Frau*, and all of our young ones. Next, King Geron welcomed us with clansfolk responding in full measure. Before the greetings ended, I asked Geron, "Why such a different attitude than when we were here before?" He answered, "All is well with your cousins except Ansgar who has joined raiders preying on riverside settlers. He has sworn to harm you if you don't capture or execute the tribune who killed Fulko." I responded,

> I've not forgotten my oath. However, I've been far from Sabatini for three years. The last I heard of him, he was with the *Picts* in *Caledonia*. If I get assigned to Britannia (as our legions move northward), I'll return him to you before he can harm other girls or boys. If Ansgar returns, tell him I'll honor my obligation. I'll reaffirm my pledge with my other cousins even though I'm a Roman officer.

We spent two days feasting while the women talked babies, the children played games, and we drank beer and sang *Volkslieder*. Soon it was time to depart as November storm clouds hastened farewells and we mounted our horses (with each child enshrouded in woolen mantels and soft deer skins). We'd ridden about halfway when heavy snowfall began, whereupon we dismounted to consider our options. Since we were equidistant between the clan's village and our riverboat, we chose to press on until an even heavier snowfall obscured the trail completely.

Although each child was snug under his or her heavy coat and Hirsh skins that the clan had presented before we left, Aurelia, Sabina, and Acacia were shivering and appeared distressed from exposure. At that point, I said, "We've no choice but to construct a windproof shelter and start a fire to counter the stultifying effects of the cold." Since Marcus and I were trained for winter survival, we cleared a spot in a thick birch grove and assembled a lean-to shelter under which we built a low fire to avoid dumping large accumulations from snow-burdened trees onto our incomplete shelter. Meanwhile, Milo collected semi-dry branches and kept the fire controlled while Marcus and I added damp deadfall limbs to the fire that slowly relieved the womens' pains. Fortunately, the children remained bundled and slept warmly packed tightly near the fire.

Marcus and I remained awake all night adding a stick-and-snow wall to deflect the wind and to reawaken Milo periodically to attend the fire. Near midnight, the snowfall ended, allowing me to look after our horses that were all eager to chomp handsful of millet from leather nosebags while Marcus and I warmed our hands beneath their shaggy winter manes.

With the women and children sleeping beneath snow-shrouded skins, Milo attempted to boil coarse gruel to feed them when they'd awaken. At first light, Marcus and I walked in opposite ways in search of the trail or anyone who could help us recover from the night's trauma. When I circled back to my outbound trail and into camp, I saw Marcus grinning and announcing, "I've found a tiny farm village where I alarmed an early riser by my ghostly appearance as a Chatti-speaking Roman officer."

A young clansman led us on to his farmstead where their women cooked a warm meal and fretted over our children, even though none had suffered from our night in the snowy woods. We spent four hours with our hosts before tramping onward through slumping mounds of wet snow. We finally arrived at the dock where the boat captain had waited long past our scheduled arrival time. We then floated down the *Logona* to the Rhein where an upstream boat took Marcus' family to Mogoniacum, while the rest of us continued downstream to Colonia.

After telling him about our favorable reception by my Chatti clan, the governor wrote to *Aulus Gallus* (Britannia's governor), recommending that Milo and Spur journey to Rome to tell the emperor and senators details of their border survey. Since it was deep winter, both overland and maritime travel to Rome were deemed, "too risky." A dispatch from Britannia's governor arrived a week later announcing,

I consider winter travel of my engineers too difficult at this time. Since you've already won praise from Roman authorities for your diplomatic efforts, both Milo and Spur can travel to Rome next spring if the *Limes* plan is still of interest to the emperor and senators. You must realize that I have many engineering problems with which I must deal here in Britannia since Nero became emperor.

Much to Aurelia's relief, we moved into renovated quarters with warm *hypocaustum* floors. Since I'd ordered my troops into winter quarters, my sub-commanders and my *Primus Pilus* directed *winter works* for hundreds of cavalrymen, infantrymen, auxiliaries, retirees, tribesmen, and slaves (who'd spent the autumn preparing for winter). We kept them active and disciplined by building or improving structures, training for future battles, and caring for horses, weapons, and personal equipment.... So, went the hard winter of AUC 808-809 (AD 55-56).

CHAPTER 15

AGRIPPINA

After Nero had been emperor one year, we began hearing about his strange relationship with his mother, *Agrippina*, who'd become Empress of Rome in AD 49 when she'd married her uncle Claudius (her third husband) to become the most powerful woman in the Empire. At that time, she also became stepmother of Claudius' daughters, *Claudia Antonia* and *Claudia Octavia*, and his son, *Britannicus*.

In her quest for power, she removed anyone from the imperial court who was loyal to the late *Valeria Messalina* (Claudius' third wife––the mother of Octavia and Britannicus). I could see that Agrippina was behind the removals of anyone whom she considered a threat to her position and her son's. One of her early victims was Britannicus' maternal grandmother (Messalina's mother, *Domita Lepida the Younger*). A few years ago, Marcus had told me,

> Agrippina was with Claudius at a parade of captive Britons where King *Caratacus* paid homage to her. A year later the title of *Augusta* was granted to her, only given to two other imperial women. That same year, Claudius founded our Germanic colony, *Colonia Claudia Ara Agrippinenium*, where she'd been born. The next year, she was given a ceremonial carriage, used only by priests and Vestal Virgins. She sponsored *Sextus Afranius Burrus* as commander of the Praetorian Guard, replacing *Rufrius Crispinus*, whom she couldn't control.

I remembered Agrippina had convinced Claudius to adopt her 13-year-old son *Nero Lucius Domitius Ahenobarbus*, after which she betrothed him to Claudius' ten-year-old daughter, *Octavia*. Agrippina then recalled *Seneca* from exile to tutor the future emperor about imperial power secrets. Gradually she deprived *Britannicus* of his heritage, isolating him from his father and his legitimate pathway to the emperorship. In AD 51, Agrippina ordered the execution of *Sosibius* (Britannicus' ex-slave tutor) because he'd expressed outrage by Claudius' naming Nero the imperial successor, instead of *Britannicus*. Nevertheless, Nero married his 13-year-old stepsister, Octavia in June 53. I'd heard later Claudius had said (a month before death), "I regret my marriage to Agrippina and my adoption of Nero. I again favor Britannicus for the throne instead of Nero." That reversal must have motivated Agrippina to eliminate Claudius, who'd become a threat to her son's march to power. Rumors abounded that Agrippina had poisoned her 63-year-old husband on 13 October 54, enabling 16-year-old Nero to rise——long before he was prepared for the position that Agrippina expected to dominate.

Power Struggle

Nero turned 17 only two months after becoming Emperor, but began exerting imperial power, naming Agrippina *Priestess of a Claudian Cult*. I also heard, "She sits in the Senate (behind a curtain) from where she exerts indirect power." It was further rumored, "She controls her son and the whole Roman Empire, but is losing control after Nero started an affair with slave-girl *Claudia Acte*" (of whom Agrippina strongly disapproved). The over-mighty mother was rumored to have excoriated her headstrong son and shifted her support to *Britannicus* in a mock attempt to make him emperor. In April 55, Britannicus died of poisoning, revealing the beginnings of a bitter mother-son power struggle. That same month I heard, "Nero forced Agrippina from the palace and deprived her of all honors and powers. He threatened to abdicate and move to Capri like Tiberius had done, *and* dismissed Burrus and Seneca, expressing hostility to Agrippina's influence."

He made her an outcast, with many calling her a danger to anyone who opposed her. We learned of senators who'd spoken against her becoming victims of her wrath. Marcus got a note from Senator *Aquilus* saying, "Empress Agrippina has begun court actions to reclaim land that had belonged to her second husband, *Gnaeus Domitius Ahenobarbus*, the father of Nero. Senator Aquilus included court records of Nero's unworthy father:

> *Consul Gnaeus Domitius Ahenobarbus* was the son of a renowned charioteer who'd become an *aedile* in 22 BC and *consul* in 16 BC. He then served as Governor of Africa and succeeded Tiberius, commanding the army that penetrated deep into Germania Magna. He was cruel and extravagant, whom many called the troublesome grandson of *Mark Anthony* and *Octavia Minor* on his mother's side. He'd been an imperial staff member, but later was ruled a murderer by Emperor Tiberius who charged him with treason, adultery, and incest. That infamous father of Nero died 15 years ago when his son was two.

Senator Aquilus added,

> The southern part of the land I'd acquired had been granted by Emperor Tiberius to Nero's great-grandfather. The title of that land had passed from debt-ridden *Gnaeus* to my close friend who sold it to me when he became too old to manage its many acres. The embittered Empress is now attempting to grab that land and all of mine, which she claims to have been granted by Emperor Tiberius.

He urgently addressed Marcus, concluding,

> Since you're now a junior senator, I need you here in Rome to protect your inheritance, which I'm ready to pass to you because of my advanced age and the recent pressures of this situation involving the powerful Empress. Although you and Ivo haven't completed your full terms as commanders on the Rhein, I might convince the emperor and his senior military staff to grant you a three-month leave of absence or a change of command so you can get here as quickly as travel permits.

Immediately, I consulted Governor Paulinus who showed no sympathy for a long leave of absence. Soon after, Marcus arrived from Mogontiacum, adding his concern about losing our vast holdings near Rome. In response, Paulinus groaned,

I can't allow both of you to be gone for three months during summer when some tribes are establishing new settlements, especially when our farm crops need to be guarded. Because Ivo has proven to be a successful negotiator, I need him here because he speaks Germanic languages better than any of my Roman commanders.

Marcus then appealed,

Governor Paulinus, we must support our other 598 senators against predatory actions by imperial-family outcasts. Because you know Senator Aquilus, you must realize we must protect senatorial lands from which our personal wealth arises. May I suggest you post Ivo as acting Legatus of *Legio XXII*. Then, I can speed to Rome to forestall my land crisis that may become a legal precedent if Agrippina wins.

Because the governor's family held a similar *latifundium* near Rome, he agreed, announcing, "Prepare to leave tomorrow, Marcus; Ivo can care for your family while you're gone." He then asked, "What will be your preferred route of travel?" Marcus replied, "On horseback up the Rhein past *Argentoratum* (Strasburg) then 240 miles to *Cabillonum* (Chalon) in Gallia, where I can float down the *Rhodanus* (the Rhone) 250 miles to *Arelate* (Arles) and across to *Massilia* (Marseilles), then by sea to Rome."

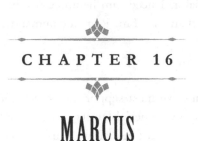

CHAPTER 16

MARCUS

Before Marcus and I left for Mogontiacum, I left my *optio* in command at Colonia and ordered him to move Aurelia and my sons upriver to temporary quarters next door to Sabina and her daughters. As soon as Marcus and I arrived at *Legio XXII's Principia,* a quick change-of-command took place, after which I picked six top cavalrymen to accompany Marcus (each riding a fast horse and leading a top quality spare).

Early the next morning, Marcus and his retinue headed south on the Roman road west of the Rhein, anticipating 40-mile-per-day legs on his 600-mile *ride-and-float trip* to the *Mare Internum* and another 400-mile water passage to Rome––a trip that could take 22 to 25 days depending on horse stamina and summer sea currents. At that point, I lost touch with Marcus, except by a report that said, "I arrived in Rome six days after leaving my horsemen in Gallia with *Flavius Quintilius"* (our Gallic friend). Weeks later another report told me,

> Actions against Empress Agrippina's land claim haven't gone well; we may lose your upland farm. Meanwhile, Senator Aquilus' lands also remain in dispute. The final decision will be Emperor Nero's in support of his alienated mother––or the Senate's in my favor.

A fortnight later another report told me,

> Little progress has been made since the Emperor and most senators have gone to their sea-breeze-cooled *villae* on Capri or up in the *Pennine*

Mountains. It appears I may remain here into the winter to settle this agonizing issue and assist our remarkable stepfather who claims he won't go to the underworld before that deadly viper who's made his late years an unending misery. Please tell Sabina and my girls I love and miss them and hope to be home soon.

Acting Legatus Ivano

Since Marcus had been gone 100 days, Governor Paulinus decided to make my temporary appointment permanent—at least until overridden by the Emperor or his generals (who exert personal views in the absence of Nero). Not long later, the governor's decision was approved, showing I still had friends in court, perhaps from my days as a member of the *Custodes Germanicus* imperial guards. However, the grizzled old *Primus Pilus* (the longest-serving member of *Legio XXII*) snorted, "Hold onto your gold-brush helmet, *my fine feathered friend*; you're not from Rome's equestrian class, so don't be surprised if some smug little *culus* (anus) from Rome comes out here with orders to replace you."

The next report from Marcus told me of his welcome to the Senate along with a score of young equestrians who'd completed much of their *cursus honorum* (ladder of offices), but had never served as commanders nor experienced combat. Since Marcus had already done both, he said,

> I've been granted seniority over the other 19 new senators and will be returning to Germania only to escort Sabina and the girls homeward; however, I can't leave Rome until this land issue is settled. Since late autumn is already on us here, you must be experiencing snows in Germania. If it's possible, Ivo, please arrange to move my family southward so I can meet them in warmer Gallia.

When I told Aurelia and Sabina of Marcus' proposal, they both blushed and giggled as Sabina slowly admitted, "You must tell Marcus I'm five months pregnant, and long-distance travel will be too risky for the fetus now." After I considered her condition, I replied to Marcus,

> Sea travel will be too rough this time of year, so it appears that each travel option is nearly impossible in the child's current stage of

development. Therefore, Sabina must remain with us 'til spring when our Germanic midwives will deliver the bambino or bambina.

When Marcus received my dispatch about Sabina's need to stay here, he answered, "I'll attempt to meet Emperor Nero and Senator Aquilus in an effort to resolve this land issue so I can return to Sabina." The old senator added this subscript, "The Empress has moved into my town villa and is claiming all of our farmlands and my 2,000-man workforce. It will be even harder to remove her unless Nero accepts the Senate's ruling in our favor."

As winter overtook Germania, Marcus' dispatches became fewer, leaving us to wonder if he'd attempt to travel around the Alpine Mountains to be with Sabina during her final pregnancy. Meanwhile, most of my attention was focused on my 4,800 restless legionaries and 1,600 auxiliaries who needed to be kept busy during four months of winter encampment.

Resolution

In December 56, Marcus reported, "Agrippina tried to move back into the palace in another effort to exert her influence over her 19-year-old son. As a result, the hostile young emperor expelled his mother again and sent her to a riverside estate in *Misenum*. While Agrippina lived there, or whenever she visited Rome, Nero sent people to annoy her because she'd remained too influential." Marcus aso wrote,

> Agrippina visited Nero the day before Senator Aquilus took me to the palace. Apparently, she'd riled young Nero to the degree that he agreed to allow us to retain the original latifundium and keep its work force; however, he chose to keep your land, knowing it had been his father's before Aquilus acquired it and built the beautiful new villa on it for Aurelia and you.

Another dispatch from Marcus arrived two days later telling us,

> Before we arrived, an officer from Nero's military staff briefed him about my *cursus honorum*, which led to questions as to why I'd vacated

my *Legatus* position in Germania. When I explained my relationship to the aging senator and the urgency of retaining our Tusculum farmlands, he asked if I wished to continue a military career or live at Tusculum. I told him I'd serve anywhere he desired, but would like you, the most effective officer in our dealings with tribal leaders, to continue in command in Germania. He then asked me to return later to discuss other postings.

Marcus Returns to Germania

As the heavy Germanic winter wore on into January and February of 57, dispatches became infrequent, leading us to believe Marcus might be making his way north. In late February, after dozens of stops at legionary outposts across Gallia, he arrived though a heavy overnight snow––without military escort. Although fit and warmly clothed, he looked more like a tribal warrior than a senior Roman officer, especially when riding a short but hardy Iberian *Pottoka* that "Looked like ancient images on cave walls."

When a guard escorted him into the *principia*, few staff members recognized him behind his untrimmed beard. After drinking a steaming cup of honey tea, he asked to go directly to Sabina nearby. I went to fetch Aurelia, but found she was already next-door with Sabina and a matron who said, "Master Marcus, our dear Sabina's likely to deliver a early."

We tiptoed quietly into the quarters where Sabina was sleeping and Aurelia was teaching Greek words and Roman numerals to the girls. Upon recognizing Marcus, the girls exploded with joy, which awakened Sabina who gurgled a happy welcome as she hugged him tightly with tears streaming. Moments later, we left them alone to talk, but Marcus soon rejoined us to enquire about Sabina's condition, which *"apparently requires lots of bed rest."*

At that point, Aurelia smiled and whispered, "My dear brother, the *matronae agree Sabina is carrying twins again* whom she hopes to be boys. Are you prepared to name them?" He burst into a wide grin, but didn't answer as he returned to Sabina's bedside, hugging and kissing her, and saying repeatedly how he'd missed her during his long absence, especially as he'd plodded through the dark and cold Gallic forests.

A week later, just as the *matronae* had predicted, premature boys were delivered without Sabina experiencing prolonged labor pains. As the first one was handed to Marcus (who'd been waiting in the adjacent room), he announced to Aurelia and me, "This one is *Gnaeus Cornelius Aquilus* after my father and our grand old senator; the other one shall be *Maximus Honorious Aquilus* after Sabina's father." Seeing how small each one appeared, he added, "Since the first one looks like a little wet rat and appears to be left-handed, I'll call him *Sinistro* (Wily). If the second one is right-handed he'll be *Dextro* (Ready)." He then returned to hug Sabina and to thank her for producing boys. When he told her the *cognomens* he chosen, she objected, claiming, "the first is unlucky, perhaps disadvantaging the little one."

As word spread that the former commander had become the father of two new warriors," a fast-assembled legionary choir sang praises to the goddess of motherhood and shouted, *"salve, salve, neonates Parvuli!"* A gathering of loyal legionaries then offered congratulatory wishes, shouting, *"Bona diem et valentudo, amicus."* (Good day and good health, our friends).

CHAPTER 17

AD 57

Governor Paulinus assigned Marcus as his *special assistant* during the next two months, while Sabina and her *matronae* got accustomed to handling the two tiny infants. Marcus' principal job was to oversee even-handed dispensing of grain and early spring imports from Egypt, Hispania, and Mauretania. In addition, he joined me in a springtime circuit of the tribes east of the Rhein, including a brief visit with Uncle Geron, whose clans had overwintered satisfactorily, and were re-plowing meadowland plots that had produced much of last year's vegetables and new spelt varieties.

King Geron looked quizzically at my legate's uniform and my shiny golden helmet with its high ornamental brush and then at Marcus' less impressive one asking, "Have you reversed your roles?" Our awkward explanation seemed to satisfy him, but left him asking, "Will you ever capture or kill the violent one who murdered Fulko?" To which I replied,

> You may remember, Milo told you he'd led road-building projects as Rome's occupation advanced northward in Britannia. Before he left here to continue his engineering projects, I asked if he knew of Sabatini's whereabouts. He later told me, "The evil one was last seen among the wild *Picts* with whom only a few Roman sea-merchants have traded. Someday I'll find him even if it takes the rest of my life. Now I'm fully committed as a Roman officer, but I'll honor my pledge when I'm back across the *Fretum* at *Camulodunum* or farther north at the new fortress Milo is building at *Lindon Pool* (Lincoln).

Geron replied, "I'm getting old fast and hear complaints from *Ansgar* that you'll never find Sabatini now you're *'the big man'* at Mogontiacum. Many call Ansgar a hothead, who's proposing a raid to flush out Sabatini before he kills again." To which I countered,

> Beware of the Picts; they'll slaughter his raiders before they're a mile inland. Tell my bold cousins to wait for a force of legionaries who're better equipped than your warriors. In addition, your in-landers have no watercraft suitable for a raid across the *Mare Germanicum.* Tell those eager warriors, "Don't make your wives into widows!" Sabatini will surely blunder within my reach because he outstays his welcome wherever he goes because of his warped sexual appetites.

Marcus Leaves Germania

In May, when Germania was lush and northern *Europa* was at spring's flowery finest, Nero's Inspector General *Antonius Camillus Bibaculus* arrived to review our readiness for combat. During his week-long inspection of *Legio XXII,* we performed mock battles, ending *Bibaculus'* intense scrutiny in a full-dress parade under the critical eyes of a dozen former *Primus-Pilus* legionaries who'd finished evaluating the strength and security of our fortifications, the quality of our support services, and the strength, skill, and fitness of my 4,800 legionaries, 1,200 cavalrymen, and 1,000 auxiliary infantrymen. Before the inspectors departed, *General Bibaculus* told me he'd rated my legion as one of Rome's finest, praising Marcus and my exacting *centuria* for having followed all of Rome's directives and leaving other legions with *"a tough act to follow."* At a small post-inspection dinner, *Bibaculus* criticized me for having a top-heavy officer structure, saying, "You must relieve *Tribune Marcus* from duties here because his talents will be underused now. Therefore, I'm recommending he be transferred to a post that needs disciplining (like you've done here). Awaiting Nero's concurrence, I can post him to Hispania or Judaea."

As a result of his offer (likely influenced by Senator Aquilus), Marcus calculated what might be a location for professional and family advantages. After thinking about Hispania's proximity to Rome and remembering Sabina's praiseworthy remark about the warm *Balearic*

Islands, Marcus asked, "Where in Iberia do you expect a command vacancy this summer?" He replied, "At *Legio* in northern Hispania––the 6th Legion did poorly in our recent inspection." Quickly switching to the history of *Legio VI*, he added,

> Until recently, the 6th was one of the finest old legions. It fought in the final stage of Rome's conquest of the Iberian Peninsula, participating in Augustus' ten-year war against the *Cantabri* tribes from 29 to 19 BC, finally bringing that northern region under Roman rule. It's been posted there for 80 years now and has carried its *Hispaniensis* cognomen for a long time. Its former soldiers and those of *Legio X Gemina* provided the first Roman settlers at *Caesaraugusta* (Zaragosa).

When *Inspector Bibaculus* concluded, Marcus replied, "Sir! I'd be honored to lead that legion, especially since I've served two years in Mauretania and understand Iberic languages that had crossed into *Tingitana* at the *Pillars of Hercules.*" The inspector replied, "I'll send a dispatch recommending you for that position. It needs confirmation by the Emperor; meanwhile, you must hold this idea close until Nero chooses to announce it. Then you can move your young family during summer when the sea is calmest."

Since Marcus and I knew little about that part of Hispania, I asked Antón to tell us about northwest *Hispania Tarraconensis*––150 miles northeast of his family home in *Lusitania.* When I asked about the town of *Legio* and the *6th Legion,* he began,

> I was recruited into the auxiliary cavalry squadron of *Legio VI Victrix* in AD 39. The legion began service in that area under *Augustus* during the *Astur-Cantrabrian Wars* (the final stage of Rome's conquest of Hispania). As a young recruit, I was told the Romans established the fort to protect the territories from hostile *Asturi* and *Cantabri* tribesmen, and guard gold bullion being shipped to Rome from *Las Médulas* via *Asturica Augusta* (Astorga).

Antón continued about *Hispania Tarraconensis* where I'd first met him when I was there ten years ago to collect horses for *Vespasian* (then commander at Mogontiacum). Antón continued,

The Romans entered Hispania over 200 years ago. A century later during Augustus' reorganization, *Tarraco* became the provincial capital. The Cantrabrian Wars finally brought Iberia under Rome's domination as the *Asturi* and *Cantabri* became the last Hispano-Celts to be pacified. The conquest provided gold, silver, and tin from rich diggings at *Las Médulas* where Roman aqueducts brought water from the nearby mountains. Thousands of slaves extracted nuggets and flakes of gold by running torrents of water over soft rocks. Hard-rock miners tunneled into gold-bearing seams, using fire to break auriferous rocks. Other exports from the region included timber, cinnabar, iron, lead, marble, wine, and olives.

Antón asked, "Why are you interested in that region, Sir?" To which I asked, "What sea route would you take to reach the road system in *Tarraconensis?*" He answered, "I'd sail to *Brigantium* on the northwestern tip of Hispania and head inland through *Favia Lambris, Lucas Augusti, Bergidum, Asturica Augusta*, and finally to *Legio*. The roadway was excellent when I was last upon it. Do you want me to gather more horses?" I answered, "No, I want you to accompany Marcus and his family there and arrange oceanic movements for them and their support people and guards. You shall be their overland guide across the final 150 miles to Marcus' new command. You can stay as long as needed and can find some special horses for them."

CHAPTER 18

DISPATCHES

Early on a mid-July morning, we loaded Marcus, Sabina and their five children onto the light craft we'd often used to move up and down the Rhein. Their supporting retinue also boarded, followed by Antón and six special guards. Finally, Aurelia and I boarded for her tearful farewell with Sabina and the children. Then my regular oarsmen from *Colonia* rowed the red-and-grey actuaria riverboat quietly onto the Rhein for a smooth downriver cruise to *Lugdunum* on the *Mare Germanicum* shore where they'd transfer to a big equestrian-class bireme for their summer trip to Hispania. Ten days later I got this dispatch from Marcus:

> We arrived safely today, after which I immediately took command as my predecessor rode out with four legionary retirees, each leading large mules laden with what Antón suspected to be a heavy load of nuggets sluiced from nearby mines. Antón has been most helpful; I'd like to keep him with me until I sort out loyalties among my staff members and my undisciplined legionaries. I certainly need *Barbartus*, your hard-assed *Primus Pilus*, if you can loan him to me to shape up my legionaries and auxiliaries.

Three weeks later Marcus reported *Barbartus* had arrived and had restructured the centuries, appointing those he deemed reliable to compete for honors as true Roman warriors. He added,

I've inherited a bloody mess here. Your top warrior recommended we decimate the legion, but he relented after finding lots of good men who needed strong leadership in this slack outpost. We've carried out six executions after we found big stashes of choice nuggets and located connections to tribal raiders who'd intercepted gold deliveries intended for our strong room. I reported the former legate, *Calidius Galerius Franco's* misconduct to the governor at *Tarraco*, but got no reply. I suspect I may have erred in doing so and may not be here long.

Meanwhile, back along the Rhein's hillsides, our new vineyards had produced a rich array of wine grapes for a large autumn harvest ready for aging in fresh-cut oaken vats in which some of our wines will be aged for us to share over the winter. Our brewers had made oversized barrels for brewing *stark dunkelbräu* (strong dark beer) for autumn festivals and winter celebrations. Between my command duties and my diplomatic visits to tribal chiefs, I'd found more time to spend with Aurelia and the boys. Marco was eight years old and could read and factor better than all of his friends (thanks to his teacher, *Solon Dorotheos*). Adults and children recognized Marco as polite and unaffected, knowing I was the top officer at the *castra*. Vespan seemed slower, but was more adept at ball handling. He loved watching the legionaries train and would emulate their combat exercises, announcing, "I'll be a great warrior like my father and Uncle Marcus."

The Plague

All seemed quiet across the empire until word arrived that a new form of an old disease (called *plaga*) has been spreading from the *Pontus Euxinus* (the Black Sea) into *Cappadocia* (eastern Turkey), *Cilicia* (southeast Turkey), and to *Salamis* (on *Cyprus*) at the eastern end of the *Mare Internum*. By the time those rumors reached Germania, dispatches followed from Rome reporting hundreds of deaths at seaside cities, causing panic in Rome and ports across the *Mare Internum*. As a result, we began preparing for the disease's arrival and awaited reports from Marcus of the *pestis'* reach into Hispania.

To understand the disease, I asked *Vibi*, "What do you know of this scourge that has roots in ancient cultures?" He replied, "I've heard little of its nature; perhaps *Solon Dorotheos* can tell us." When I asked Solon (a Freedman after ten years a slave), he told us,

As a student of history, I learned my people had faced catastrophes from which some survived despite the event's magnitude. The most incomprehensible disasters had been these *pesti* sicknesses, sent by an angry god. The most devastating *plaga* was the *Great Athenian Scourge* that fell upon that great city 500 years ago during the *Peloponnesian War* (between Athens and Sparta from 431 to 404 BC). Because of overcrowded wartime conditions in Athens, the disease spread quickly, killing ten thousand. General Thucydides had written an account of a *plaga* event in his *History of the Peloponnesian War.*

Solon continued,

The sickness originated in Ethiopia and spread over Egypt and Greece. Having experienced that infection, the general told of his body rash and high fever. Victims coughed blood, suffered stomach cramps, and vomited. Most people experienced insomnia and unquenchable thirsts that drove some to jump into wells. Most died by the 8th day; any who survived had uncontrollable diarrheas that led to desiccation and death.

Vibi spoke, noting, "The symptoms you've described differ from ones dispatched from Rome called *a black-bile illness* found in corpse livers. Some say it's similar to *Vibrio vulnificus* found after eating oysters in the wrong season." Solon philosophized on the consequences of the devastating event,

Thucydides told of the plague's effects on Graecian society. Even our doctors died while trying to heal others, resulting in a despair that led people to disregard laws and plunge into self-indulgence. No one observed funerary rites, civic duties, or religions. Thucydides admitted supporting hedonism with the plague illustrating the futility of believing in our Olympian gods.

As a result of that report, I asked, "Do we have cause for concern, living far from the big cities?" Solon answered, "Of course, Sir! Many great illnesses are shipborne from afar." Vibi added, "The growing *plaga* may reach the Rhein next year; therefore, you should disperse our people into the countryside and order wastes carried far from our water sources." Solon agreed, noting,

> I've read contamination of wells may've been the source of poisoning and suggest that if a *pesti* arrives downriver, you should move your family near uncontaminated water. You should also prepare to move your legion to a mountain tributary until the misery passes, as it often does within a year.

Vibi joked, "My grandfather justified his use of strong drinks to override the nauseating effects of tainted foods eaten afield." He claimed, "Boiled tea's scalding liquid would kill anything that might crawl into my pot." Strong "burnt" wine (like brandy) would surely do the same.

Two days later, I got a dispatch from Marcus that dozens of people had died in Hispanic cities. He asked, "Might it be better to send Sabina and the children to Mogontiacum where it's cooler? Sabina says she wants to move from "this stinking rat's nest in the Iberian wilderness." Before my answer reached him, another dispatch arrived that told me, "The disease arrived in the nearby *Las Médulas* gold mines where a dozen slaves died suddenly."

I fired back an urgent dispatch covering Solon's points of sanitation and pure water, and suggested Antón should lead Sabina and her retinue to a secure hideout in the *Montes de León* between the *Cantabrian* and *Macizo Galaico Mountains* whose summits are snow covered in winter. I told him, "I'd heard *Monte Teleno, Cabeza de la Yegua, Pena Trevinca,* and *Vizcodillo* all send lots of fresh water to streams below where the sickness wouldn't be found." Two weeks later, I received this answer from Marcus,

> I've sent my family with Antón and ten others into the mountains north of here to live among the *Asturi* with whom Antón had been associated since his first cavalry posting here more than 15 years ago. I rode with them to the tiny village of *Valporquero de Torio* in the municipality of *Vegacervera* (30 miles north of here) where the tribe controls an enormous cavern they call *"La Cueva de Valporquero,"* little known beyond their remote settlement. Antón assured me the cave's river is pure and the tribesmen allow few outsiders to enter its endless darkness. If I remain uninfected, I'll visit them fortnightly.

CHAPTER 19

AD 58

The autumn of 57 had been a deadly one around the *Mare Internum* with a *one-in-six death rate* in major cities, but far less in the countryside. Because of that difference, harvests were near normal in rural regions, leaving my legion in better condition than others across the empire. Marcus wrote,

> I've lost 192 men to the debilitating sickness, while the nearby mines lost triple that number. Fortunately, the huge quantities of clean, fresh gold-sluicing water from the *Montes de León* (arriving on recently extended aqueducts) appears to have washed away the contaminants that have caused so many late-summer deaths.

In November, he wrote,

> I've lost no more men, nor have more *Asturi* tribes-folk died near the fort. Antón has reported good health at his encampment where Sabina and the children are eager to rejoin me. Despite this sharp change from late summer, I've withheld permission for them to return until early snows begin in the higher elevations.

As a result of good news from Hispania, *Solon* and I concluded that sanitation is all-important in crises like this one that most Roman cities had faced during the summer's mysterious *miasma*. Aurelia and I were thankful Marcus' family had avoided the deadly outbreak by living away from contaminated centers. In his next dispatch, Marcus told me about the high death rate in *Tingis* and how Sabina was concerned about Flavia's brother she'd purchased for *Rhoati* at the slave market. Since Marcus had contacts in *Mauretania Tinginita*, he asked if I'd allow Antón to travel to *Tingis* to learn if *Trupo* and *Rhoati* had survived. After I agreed, Marcus wrote,

> Antón departed on "a 500-mile ride along the *Astura River,* then down the principal north-south Roman road through *Salamantica, Trumuli, Emerita Augusta, Hispalis,* and *Mellaria* where he'll cross the *Fretum Gaditanum* to *Tingis*. He's expected to be gone six to eight weeks, where he'll attempt to purchase *Trupo* if he's still alive and if Rhoati hasn't survived the *plaga*.

Therefore, we waited into January until we heard about Antón's thousand-mile mission. Finally, in late January, Marcus reported, "Antón has returned with Trupo who's now nine years old and speaks only the difficult *Fezzian tarafit* dialect and bits of *Gallego* from his early childhood." Marcus also described Trupo's arrival at Legio,

> He's a skinny little blond who was overjoyed to see his sister after two years apart. Antón told us of his unsuccessful search around *Tingis* and *Gaditanum* until he found *Aduzi Mazak* at the city market and was taken to *Hami*, who'd kept the unwanted waif after *Rhoati* and other clan members had perished from *"the Egyptian curse sent from the east."*

Antón confided,

> *Hami* was a hard bargainer, asking twice the 500 *denari* you'd sent with me. After two days of haggling, we compromised, settling on 400 denari and a second horse I'd bought in *Baetia* while coming south, meaning Trupo had to ride double to my home near *Bracara Augusta* where we spent five days eating, sleeping, and teaching him Lusitani and army Latin words. While there, I bought two *Nafarroaka Zaldiko* colts favored for easy riding.

Finally, Marcus wrote of Trupo's transition to life among 4,800 legionaries and how he'd learned enough Latin to express appreciation for becoming our newly adopted son. Sabina added, "Flavia often translates for Trupo because they both speak childhood *Tarafit* and *Gallego* phrases. Now she's his best Latin teacher. We hope he'll forget his hard time as a captive."

Tribune Lupis Arrives

On the 20th of May, Governor Paulinus arrived with a young political tribune from Rome named *Decius Fenius Lupis*, whom the governor called *Lupo* (wolf). He'd been assigned as my *tribunus laticlavius* (second-in-command), requiring me to indoctrinate him in the legion's strengths and introduce him to a dozen tribal chiefs east the Rhein.

His arrogant attitude quickly poisoned his relationship with my legionaries and troubled our diplomacy with the Germanic tribesmen, influenced by *Ansgar, Lanzo,* and *Vulfgang.* At lunch in the *Principia, Lupis* asked scornfully, "How did you become a *legatus legionis* having never undertaken the prescribed *cursus honorum?*" To which I politely answered, "By leading six cavalry *turmae* into combat in *Cymru,* by finding *King Caratacus* for Emperor Claudius, and by negotiating peaceful relationships with a dozen tribes beyond the Rhein."

He started to brag of his equestrian lineage, but was interrupted by the governor who told me, "I'll explain later." As I introduced *Fenius Lupis* to my staff officers, I saw how uncomfortable each of them were, knowing that political *tribunii* are sent to spy on powerful *Legatii* who might threaten unpopular emperors. Over the next six weeks, this new *'broad-stripe tribune'* began issuing orders beyond his authority, putting me in the awkward position of having to negate many of his senseless actions. Near summer's end, the governor returned to ask me about reports from *Lupo,* telling him to replace me with an equestrian *Legatus.* When he learned more of my conflicts with the tribune, Governor Paulinus told me,

> It's inevitable an insider from Rome will replace you, but I've withheld Lupo's complaints against you. I'm certain he'll circumvent my efforts; therefore, I'm moving him to Colonia and will report to Rome that he's completed his laticlavian training. Unfortunately, he'll still trouble you.

That welcome effort by the governor appeared to have sidelined the "Black Wolf," as I called him; however, if he were returned to Rome he'd become too closely associated with Nero, which would leave me vulnerable to the whims of insiders on the imperial staff. As I'd been anticipating, notification arrived that a favorite young senator who'd filled all his military and political requirements for a major command would arrive at Mogontiacum in the autumn. At the same time, Governor Paulinus told me, "Come to Colonia to discuss your tenure at the 22nd Legion." At that meeting, he told me, "A mid-senior senator named *Numerius Gratus Crito* will soon take your position. I suggest you move your family south before winter prevents oceanic travel." When I enquired if he had a posting for me, he replied,

> Not yet, Ivano, but I expect you to introduce *Numerius Crito* to your staff and some tribal chieftains. Like most newcomers from Rome, he'll likely want you gone from your loyal legionaries as soon as possible so he can invoke his own policies and command practices.

I suggested, "If I'm here with you at Colonia for a while, Governor, you can send me upriver as your tribal negotiator until I get Aurelia and the boys settled back at Tusculum or down on the warm Balearic Islands."

CHAPTER 20

AD 58 AND 59

Since it was mid-November AD 58 and North Europe's winter was again underway, I studied four ways to move Aurelia and her retinue southward. The first was a float downriver to *Lugdunum* and over the *Oceanus Atlanticus* to *North Hispania* where they could stay until spring with Sabina and Marcus. A second way would be across Northern Hispania to *Caesaraugusta* (Zarragosa) then down the *Iberus Fluss* into the *Mare Balearicum* and on to *Palma* or *Pollentia* on the largest *Balearic Isle*.

A third consideration was a boat trip up the Rhein to *Mons Brisiacus* (Tarodunum) and then on a hundred-mile horseback ride to *Vesontio*, followed by a 250-mile downriver float to *Arelate* (Arles), and a short trek to *Massilia* from where an overwater passage to Rome could be completed in December (dodging winter storms). Least desirable (and most risky) was a long oceanic trip west of *Iberia*, passing through the *Pillars of Hercules* again, reaching Rome at some unpredictable date in January.

When Aurelia and I discussed those choices, she favored the second that combined a visit to Marcus and Sabina, then continued to the island of *Majorca* where they'd remain 'til spring, living near *Captain Val*, who owns a sunny whitewashed villa there. With that option accepted, I sent word to Marcus that "Aurelia (with our two boys and seven others) would arrive within ten days in *Portus Victoriae* on the *Mare Cantabricum* coast of North Hispania. I also asked Antón to lead Aurelia to *Legio* where she wants to remain while I await reassignment.

The next morning, she and her retinue were afloat on the Rhein. Two days later, I learned they'd left *Lugdunum* on a bireme to Hispania.

A fortnight later, Marcus' sent signals telling me, "They've arrived safely, but exhausted from the final 150-mile overland trek around the mountains." With that difficult move completed, I could concentrate on my final duties in Germania, including Crito's introductory visits with Germanic tribes, including a meeting with King Geron, where Cousin Ansgar was unusually civil, saying, "We regret your departure, Ivo; please return to help us remain friendly with your legionaries. We hope this one you call *Crito* will treat us fairly."

After our four tribal visits, Governor Paulinus officiated at my departure dinner, lauding my diplomatic efforts with the tribes and for keeping *Legio XXII* at its highest standards. The next morning, he conducted a full-dress, change-of-command ceremony with trumpet blasts during my handover of the legion's golden *Eagle Standard* to Crito. Immediately afterward, legionaries and auxiliaries lined the riverbank, highlighting my departure, waving and saluting while a harmonious choral tribute was sung. Finally, I heard *cornicen* blasts long after I was out of sight as the governor's river craft swept me away. I thought, *Farewell to Mogontiacum and to my hard-eaned legionary command.* As I reflected on my tribal-diplomacy works, I wondered, *Will I ever return?"*

Back at Colonia and on to Britannia

That evening we docked at Colonia where I spent two days writing a summary of my command and sending dispatches to Marcus, Milo, and Senator Aquilus (whom I'd not seen since I left Rome over three years ago). Since I was serving as an assistant to the governor, I had little to do while awaiting a new posting somewhere across the empire. One of my first priorities was to convince Governor Paulinus to be rid of the "pain-in-the-ass" tribune (*Lupo*) whom he'd sent upriver to Legatus Crito, not as second-in-command, inflaming his equestrian arrogance to the degree that Crito sent him back to Paulinus who told him, "Pack your kit, *Wolfie*, you're unfit for any command in my province. Perhaps you should learn humility before you're offered another *laticlavius* opportunity."

With no re-assignment orders, I requested a leave-of-absence to travel to Britannia to visit brother Milo, who was building a legionary fortress at *Lindum* (Lincoln) garrisoned by *Legio IX Hispana.* With leave orders signed by the governor, I sailed across the *Mare Germanicus* to

Camolodunum where I visited Spur's and Milo's families. I then proceeded northwest along Milo's well-traveled military roads through *Grantchester, Godmanchester, Chesterton, Durobrivae*, and *Great Casterton*, and then along the newest segment of the *Ermine Way* through *Coritavi* territory. I finally arrived at the growing *Lindum* camp at the end of the *Fosse Way* that now stretched 210 miles northeast from *Muridunum* (Seaton) in the *Oceanus Britannicus* littoral region where I'd served under Vespasian during our capture of southwestern Britannia.

As expected, Milo was making early morning inspections of various construction projects where I found him ten miles north of Lindum on an *Ermine Street* extension toward the *Abus River* (the Humber) where a ferry boat would soon be crossing the wide estuary. When I caught up with Milo, he summarized his projects, repeating his concern about *"working all my life in Britannia,"* After we told each other about our youngsters, I explained my loss of command, finally coming to the subject of *Tribune Sabatini* and my Chattian promise to avenge the death of Fulko. Milo responded,

> I've heard rumors Sabatini has overstayed his welcome with the Picts and is living farther south among the *Veniconti* and *Horesti* tribes about 250 miles north of here, just beyond the *Bodotria Æstuar* (Firth of Forth) and the *Tava Æstuar* (Firth of Tay). The best way to get there would be overwater from the *Abus Æstuar* (the Humber estuary), paralleling the *Oceanus Germanicus* coast of Britannia to its northeastern inlets; however, I must warn you it's a rotten time of the year to travel there and I know little about the northern tribes' attitudes toward the Romans.

Milo continued,

> You should forget about trying to find Sabatini there because he's said to be on the move. One of my *Otadeni* road-workers from *Habitanicum* (about a hundred miles from here) told me he'd heard of a rabblerousing Roman whom some people call *Sabat*. He promised the northern tribes they could throw the legions out of Britannia before they reach the island's throat between the *Ituna Æstuar* (Selway Firth) and the mouth of the *Vedra Fluss* (at Newcastle).

I responded,

> You know I'm committed to avenging Fulko. There's no better time
> for me to pursue Sabatini than right now. I'll need a dozen armed
> volunteers with horses and equipment. Do you have enough influence
> with your legate to provide support for my winter raid?

Milo answered, "I'm just a builder, Ivo, but I'll take you to my
boss, who'll listen to you, since you've been a legate. If he agrees,
I'll ask some of my *Damnii* and *Otadeni* workers to help you find the
slippery one." When Milo introduced me to Legate *Quintus Caesius
Rufus,* he said, "I've heard of you *Ivano* and of your dealings with *Queen
Cartimandua* and the capture of *King Caractcus*. I was serving at *Glaevum*
then." He then asked,

> Are you aware that *King Venutius* turned his *Carvetii* tribe against Queen
> Cartimandua and became the leader of a new resistance against Rome's
> occupation that's pointing north into their region? The Briganti queen
> rejected her consort-king *Venutiu*s, and married *Vellocatus*, whom she's
> elevated to her kingship in place of *Venutiu*s, who has turned against
> us. My predecessor defended Cartimandua, which weakened Venutius'
> revolt.

When I acknowledged my part in earlier negotiations, he
commented, "You're certainly an adventurer, Ivano! Your Engineer
brother tells me you want to lead a raid into the North where few
legionaries have ventured."

We spent an hour discussing the difficulties of finding, capturing,
and transporting the tribune. At the end, *Legatus Rufus* agreed to provide
me with auxiliary warriors, all horses and supplies, and sea transport up
and back. He added, "I'll have Milo build us a stockade for your escapist
here at Lindum. How soon can you be ready to depart?"

I answered, "Perhaps in a week. First I need to find where Sabatini
might be. Next, I need to reaffirm permission from your governor.
Meanwhile, I'll train some tribesmen as my raiding force." After those
elements were satisfied, we waited for reports that told us Sabatini has
been seen by *Damnii* tribesfolk. One *Otadeni* lad claimed, "The man
called *Sabat* was seen heading south along *Dere Street* toward the *trium*

montium region and will likely be near the *Tweodum Flu* (the Tweed River) to rally support from *Otadeni, Damnii,* and *Gadeni* chiefs against incursions in their tribal areas." At last, we were ready for my raid to capture the runaway tribune.

CHAPTER 21

RAID

By the time we'd completed our preparations, my plan had slipped into February and the weather had turned from occasional snows to frequent rains, meaning our effort would likely leave us little chance of staying dry. Therefore, we wore waxed cloaks, full-length leather trousers, and scalloped winter sandals with wool leggings that could be dried twice a day. We also found a warrior who could cook, staunch wounds, and treat illnesses.

We seemed prepared when we left *Lindum* on February 18th on a rainless day and rode up *Ermine Street* to the *Abus Æstuar* where we loaded 15 horses, three burden-bearing mules, and all of our support equipment. By noon we'd passed the *Ocalum Prominatory* as we exited the *aestuar* and turned north, passing the *Gabrantuicorum Sinus* four hours later, after which we slept at a pre-existing Roman marching camp called *Filey*. Early the next morning, we sped along coastal *Brigantia,* landing near the *Vedra Fluss* (the Weer River) where all but the cook took quick swims, after which we feasted on roast venison he'd cooked the night before while we'd slept.

Since we were 70 miles short of an entry point to the *Tweodum Flu* (the Tweed), our *Natum* told me, "We'll camp on an uninhabited island (Lindisfarne). From there my crew can row your party 20 miles upriver or put you ashore before daylight opposite this island. What do you prefer?" I answered, "As much as I'd like an upriver ride, I want you to drop us across from this island where few tribesmen can see us. I need secrecy to avoid flushing my 'gamecock' from his nest." The *Natum* then added,

> I've been up here before so I'll tell you of your path to *trium montium*. After you've unloaded and headed west, you'll see three low mountains about 20 miles away––that's your target. You'll cross an old trackway a few miles inland called *The Devil's Causeway*. Three or four miles farther you'll cross a small river that joins the *Tweodum* (at Coldstream). Then you can follow the river to *Watling Sreet* that enters the village (near Selkirk).

A mile from the town, I hid my team in a grove and sent my two *Gadeni* lads (from *Horcovicum*) into town to ask, "Is the famous Roman still about whom we wish to meet?" Since it was a wet morning, few people were about, but the first person they asked replied in a local dialect, "Aye, me laddies, he be someres doun the *Watl Stras* ging'n na *Habitancum* 'n *Corstopitum*." Another agreed adding, "Bout nouw, he be near ta *Bremenium* (Jedburgh)."

When the lads reported what they'd learned, I sent another lad back to the ship, requesting it be moved south to wait a day at each successive river mouth until contacted. We then headed down Watling Street with the same lads (now in their home area) repeating questions about Sabatini. As they entered *Habitancum* in the *Chevium Hills*, they saw a cluster of tribesfolk listening to a central spokesperson, about whom one lad told me, "I do b'lieve we've foun 'im, Sir!"

Since there were too many tribesmen about, I led my team on a wide circuit around the site to await Sabatini's move toward *Bunnun* in *Redesdale* where we'd encircle his foursome on the open road. In mid-afternoon, we saw four riders coming toward us as we rested in a roadside grove. As they stopped to chat with our *Gadeni* lads who'd asked a question, we moved to join them. Since they'd drunk too much ale at their long lunch, they made no attempt to escape because we weren't wearing legionary uniforms, and it took a full minute for the weatherworn tribune to recognize me.

When it finally sunk in that he was my captive, he croaked, *"Endlich hast du mich gefunden, mein alter Germanicher Feind."* (Finally, my old German enemy you've found me). "Where do we go now?" I answered, *"Nach Rom, Tribunus Hosidius Mallius Sabatinus. Nach Rom!"* (To Rome! To Rome).

Return to Lindum

After an easy capture, we headed east through the *Rothburgh Silva* (Rothbury Forest), moving toward the mouth of the *Coccuveda Flu* (Coquet River) where I planned to release Sabatini's companions. When we arrived at *Amblium* (Amble), I found our reliable *Natum* had anchored his ship as instructed, but had moved onward. Because of our long ride back, our preplanned meeting time had expired. Therefore, we had to unshackle Sabatini for a faster ride toward the ship we'd seen moving away over a mile ahead.

From *Amblium* we struggled through the *Wilds of Wanney* to the mouth of the *Wansbeck*, where we finally boarded the ship. The exhausted tribune feigned illness, but rested as we floated a hundred miles south. We then rounded *Spurn Head* back into the *Humber's* broad tidal waters onto the *River Ancholme*, and up its channel to Milo's road that took us back to *Lindum*.

Legatus Rufus and his *Primus Pilus Callus* greeted us at the fort, but when their guards started moving Sabatini into an unheated guardhouse; I realized our prisoner would require medical attention and warmer quarters to recover. Although he was 57 years old, he appeared ten years older in his degraded condition. As a result, *Legate Rufus* ordered, "Bed this ragged tribune in the infirmary, but keep him guarded."

Rufus asked me at dinner, "What do you plan to do with your prisoner after he recovers enough to be moved." I replied, "I must take him to Rome to be retried by the Senate, but first I must get permission from my governor so I can escort Sabatini to Rome." Rufus then offered his help through Governor Suetonius, adding,

> He'll surely want to help and may request your transfer to Britannia to authorize your month-long trip to Rome with Sabatini. Since he'll be at Lindum next week, I'll introduce you so he can transfer you to Britannia, and arrange your travel to Rome.

Meanwhile, Sabatini was recovering and was arguing for his release from "illegal confinement." When Suetonius arrived, he was eager to visit the accused to determine if he should honor my request to take the captive tribune to Rome for judgment by the Senate. After a lengthy interview with Sabatini, Suetonius joined Rufus and me at dinner where little was discussed but his recent *Cymruian* problems where a large legionary force might be needed to quell another uprising.

After dinner, the governor asked about my tribal heritage in Germania and my Chattian obligation to bring Sabatini to justice. After my explanation, he said to me,

> I've heard of you *Ivanus*; you were with *Legatus Vespasianus* during the invasion. Rufus told me of your diplomacy with *Cartimandua* in Brigantia when *Caratacus* was captured. I've also read of your peacemaking successes with some tribal chieftains. Therefore, I'll ask *Governor Suetonius* to release you to join my campaign in *Cymruia*.

The discussion then turned to Governor Suetonius, in which he told me of his years of service to Rome,

> I was born at *Pisaurum* on the Adriatic coast and was educated in Rome during the reign of Tiberius. Caligula sent me to Mauretania as *praetor* in 40, after which he appointed me governor. In collaboration with *Geta* (whom you must remember from the invasion), we suppressed a revolt in that mountainous province. The next year, I was the first Roman to lead troops across the high Atlas Mountains. Years later, Nero appointed me Governor of Britannia, replacing *Quintus Veranius*, who'd died in office not long ago. I continued Quint's policy of aggressively subduing the hostile *Cymruians*.

I then told him of my unpleasant experience in Mauretania to recover my kidnapped son and of my long trek through the Atlas ranges to find him. Finally, the discussion turned to Tribune Sabatini, who'd recovered sufficiently to be housed in quarters awaiting our move to Rome (mostly by sea). In that discussion, Governor Suetonius asked, "Is it necessary for you to make that difficult journey, only to have that *mingo*-eyed Boy-Emperor pardon him for long-ago misconduct?" I replied,

> Sir! I'm under a triple obligation to punish him. First is my promise to fulfill an oath to my uncle, *King Geron* whose son *Fulko* (my cousin) was rape-murdered by Sabatini 24 years ago. Second is my personal vengeance for an attempted rape on my bride-to-be 16 years ago. Third

is an obligation to return him to the senate to face *rapta* charges for depraved acts unbecoming of a legionary officer.

Governor Suetonius concluded our discussion, barking,

I'd've killed that vile pig many years ago and left his stinking carcass for the vultures. Why waste months of your precious youth far from your family in an honorable pursuit only to be thwarted by some clever misuse of Roman law? I'll let you go to Rome now, but hurry back to help me in my *Cymruian* campaign.

CHAPTER 22

ROMA

I thought, *so much to do in so little time!* First, I sent Marcus this request: "Would you send Aurelia and her retinue across to *Caesar Augusta* (Zaragoza) and down the *Iberus Fluss* to *Pollentia,* then on to the biggest *Balearides Isla?*" I received this answer: "I've moved both families to that warm site."

Soon after, I began my trip with Sabatini and four guards to Rome. We swept west past Gallia's northwestern corner then south to the *Garumna Fluss* estuary, passing through *Burdigala* (Bordeaux) and on to *Aginnum* (Agen) where we rented horses to ride the *Via Aquitania* to *Toulouse* where *Flavius Quintilius* accompanied us to the port of *Agathe* (Agde). From there we floated to *Majorca* where I expected to find Aurelia and Sabina, and six sun-tanned children fully recovered after an overland trip from north Hispania.

Instead, I found Aurelia and Sabina had already sailed toward Rome. While in *Pollentia,* she'd contacted *Captain Val* who'd been transporting goods between Hispania, Italia, and Egypt, and asked, "Will you take us to Rome?" He replied, "I'd be honored to carry ye to the *Port of Ostia.*" On learning that news, we hastened our departure, hoping to catch Val's ship.

Two days after we left Majorca and passed between Sardinia and Corsica, I spotted a familiar-looking craft. As we drew near the smaller ship, I heard a stentorian voice boom out, "Welcome, Sir Ivano!" To which I echoed, *"Good day, my old friend!"* As both captains rested their rowers, I transferred to Val's craft where Aurelia jumped with joy to greet me much sooner than she'd expected. Two days later as we docked in Ostia, I saw a crowd had formed to see the notorious tribune. Because of that gathering, we hustled Sabatini to the legionary fort while Captain Val hosted us at what he called "the finest restaurant in town." While we were dining, a crowd of *plebian tribunates* had gathered to support the exiled tribune. As we were leaving, six of these aging *plebians* confronted me, claiming, "We're non-aristocratic plebians, formerly held sacrosanct in Rome who invoke our ancient pledge to kill any person who harms a tribune. We of the *Augustan tribunate* reclaim our *Tribunicia Potestae Powers* to protect the accused."

Fortunately, my guards had taken Sabatini to temporary incarceration until we could move him to a *gabiola* (jail) near the senate. We then rode to *Villa Antigua Rustica* to visit Senator Aquilus, who was unable to leave his bed because of a recent fall. He was strong-minded and pleased to see us––after warm greetings, he spoke sharply against Sabatini, recalling,

> We should've executed that two-headed viper years ago. I hope the Senate will set a powerful precedent against sexual depravity with many senators enforcing our *Lex Scantinia* laws that penalize *stuprae* against male *ingenui* or *praetextati* (minors). I hope our judgment will succeed, but I'm concerned our emperor may reverse any decision.

He then told me, "I deeply regret losing your land and the special villa I'd built for you that Agrippina has stolen." He added,

> I believe the disputed property might be recoverable because of Agrippina's disaffection with her son who's cast her from her position of influence. Differences have become so embittered that she may leave Italia. Rumors speak of her departure to her *Misenum* villa on Naples Bay.

He then returned to Sabatini's prospects, speaking more softly,

> As you can see, Ivo, I'm too crippled to journey to the Senate. As a result, I've filed my testimony to be read to the body, recommending execution. I've also told my close friends to accept nothing less than *castrata* and banishment to the farthest end of the empire. I want you

to attend the proceedings as my representative and repeat your former testimony of your cousin's rape-murder, and report the details to me.

During the week, a senatorial quorum heard earlier testimony, including those from mothers whose children had been raped by Sabatini. Although many arguments were repeated, new cases of homoerotic rapes came to light. When final judgment was voted, a clear majority called for *castrata* and hard labor in the mines in Hispania, Britannia, Dacia, or Noricum. When I reported back to Senator Aquilus, he seemed pleased with the outcome, but told me, "Don't count on justice in these politically charged times when that *pedere*-brained emperor is distracted by his own troubles." He added,

> Nero may negate our hard-won judgment. He's fighting with his mother who wants to dispose of *Poppaea,* with whom he became enamored last year. Nero wants to dump *Octavia* and marry *Poppaea,* but his mother won't allow it. Their fight is poisoning my actions may help Sabatini.

As Senator Aquilus predicted, when Nero reviewed senatorial actions, he objected to our severe judgment, ordering the removal of the *castrata* penalty, but confirming "Hard labor in Britannia's lead mines." When Aquilus and other senior senators wrote concerns, Nero answered, "The Emperor's decision stands; move your prisoner back to Britannia!"

When I told Senator Aquilus, he grumbled, "You'll have to tell your Chatti king about Roman justice that'll be hard to explain. Please tell your Uncle that real justice will prevail, even if we must outwait this bungling emperor. Tell him, "We will assure a deserving end to Sabatini."

When Nero learned I'd been the one who'd captured the tribune and had brought him to Rome, he told his generals, "Bring that Chatti-Roman cavalryman to me. I want him to take Sabatini back to Britannia and to take command of one of my legions."

The tall Batavian commandant, *Orthus Opitzimus Vasso,* met me when I reported to the palace. He was the current *Corporis custodes* boss who'd replaced *Cornelius Sabinus.* Orthus asked me, *"Warst du einmal ein Custodes Mitglied?"* (Were you once a Custodes member?). I replied, *"Jawohl, Herr Kommandant, unter Sabinus."* We proceeded past the Claudian library and the emperor's map room to a garden atrium where we joined the Emperor and two general officers who knew Marcus and had heard of my diplomacy in Germania. After introductory comments, Emperor Nero remarked,

> I remember you after mother married Claudius. Britannicus and I often saw you in the library. I'm pleased you're still serving, but I want you to return to Britannia to deal with tribal leaders like Queen *Cartimandua* and the Iceni King *Esuprastus* (Prasatagus) whose people are becoming restless.

After I agreed, he added,

> I'm told you brought our troublesome tribune to Rome. To avoid further controversy here, I want you to take him to our Cornish mines as punishment for his unlawful acts. I want him out of here tomorrow to get hostile senators off my back. As soon as a legionary vacancy occurs, I'll consider you for a command position somewhere across my empire. Meanwhile, I want you to help *Suetonius* keep peace in Britannia. I'll send him a letter to use you as a negotiator with those rebellious Britannic tribes while he's fighting those Cambric devils he wants to destroy.

When I told Aurelia I'd be returning to Britannia almost immediately, she burst into tears, muttering, "How many more of these long separations must we endure? We should be together as Marco and Vespan grow into handsome young Romans with you serving as their heroic, at-home father." I answered,

> After Marcus and I complete one more provincial assignment, we'll likely earn a staff position here in Rome. Marcus will serve in the Senate, but my opportunities have declined after Emperor Claudius was assassinated and Nero's mother stole our land. I expect I may end up being land manager for Marcus when he occupies *Villa Antigua Rustica*.

Aurelia responded despondently, "Since we've lost of our *Tusculum* property, we'll wait for you at Sabina's father's villa where the children can be together. Please stay safe and hurry home to me.

CHAPTER 23

BRITANNIA

With imperial orders in hand, I rushed to *Villa Antigua Rustica* to spend one more day with Aurelia and our fast-growing boys before starting another long journey to Britannia. While at Tusculum I visited Senator Aquilus (perhaps for the last time) where he was breathing with difficulty and muttering about leaving important tasks unfinished. He told me,

> Because I can't leave this stultifying deathbed anymore, I've asked the general staff to return Marcus from Hispania to take over my farming works. I was expecting to have both of you smart young warriors with me to the end, but that *dumb-ass* emperor is keeping both of you fine lads away from me when I need you most.

When I mentioned Nero's letter to Suetonius, the old senator added,

> I've known that bull-headed viper for years. He gained notoriety years ago when he put down a violent revolt in Mauretania. Because he'd solidified his strongman reputation there, he was the obvious choice to govern Britannia when *Quintus Veranius* died last year. He has already launched a mean campaign against the druids on Mona Island. Be careful! Old Suet'll get you mixed up in the mess he's certain to create and our donkey-brained emperor will make matters worse. Too bad old Claudius is gone!

Before I left, he explained differences among legate positions across the empire in *near-and-far* and *stable-and-unstable* provinces:

There are two kinds of provinces––Senatorial and Imperial––with different levels of governors and legates who enforce Roman law there. The highest legates are *promagistrates* that include *proconsuls* and *propraetors*. Back in the Republican Era, we senators appointed provincial governors. Now, the Emperor governs through appointees. Although early emperors didn't eliminate our system of selecting proconsuls and propraetors in stable provinces near Rome, imperial appointees now rule provinces farther away to prevent powerful legates from usurping the throne.

I understood that troubled provinces (like Britannia) were commanded by experienced legates with *Consular Imperium* controlling a multi-legion army while governing the entire region. Appointment of these heavyweight governorships is Nero's whim of now. The old senator continued,

We have ten *Public Provinces* where I've helped appoint our governors. These provinces (free from rebellions) are allowed a single legion so we won't try to restore the *Republic*. Hence, we've kept these *Public ones* under our proconsuls' authority with no need for the Emperor to intervene. Since these provinces aren't Nero's, he won't grant us full legions––only *vexillationes* or cavalry *alae*.

I asked, "What must I do to regain legatus status?" Aquilus replied,

Since you're not part of Rome's elite and haven't fulfilled the progressive *cursus honorum* requirements, I doubt if you'll ever become a legate again unless Nero mandates it. Nevertheless, you'll be valuable to Suetonius as a multilingual mediator––if that rasp-tounged war-horse will listen to you. Because he knows me, I'll write an addendum to Nero's comments about you, which may gain you a cavalry-command or service as a staff member for my fierce old friend.

Northward Bound

The following morning, I gathered my four legionaries to accompany Sabatini back to Britannia. All the young lads agreed they'd enjoyed their first visits to Rome and now regretted another long journey guarding our hostile prisoner. The reverse course was no pleasure trip, but we accepted that dull duty as we moved across familiar waters and lands.

Weeks later we reached the *Oceanus Vergivius* (the St George Channel) that led us into the *Sabrina Aestuar* (the Severn) and up the *Usk River* to *Isca* (Caerleon) where I met *Legio II's* legate to arrange the transfer of Sabatini to the lead mines 20 miles southwest of *Aquae Sulis* (Bath). As the tide was rising, we proceeded across the estuary to *Uphill Harbor* and onto the *Axe River* where a high tide floated us 12 miles inland to the settlement of *Weare*. There we met two legionaries who oversaw a large mine near *Charterhouse* in the *Mendip Hills*. After securing Sabatini in a military stockade, we ate lunch with the long-serving soldiers as one told us of Rome's principal source of lead for the past ten years, adding,

> Our settlement here at *Vebriacum* grew around these lead-and-silver mines that had been tribal sites for a thousand years. Some ores are low in silver, but high-temperature smelting releases enough of the shiny metal to pay our wages and send bullion ingots to mints that produce *denarii* for stimulating trade across this province. Despite the monetic value of silver, our lead production is more important because tons are used to line water-delivery systems. Builders use this malleable metal to seal thermal baths and leaky roofs, while *mortici* use it to seal equestrian coffins.

Before we left, they showed us the cell where Sabatini was held before moving him underground. While I was there, a sullen guard grunted, "He won't last long down there." I said farewell to my old enemy, who responded, "This isn't the end, Ivo! We shall meet again, even if it's down by the *River Styx* where I'll wait for you!"

After my final confrontation with the gloomy tribune, a cheerful soldier took me to a civilian smelter where silver was being refined for transfer to a *Fosse Way* fort. At the smelter I saw *hundred-libra lead pigs* awaiting movement to the nearby *Cheddar Port* for transport to cities across the empire.

With Sabatini out of mind, I was ready to hurry on to *Londinium* where the province's administrative headquarters was being moved. From the mines at *Charterhouse,* we rode company horses to *Aquae Sulis* where we soaked in the *Dobuni* tribe's hot springs before heading on to *Calleva Atrebatum* (Silchester) and then to *Londinium* where I expected to serve a year.

When I arrived, I learned of the deaths of *Senator Aquilus* and *Agrippina Minor.* Details were few, but the death of our dear old senator was not unexpected. Transferring his properties would be complicated by Marcus' absence to fight counterclaims by those he called "*parasites* that hovered about like evil spirits." Because I'd just returned after a lengthy absence, and was needed for tribal diplomacy, the governor told me, "Your friend Marcus must be granted leave to deal with your legal matters in Rome."

Of interest to most Romans was the death of Nero's mother, *Agrippina,* because it was known that he'd cast her aside as an unwanted advisor. Knowledge of her involvement in political affairs had amplified the belief that the "vindictive boy emperor" had his mother assassinated to be free of her oppressive dominance. Since I'd barely known her when I served in the palace, I attempted to understand what may have motivated the vile act of matricide by reading every dispatch from Rome. One praised her highly,

> Agrippina saw "family as an instrument of power." Since Nero was the last survivor of the Augustan family, many believed it was impossible to oppose him. By the lofty qualities of character with which she'd been endowed, Agrippina held power as long as she kept Nero under her influence. After he turned against her, such power diminished. Although Nero was young and weak, those who wanted change supported him. Agrippina tried to dispose of Poppaea, which sealed her doom.

We later learned Nero's fleet commander had presented a scheme to eliminate Agrippina in a sinking ship to hide her body in the Bay of Naples. Nero may have consented to the plan, but Agrippina escaped, only to be slain by another naval officer, ending the power and infkuence of "a remarkable woman who'd defended the social and political traditions of Roman aristocracy."

During the next months, we received dispatches from Rome telling of the two funerals. The first told of Senator *Aquilus'* memorial that was overshadowed by Agrippina's state funeral and Nero's claims that, "She'd plotted to kill me, but chose suicide instead." It was further rumored her last words were, "Smite my womb from where I'd birthed an abominable son." Before her cremation, Nero viewed her corpse, commenting, "How beautiful she is." At her hasty funeral, he remained speechless. When news of her death spread, self-seeking people sent letters to Nero stating, "You've been saved from her plots." It was also reported her death laid heavily on Nero's conscience with nightmares haunting him and *Persian* magicians hired to scare her ghost away." As a final insult, her household servants paid for her plain tomb at *Misenum.*

Because Marcus had to return to Hispania before Aquilus' estate could be adjudicated, he'd appointed his father-in-law (*Consul Maximus Carpentius*) as executor to protect the estate from Agrippina's claims.

Prosecuting Gold Thieves

Marcus then wrote, "I rushed back to my troubled command where we'd begun rooting out gold thieves within my legion. Upon my return, I met with five reliable legionaries led by your trustworthy Primus Pilus, *Amulius Fenius Barbartus,* who'd been conducting my investigation during my absence." He added,

> Led by *Barbartus,* my team included *Aurgurus* (the *praefectus castrorum*), *Antón* (your Lusitanian), and *Archarius* and *Blandus* (my best *tribuni angusticlavii*). While I was gone, they'd discovered corruption involving the former legate and ten legionaries connected to mining officials who'd been skimming the best nuggets for years.

With evidence in hand (and former *Legate Marvelos* located) Marcus told of a "Commanders Meeting on *Majorca.*" While he'd been in Rome, Marcus alerted Nero's *Inspector General* of his discoveries and suggested exposing senior *Tarraconensian* officials while they were away from their capital at *Tarraco* on the east coast of Hispania.

The imperial inspector arranged a conference where he'd inform the provincial governors and legates about the strengths and weaknesses of

Rome's 30 legions, pointing out the best and worst units. Little did the *Tarraconensian* governor know he'd be ambushed after his former legate and retired legionaries had been arrested with big collections of grape-sized nuggets. At the same time, Marcus wrote,

> A score of my trustworthy legionaries had ridden south to *Salamantica* where they'd captured *Decius Stentius Marvelos* with two retired legionaries, confiscating 20 heavy bags containing thousands of nuggets that Barbartus brought to Pollentia.

Marcus later reported, "When *Governor Fortunius Altuneus Gordus* arrived and saw *Legate Marvelos* in manacles, he realized he was finished as a Roman nobleman. Since the conference had been a ruse to expose the gold thieves, the inspector's findings were referred to Rome for review and punishments. Immediately dozens of super-wealthy senators absented themselves from the debates, implying much of their personal wealth may have come from tax-skimming, pirating, slave-marketing, and grain-hoarding schemes. As a result, Gordus' and Marvelos' properties were seized and both were sentenced to imprisonment in Britannia's lead mines." Nero concurred, demanding, "All recovered gold will help pay for my *Capitolinus* projects."

Soon after, Barbarbus and 40 legionary guards brought the gold-thief prisoners to the *Mendip-Hills* lead mines where Sabatini had been imprisoned. Meanwhile, I headed north with Antón, Barbartus, and Vibi so we could join Governor Suetonius in his campaign against the Silures.

Governor Suetonius

After riding to *Glevum* and on to *Verocomium* (Gloucester and Wroxeter), we found *Old Suet* (as Senator Aquilus had called him) leading *Legios XIV, II,* and *XX* toward a forward position in *Cymruia*. As we arrived to report for duty, I told my companions,

> Swventeen years ago, during the invasion, Governor Suetonius had been a mid-ranking commander under *Vespasianus* when Marcus and I were junior cavalry commanders. In the intervening years, he had a

reputation of "the most-determined and battle-proven warrior." I'm looking forward to serving him.

I attempted to make an appointment to meet him, but was told he had no time for visitors because of important strategy and logistics meetings. Nevertheless, I mentioned a dispatch from Rome that said I was available for cavalry command or staff duty. Therefore, I left word that I'd wait for further instructions. Late that evening when the governor returned to his *principia*, he asked, "Where's that cavalry officer with the fancy horse?" Since no one could answer, a runner rushed to our tent, shouting to Barbartus, "Report to headquarters immediately!" Meanwhile, I'd been visiting fellow cavalrymen and was unaware of Barbartus' urgent call. As a result, he met Suetonius who recognized him as a long-serving *primipulus* (senior centurion). When I returned he told me,

> You probably won't like it, but I've got an assignment. The governor asked me to serve as his inspector, and wants you to go to Londinium to deal with troubling financial matters. I made an appointment for you to meet him at supper tomorrow.

When I reached his tent, Suetonius looked me over feigning anger, saying, "Where were you last night, sleeping with that showy horse? I remember you gave *Vespasianus* one of those superb studs years ago," and in a brighter tone he added,

> It seems our fat-assed emperor wants me to give you a command. Unfortunately, I've got all his petty equestrians I can tolerate now. I'd gladly give you a cavalry squadron, but Aquilus tells me you're a good negotiator and have tribal friends here and in Germania. Since it's too late for me to stop my drive to wipe out these wretched *Druidae*, I want you to go to the fen country north of Camulodunum and quiet that loud-mouthed Iceni queen who's raging about my *Cymruian* campaign. I also want you to stop the emperor's mindless procurator in Londinium from recalling Seneca's big Roman loans to the tribal kings.

Governor Suetonius also ordered, "Before you leave, I want you to meet with some of the local chiefs you knew to settle issues about the rich mines we've taken, but don't try to deal with their druid's human-sacrifices of our captured centurions."

Because I'd been away for three years, I hadn't assisted the former governor, *Quintus Veranius* (who'd died in office), but I learned he'd attempted raiding the *Silures*; however, his death had ended actions until *Suetonius* arrived. Governor Suet complained, "I hate campaigning in these dark forests, but my march has taken us to its far northwest corner where I'm preparing to attack *Mona Island*, which is *a haven for refugees.*"

When I attempted to reach tribal chieftains, I was greeted with a hail of arrows and was fortunate to escape alive. On my return, Suetonius told me, "I've little use for you here, since your angry chiefs are unbending." He added, "The main incentive for my campaign is Rome's desire to destroy the druids. Mona is the center of their power and their last outpost that I'm charged to destroy, even if I must employ a level of brutality rarely seen in Roman conquests."

I'd only been with Suetonius two days, when he said, "Get over to Londinium to restrain that simpleton procurator *Catus Decianus* whom I don't trust dealings with our client kings, especially the Iceni.

CHAPTER 24

PRASATAGUS

In the spring of 60, I went east to visit Iceni *King Esuprastus* (Prasutagus) who'd become concerned about the presence of Roman merchants and legionary retirees who'd been reaching north from Camulodunum into his region. I'd been authorized by the governor to offer continuing client status to the Iceni king if he'd agreed to donate part of his lands to us for military land grants. As our talks began, Esuprastus became ill, ending negotiations.

When I attempted to return in April (with Antón and Vibi), ten Iceni warriors intercepted us who obviously disliked Romans. I presented a document with their king's seal, but none would accept it, demanding us to yield our horses and leave on foot. Since Antón had been a battle-proven warrior, he charged headlong into their cluster of shaggy ponies, scattering the group of youthful assailants without killing any, while shouting for me to flee into the reedy fens.

Since I knew little about the vast wetland and was separated from the others, I headed eastward to exit the region on its far side, or to find higher ground on which to rest my horse. After finding a spot covered with ancient oaks, I attempted to climb one to make sense of my predicament. However, low-hanging clouds obscured the sun, leaving me with little awareness of where my destination might lie. Therefore, I proceeded downwind remembering *most rain clouds move eastward across Britannia*. Since we'd ridden well north of Londinium and had missed an unimproved tribal track called the *Icknield Way*, I calculated I was somewhere east of *Durovigutum* (Godmanchester), just below the *River Ouse*, and not far from a multi-clan sanctuary called the *Isle of Eels*.

Moving eastward, I saw woodsmoke rising from a low island that held seven family huts and a common room where I was greeted suspiciously, but fed roasted eels and served strong drinks. After an hour of questions in an odd dialect asking why I'd come to his fenland retreat, I seemed accepted by that isolated clan whose leader warned me of Iceni hostility toward land-grabbing Romans, since "a fat lad in Rome now ruled most of Europa, 'cept our reedy fens." He added,

> Those *Durovigutum* lads oo'd threatened ye be a troublesome lot; they claim ta guard our wetlands, usin' *Ermine Street* as a *Grenze* (boundary). If ye be 'eadin' ta our king's 'ouse, me lads'll take ye on 'idden dikes ta the fen edge 'n through 'ostile Icklanders 'oom ye may find less friendly than we.

He concluded, "Ye may sleep 'ere tonight in our meetin' 'all. Doan' be 'larmed if one o' me nieces joins ye, *Mein schöner Chatti Krieger"* (My pretty Chatti warrior). Later that night I awoke with a warm body snuggling closely, but didn't object for fear of insulting my host. We both slept well despite her arousing squirms.

King Esuprastus Dies

When I finally arrived at the tribal fortress (three days later than planned), I learned of the death of the Iceni king, with whom I'd expected to develop a favorable client relationship and make profitable trade arrangements between his big tribe and aggressive Roman merchants who'd already been marketing Britannic goods throughout the empire.

I then sought a senior official with whom I might continue my unfinished tribal diplomacy. Without my knowledge, Seutonius had received instructions from Rome to reject the King's will that had reached Rome before I'd entered discussions with his advisors. I later found that those instructions had said,

> Since the Iceni king is dead, the Emperor wants the entire kingdom instead the part offered in the king's will. Although *Ostorius* had

defeated much of the tribe 12 years ago, the emperor believes you can conquer all of its warriors now, should they choose to challenge us.

When Antón and Vibi joined me at the fortress, they told me they'd been asked to estimate the fighting strength of the entire tribe, in light of a negative response to the emperor's claim on all of the tribe's land.

Other Problems

Meanwhile, I learned Sabatini had been released from the Mendip mine and was expected to rejoin friends in Londinium where he hoped to regain his health that had eroded when working underground. Later when Vibi enquired how the release came about, this answer followed,

> A wealthy merchant named *Lucius Aemilius Lepidus* had appealed to certain senators who believed *Sabatini's sentence was a death sentence* due to his degraded condition and the poisonous environment of the mine.

Therefore, Lucius (*Little Luki* whom I'd rescued from the Rhein years ago) had apparently "bought" Sabatini's release. Vibi told me, "A lot of money had been paid for a pardon, but I'd not learned who'd been bribed." After learning more of Sabatini's release, I was told to provide a new agreement between inflexible Roman officials and the dead King's rumored successor, *Queen Boudica*. Before I could deal with her, I asked Vibi to locate Luki because Sabatini would likely be with him. A week later he told me,

> We found him at Camulodunum where he's built a trading center using legionary retirees to deal with tribal opportunists throughout Britannia. I've asked two retired legionaries to watch for Sabatini near Luki's warehouse.

When I sought to re-establish diplomatic contacts with the Iceni queen, I was told, "Esuprastus' policies of accepting Roman settlers in Iceni territory are being rejected; your offer of continued *clientela* is unlikely." Nevertheless, I found some deals might be considered because shiny new silver *denarii* were spreading across Britannia, stimulating the sales of farm products grown on the rich fen-edge soil. Roman merchants were reaching farther north to buy cattle, sheep, goats, geese, ducks, chickens, and vegetables raised on rain-watered meadows and were seeking ship-building timbers that were in great demand because other provinces had been deforested to meet warship and transport-craft demands after centuries of *Mare Internum* wars and *Mare Atlanticus* outreaches. Unfortunately, most of that Roman silver coinage was being recalled as "unauthorized loans."

Sabatini Reappears

As Antón and I were leaving the Iceni *Breckland* fortress, we came face to face with Sabatini, apparently recovered from his imprisonment. Luki (who accompanied him) was polite and confident in his wealth, saying politely,

> Dear friend Ivo, We've been discussing new trade plans with the queen who has found my proposals better than Nero's. I expect to open a wide range of opportunities for her people. Sabatini had already developed relationships in other parts of Britannia and will assist me in bringing opportunities to Boudica's people, for which I shall win Nero's approval. I expect you and I will meet frequently, Ivo, perhaps as friends.

Sabatini remarked, "It's good to see you, Ivo. Perhaps we can ignore our differences since I've been harshly punished in that terrible mine." I answered, "Most unlikely Sabatini; you're still my enemy and will be punished by my cousins who await your return to Germania."

I then headed back across Britannia to where Governor Suetonius was preparing his attack on the Druids about whom he said, "They're calling for a nationwide revolt against me." When I briefed him about my failure to extend a clientship with the Iceni queen and of Luki's trade endeavor, he replied, "Let 'em burn their bridges like your miserable tribune does. His appetites usually overwhelm his welcomes." Suetonius then sent me back to Londinium and onward to the Iceni center to deal further with their bold new leader whom he called, *"King Boudica."*

CHAPTER 25

BOUDICA

When Antón, Vibi, and I were surprisingly unwelcomed by the Iceni people, I asked our formerly polite host, "Can you tell us about your queen who has assumed your tribe's Kingship?" To which I was told,

> Sixteen years ago, she married Iceni *King Esuprastus*. She's not of Iceni origin, but of the Trinovanti tribe. Cross-tribal marriages are necessary among our ruling classes. In Celtic society, dominant women hold power positions in politics, religion, and art. Women like Boudica own land and can choose a spouse. You'll find she's smarter than most men.

I then asked about the deteriorating Iceni relationship with Rome, getting this perspective,

> Although our tribe has geographic advantages and has remained independent of Imperial dominance, the Roman threat to all of Britannia has suddenly arisen under Nero. We'd remained passive while Claudius conquered western parts of Britannia and founded Roman towns away from us. *King Esuprastus* realized we couldn't remain independent from creeping Romanization. In his attempt to avoid conflict, he'd become a client king, which forced him to answer to Rome's ruling class. That decision enabled us to remain unfettered during his lifetime.

I then asked about Rome's rejection of a woman as their leader. The reply left me wondering if I'd get to meet her, but her advisor answered,

> Just before the king's death, he willed half of his kingdom to the emperor to ensure tranquility in this region. Unfortunately, Roman law doesn't allow inheritance to be passed to daughters or for women to rule. Under your law, our queen has no claim to succession. Nevertheless, our people see her as our leader and know the *Trinovanti* tribe will support her as our ruler. She realized that many Britannic tribes have suffered under Roman taxation and are being dominated by greedy legionary retirees. She also saw that your unfinished Claudian Temple in Camulodunum has become an object of derision by our people who are angered by your Governor's raids on *Cymruia's* Druids.

Before our discussion ended, he added,

> In the 17 years since your invasion, Rome's conquest has stretched northward, and now your Governor is attempting to destroy the Druids on *Mona*. Since that island is a hotbed of anti-Roman activity, your governor is overlooking us in the Southeast. That siege has fired us up to drive all of your settlers out of here.

Finally, I was invited to meet Queen Boudica to review what she'd called, "Nero's insult." I was forewarned she'd said, "This Kingdom will never be ruled from Rome." To ease tensions, I'd taken a pearl-white horse (as a token of good will) before attempting to open discussions. When we met the first time, her air of dominance impressed me. She was tall and spoke in a low voice while looking deeply into my eyes. She was wearing a gold torc, a multi-colored tunic, and a thick wool cloak fastened by a turquoise-and-silver penannular brooch. She listened to my proposal with continued eye contact, responding with a counter proposal that wouldn't be acceptable to Nero. Nevertheless, she accepted my gift-horse, which she mounted with ease, saying,

> My new friend, I shall treasure this magnificent animal and your friendship; you'll always be welcome in my kingdom. Let's hope Nero

will recognize me as the Iceni ruler like Claudius had accepted *Prasto* 17 years ago. Why do you, a *Chattiman*, conduct Roman diplomacy?"

I attempted to answer by telling of my language skills that included Celtic dialects. After exploring the most troubling issue about Rome's refusal to respect her position as the new "*Iceni King*," she told me,

As his diplomat, you're obviously out of touch with Nero. His treatment of my people has made your "Client" offer meaningless. Tell your Governor Seutonius, "Most Britannic tribes are appalled by his treatment of the Druids. I expect to meet him on a field of battle soon."

As she stood (signaling my interview had ended), she concluded,

My people are proud of our independence and revolted 12 years ago when *Ostorius Scapula* tried to disarm all of Britannia. Unfortunately, he defeated us and put down our tribe's uprisings. Thankfully he left us independent. When you met with the enfeebled *Prasuto* last spring, I hoped we'd continue our client status, but he'd mistakenly named Nero as co-heir that should've placed our kingdom beyond injury. The opposite occurred when overconfident centurions claimed farms and enslaved my people. That's when I moved to reclaim our independence. I'm named after the goddess of victory some call "*Boudiga*" whom I'll honor in battle if needed. As a teenager, I learned to lead men and fight for the rights we've enjoyed. Since I'm now holding the kingship of my tribe, I must face Suetonius soon.

As I stood to depart, she warned, "Tell your *Road-Builder* brother to move his family from Camulodunum. While you've been here, your associates have been assessing my tribe's warring strength and will tell you I'm preparing to reject Rome and face your legions in a battle that I shall lead soon." When I asked how she knew of Milo, she explained,

My workers have helped him build some of those long straight military roads on which we'll march to kill Romans. We'll destroy his marble temple in Camulodunum near where I was born. He must move his family to save his sons from my warriors' wrath. You must also tell Rome's tax collectors, *"Never set foot on my tribe's land again!"*

The Procurator

I hurried back to Londinium where I met *Catus Decianus* (Nero's procurator in Britannia) and sent a dispatch to warn Governor Seutonius of Boudica's threat of hostile actions—likely to begin soon. Since Suetonius was in northern *Cymruia*, Catus argued,

> As chief financial officer here in Britannia, I share command with the governor, but I'm not subordinate to him. As *procurator,* I report directly to the emperor. Although Seutonius heads civil and judicial administration and commands all military units here, I control financial affairs, including *tributum soli* (land tax), *tributum capitis* (poll tax), and *portorium* (highway tax). I also collect land rents, operate mines, and pay public servants and soldiers. Big provinces like Britannia could not succeed without *procuratori* like me.

He added, "These fiscal offices are held by equestrians of the highest senatorial orders. The reason for this split of authority is to prevent concentrating too much power in the hands of over-mighty governors and limit *peculation* (embezzlement) opportunities." As a result of his self-assurance, I finally understood why friction arose between governors and procurators over jurisdiction and money matters. I also learned the main cause of what might become a tribal war was the great sums of money Claudius had "loaned" to the foremost tribal kings and chieftains to stimulate local economies and yield more Roman taxes. *Catus* maintained,

> Some of these loans were funded by Nero's favorite advisor, the very rich statesman, *Lucius Annaeus Seneca,* and were mandated for *repayment on demand*. Seneca (enjoying high interest) had lent 40 million *sesterces* to the leading Britons. Fearing default, he told me, "Recall those loans at once and use severe measures to collect the money." Nero has demanded, "Reject the will of King Prasatagus' and take his entire domain."

As a result, Boudica's scribe sent Suetonius this dispatch,

> We are insulted by your financial officer's decision to call in loans and the harsh measures his soldiers are using to collect the vast amount money. The fury of my people may goad us into war. Since you are in *Cymruia* and may not have approved *Catus'* actions, I must know who sent soldiers to pillage our kingdom. It appears Nero authorized this violence, but your greedy veterans are driving my people from their farms and enslaving them.

I was shown an appeal from the queen's scribe that read:

> King Prasuto's attempts to preserve his kingdom are being reviled and our lands are being claimed as if we'd been conquered. My own manor house is being plundered and my people are called "prizes of war." Even my relatives have been claimed. Our chieftains are being deprived of long-held estates that are now being claimed by former legionaries. We've attempted to deal with a tribune called *Hosidius Mallius Sabatinus*, who claims to be Emperor Nero's official representative here, but he's the very one who has claimed my royal house.

After I read that appeal to Governor Suetonius, I sent it with this message,

> Further humiliating the queen and her tribal leaders, former soldiers are claiming the best lands and turning her entire tribe against us. We're being called *Brutal Invaders* with Queen Boudica saying she'll avenge "Rome's unforgiveable acts." She asked, *"Is nothing is safe from Nero's arrogance?"*

As conditions beyond the fens grew into what might become a full-scale war, I rushed to *Lindum* to exhort Milo to move his family across the *fretum* to Gallia or Germania. At the same time, I carried Governor General Suetonius' orders directing me to bring 500 cavalrymen from Lindum for his druidic war in *Cymruia*. Surprisingly, Milo ignored my warning of an uprising across Britannia trying to minimize the threat, arguing, "Acacia and our boys'll be safe because they fit comfortably into both societies." I countered, "I've seen fire in the eyes of the rejected queen who has vowed to exterminate all Romans on this island, including those who serve them."

I then met with Lindum's legate and his staff, presenting my orders to borrow 500 of his cavalrymen to fight in Suetonius' anti-druidic campaign. I also warned him of the beginnings of the tribal revolt forming beyond the lower fenlands for which his *9th Legion* must be prepared to fight. Before I left, I attempted to convince his senior legionaries of the danger to their families——with this stark warning:

> If you have family members in Camulodunum's colony, you must move them or they'll all die in *Queen Boudica's Revenge*. I've just met her and understand her anger. At the same time, my Lusitani horseman has witnessed a widening assemblage of warriors, with sympathetic responses heard of from her neighboring tribes.

After the legate warned his staff members about the danger to their families in Camulodunum, he ordered, "Ready a fast ship to the *Colony* so we can transport your loved ones to Gallia until this crisis ends.

CHAPTER 26

CYMRUIAN WAR

On the morning of 30 September 60, I departed *Lindum* leading a 512-man cavalry *alae* toward *Deva*. This auxiliary *9th Legion quingenaria* consisted of sixteen 30-man *turmae*, plus 32 officers and administrative assistants, formerly commanded by a long-serving tribune who'd been wounded in a recent skirmish. His unit included 120 *Batavi* swimmers, 120 *equiti* (messengers, escorts, and scouts) and 240 Hispanic swordsmen (with strong Iberian warhorses). At noon, we crossed the *Trisantona Fluss* (the Trent) at *Ad Pontem* (East Stoke) and headed west below the *Peak District* toward *Derventio* (Little Chester). We followed a poorer track-way to *Rocester* and *Chesterton*, continuing northwest across open country, arriving at *Deva* (Chester) after a four-day ride. At Deva, we joined legionaries with whom we moved along the coast to *Pentre* where 40 flat-bottom transport ships lay anchored ready to move part of the *20th Legion's* infantry toward Mona. I saw little of Suetonius or his senior staff since my unit was attached to *Legio XX*. While awaiting the invasion, we sub-commanders were briefed on the battle plan by *Legio XIIII's* legate who'd come from *Burrium* (Usk). He told us,

> *Legio XIIII Gemina* from *Viroconium* and *Burrium* is the backbone of this operation. Overall control is under Governor *Suetonius Paulinus* (Rome's master of strategy and warfare). In previous years, he quelled other uprisings; however, his methods have been criticized as "too brutal."

131

When a young officer asked, "Why?" The legate added,

Procurator *Julius Alpinus* protested the violent way Suetonius conducts war. Freedman *Polyclitus* examined the complaint, causing Nero to fire Suetonius. Because our tough leader had been so effective as a warrior, Nero reinstated him (after Governor *Quintus Veranius* died after only seven months as governor), temporarily validating Suetonius' harsh ways.

The legate introduced a bright young tribune who told us of preparatory activities and why Suetonius was using so many soldiers in *Cymruia*. He began,

Random fighting in the north has become too costly. We've faced the *Siluri* in the southeast and the *Ordovici* in the north. The 2nd legion has been attacking in the southeast, while the 14th and parts of the 20th are ready to press the northern tribes onto *Mona*. During two years here, we've encountered heavy resistance from the *Ordovici* and *Decangli*. I helped Govenor *Veranius* plan a campaign, but he left Suetonius the task of crushing the Druid's stronghold. We know these scrappy *Cymruians* have courage because they attack our outposts and convoys, and use the *Snowdonian* Mountains to their advantage. We plan to crowd them onto Mona Island and exterminate them.

At that point, a staff officer added,

They're fond of war and eager to fight. We must be ready to face their wild ways——only courage appears to drive 'em on. Therefore, we must outwit them and limit their range of actions. That's why we're going to push them onto Mona Island where there's no escape.

One newcomer asked, "What kinds of weapons will they use, Sir?" A combat-experienced tribune answered,

They'll be lightly armed. Their chief weapon is the sword; some will carry spears and daggers. Body armor is rare, but shields and helmets are common. We expect javelin volleys followed by hand-to-hand fighting. Light chariots will be used on flat ground to thrust into our lines. They'll strike and withdraw in hit-and-run waves of thousands of sword-wielding infantrymen. They'll charge, engage, retire, regroup, and repeat those actions, expecting us to withdraw.

The legate concluded,

Since we've fought many battles here, we know their tribal tactics and how to defeat them. *Mona* is heavily defended and separated from the mainland by the *Menai Straits*—a big problem for us is getting our armies across in light barges to make simultaneous invasions along the front.

Weaponry, Strategy and Morale

As I rode along the shore in full view of the Celts on the far shore, I saw we'd been armed with the finest weaponry, including *ballistae* capable of throwing flaming missiles, boulders, and iron bolts more than a third of a mile with devastating effect on earthworks, fortifications, and massed troops. I was told our most powerful *onagers* could cast great stones across the straits in support of our amphibious landings.

Meanwhile, I saw our legionaries practicing with crossbows and *pila*, while others were feasting and singing in full view of their opponents who boomed vulgar insults from less than a thousand feet away. Most important for our morale was the sight of a well-supplied logistics train that supported us for a long siege. The biggest problem I saw was the fast-flowing tide sweeping through the narrow strait. I was told Suetonius had said,

Bridges will be useless against the tide's destructive strength. At low tide, deep-draft boats will be grounded. I've ordered flat-bottomed craft to float my infantry across when the tide is slack. I've also told my Batavian and Iberian cavalrymen, "Swim your strong warhorses across the strait under cover of my most intense fire and stone bombardment."

Later, he spoke to each legionary element, reassuring thousands,

These tribesmen and their priests have stood against us too long! I've gathered you who've demonstrated your worth beyond question. Let me reassure you——our opponents are lightly armed and include thousands of refugees without armor and lack the support we have. They won't be easy adversaries, but we'll defeat them. First we must cross that narrow strait. Go to your boats and horses and sleep 'til our firebombing begins. I'll see you on Mona tomorrow! *May our gods be with you my faithful warriors!*

The Next Morning

When I awoke after four hours of light sleep by my horse, I saw dozens of boats being carried to the water's edge by armed infantrymen awaiting the signal to row across. The heavy *ballistae* were straining for the first volley of crushing discharges, while bowmen and crossbow archers were set to launch a rain of iron-tipped arrows and lead-weighted bolts onto thick crowds of opposing tribesmen. Within minutes, cavalry commanders formed lines of mounted horsemen ready to lead our Batavi swimmers into the shallows to cross during the slackest tide.

Suddenly, a cry arose from the far shore as tribesmen began beating swords on shields and druids moved among blue-painted warriors, invoking dark forces against us. As the twilight brightened, we could see painted women dancing wildly among their warriors, waving torches to incite their men into action against our boatloads of invaders.

I'd massed my squadron right of center behind 40 boats of *14th and 20th Legion* infantrymen who were on the water. paddling like well-timed rowers. As I led my 500 cavalrymen into the shallows, I could see in the red dawn a flotilla of 30-man barges followed by six other 500-man cavalry units.

Suddenly there was a collective gasp, followed by an awed silence, as thousands of arrows and crossbow bolts rained down on the enemy. At that moment of strained silence, we could hear scores of resounding thuds as our *ballista* and *onager* crews launched heavy stones and missiles. We also saw fiery bombards arch high overhead and fall onto packed lines of swordsmen who stood as a secondary wave ready to confront our invaders who understood legionary disgrace if they failed to earn battle honors.

The Battle

As our first wave of legionaries arrived, I could hear the screams and moans of mortally wounded tribesmen and saw scores of our own troops lying dead on the shore. As rowers reversed empty boats for additional loads, some blocked our swimming horses, but my cavalrymen dodged left and right to gain footholds so we could burst on the shore to use our height advantages to chop down onto the masses, reversing left and right slaying as many tribesmen as possible. At this most dangerous point of our charge into enemy flanks, many injured horses lashed about, downing the nearest tribesmen who stood too tightly packed to be effective as swordsmen.

Amid the melee, I heard resounding impacts of metal on metal and swords cracking shields, making sounds our old warriors called, "the mad martial music of war." As the fury of death whirred all around, I saw my cavalrymen meet massed tribesmen on the deadliest front, slowly advancing in our part of the most violent human slaughter one could imagine. Through the bloody blur I glimpsed riderless horses bolting away, mowing down bewildered *Ordovicians*. As we gained more beachhead ground, I heared the shouts of centurions ordering infantrymen into *testudo* formations of interlocking shields for protection from overhead missiles while using *gladii* short-swords to punch into the exposed bellies of the compressed masses of tribesmen struggling all around them.

I followed four of my horsemen who'd penetrated the enemy flank where we turned to attack from the rear, allowing much of the Roman front to advance. From our risky position, I saw more barges arriving and scores of cavalrymen swimming between the boats loaded with another thousand heavily armed legionaries. Because all of my men had punched through and were now fighting with little support, we were confronted by fresh waves of swordsmen who forced us to higher ground from where I saw the sky filled with another cloud of bombards, arching high from the opposite shore.

Fortunately for us, other units also began breaking through, forcing the enemy's rearguard to fight in all directions, allowing second and third waves of our legionary invaders ashore. At the same time, unarmed *capsarii* were loading legionary wounded onto empty boats shuttling them to aid stations where bandaging was performed by others who worked to save our injured.

As I tried to rest my useless right arm from having swung my *Spatha* too many times, six of my riders dashed to protect me. Since my horse was bleeding and uncontrollable, ten of my warriors formed a protective wall, while five unseated were trying to grab riderless horses for remounts. From my viewpoint, I saw capsized boats and legionaries struggling in deeper water where dozens were drowning or being rescued by latecomers. I also saw arrows protruding from legionaries, tribesmen, and horses, and could hear cries from hundreds of wounded. I also saw women dragging wounded tribesmen into sacred groves where druid priests were promising immortality.

We rested briefly, but had to re-enter the heavy action to dominate this bloody massacre before we lost too many of our own troops. Meanwhile, the slaughter continued with unforeseen ferocity. I thought, *"The memory of Suetonius' extermination effort on Mona will echo as an unforgivable atrocity among all tribes in Britannia."* I also thought, *"After hours of executing fallen tribesmen, our mighty legions must appear too awesome for the rabble that opposes us to continue."*

Suetonius had said, "Breaking the enemy's line will start a rout that'll continue to the far side of the island. That rout of this rowdy force will leave us in a position to thrust across Mona's meadows and forests and push their defeated mob into the *Mare Atlanticus.*" As our invasion was climaxing, Suetonius crossed the strait with his senior staff officers and issued this shocking order: "Kill everyone!" He added,

> Seeing that first cavalry unit break through released my tensions. Killing our enemies will be easier now than if they'd stood to fight. We'll exploit their weakness and spare no one on this bloody field, including women. Chase the druids into their sacred groves and burn 'em alive. Show no quarter!

As Suetonius had ordered, men and women were being slaughtered. Druidic priests and their retinues were driven into sacred groves and burned, with none taken alive. I thought,

> *Suetonius will surely be called "the worst Roman." He'd quelled all resistance and earned the "Bloody Butcher of Britannia" title. But had he gone too far*

in vanquishing his enemies——even after most had surrendered? During the sleepless night that followed, I saw *flashing memories of thousands of bloody-haired, half-naked men wielding leather shields and iron swords, surrounded by wild-eyed, shrieking women and white-robed druids wailing to their gods. I heard the endless clash of weapons and obscene shouts of defiance roaring in my ears. I could still hear the dying screams and final grunts as my heavy sword sliced though those who'd injured my precious horse.* Each time I closed my eyes stark visions haunted me over and over. *I'd see the cluttered Menai Straits from both sides with arching floods of whistling arrows and resounding thuds of crushing bombards. I'd see bobbing bodies of long-serving legionaries trying to save themselves in the red and grey waters of the strait. Over and over, I saw the glint of polished weapons, heard painful cries of injured horses, and saw woad-blue men being struck down in unspeakable agony onto the blood-muddy ground.*

The next day, we thought, *"All is finished!"* ——Not so——Many who'd sought sanctuary had fled into the island's forests. Those found were executed on the spot. The injured in nearby homes were torched or carried to fire pits and thrown in alive. Mona's population was shattered, their holy men murdered, and the sacred groves burned to ashes. It was later reported, "Suetonius' campaign was a total victory; his valiant legions had dominated troubled *Cymruia*."

CHAPTER 27

PROBLEMS

Not long into the campaign, Suetonius called me to his headquarters where I met Marcus, who'd been reassigned from Hispania to serve on the governor's battle staff (awaiting a command assignment in Britannia). At the same time, I was ordered to return the 419 survivors of my borrowed squadron to *Lindum* and to proceed onward to *Londinium*. There I'd continue to serve as tribal negotiator until Suetonius arrived at his future headquarters in the rapidly growing *Tamesis River* trade center, chosen for its easy riverine access due to the tidal rise that reached so far inland.

Before I departed, Marcus told me about Aurelia and my children living with Sabina at her father's *latifundium* near *Tusculum*. He also told me of the plague-like illness that had swept through southern *Europa*, which his family and most soldiers had avoided in northern *Hispania*. In addition, he explained how his team had exposed "the great gold grab" and how he'd won favor by returning most of *Governor Gordus'* stash of Hispanic nuggets to the royal treasury. In turn, I told Marcus of my meetings with the late *King Esparatus* and his bold widow, *Boudica*, of whom I said, "will surely be a trouble maker."

In a brief meeting, Suetonius complimented Marcus on his effort to restore the 7th Legion to its former high status and said, "You're first in line to command either the 20th or the 2nd whose commanders had performed heroically and will be returning to Rome to join their families soon. Meanwhile, I'll post you to a *laticlavius* position. He then turned to me,

I've heard you made the initial breakthrough on the *Ordovici* front during our invasion. When we meet in Londinium, I'll present *ornamenta* to you and the others who performed so heroically in the battle. I want you to keep me informed about that Iceni harridan called Boudica who's causing even greater trouble in the eastern fen country.

He continued,

My mission here in *Cymruia* was to punish these tribes who've stood in the way of our northwestward march. We've killed ten thousand and wiped out their druids, but I'm now being accused of exercising a level of ferocity beyond what Nero requires. Because of efforts to end the druids, Nero may fire me again because of rumored uprisings.

As I led my wounded horse to rejoin my troops, Suetonius shouted,

After you deliver your borrowed squadron back to Lindum, I want you to race down to Londinium to prevent that verp *Catus Decianus* from doing more damage than he's already done. You reported he's caused great hostility among the Britannic tribes by recalling loans to the Iceni king. He claims he'd done it to protect *Seneca's* investments, demanding the widow-queen acknowledge her late husband's debts. As a result, *Catus* has demanded immediate repayment from her and other tribes.

At Lindum I learned, "Hundreds of Iceni and Trinovanti tribesmen have been resisting collections by baliffs, tax collectors, and soldiers, some of whom had reached Boudica's fort demanding huge repayments. Meanwhile, Milo told me, "Lindum's family members had sailed from Camulodum to Gallia; thanks to your warning, my family was with them."

As Antón and I traveled down the *Ermine Way* from Lindum through *Durobrivae* and other villages, I became aware that only older men and sub-teen boys remained in the west-fen villages. On inquiring where they'd gone, Vibi told Antón, "I'd heard all Iceni warriors had been ordered to assemble north of Camulodunum."

Realizing the immediacy of the threat, we hurried to the *Icknield Trackway* where we saw even more tribesmen heading southwest.

When we reached *Londinium,* all seemed quiet, so I sent Antón east to *Camulodunum* to find Milo's brother-in-law to learn of preparations for an attack. At Londinium, I learned *Procurator Catus* had already fled downriver on a ten-oared *schifo* to *Dubris* (Dover) with three staff members and 40 large bags of golden *aurea* and silver *denari* coins. At a riverside inn, I met Luki who told me of his concerns and of troubles north of *Camulodunum.* When I asked about Sabatini, he said,

> That *idiota culus* (dumb ass) will get us all killed! When he heard of Rome's effort to collect debts and confiscate tribal estates, he asked me to join him in "the best Iceni land grabs." Since he's so excited about rich pickings, he and six legionaries went to tell the queen they'd help her. I was expecting to meet him, but I doubt if I'll see him again when an uprising starts. I know he'll do something wicked when he and his retiree friends drink too much.

When Antón joined me in Londinium, he shook his head saying,

> Those bloody fools are oblivious of the great danger about to fall on 'em. I found Acacia's brother and told him what I'd seen along the western edge of Iceni territory and of an army forming to his north. He answered, "Your legions'll protect us." Former legionaries ask me to signal the governor for help.

Before my dispatch could reach Suetonius, conditions in the Iceni region exploded, sending an estimated 20,000 ill-trained warriors on a march toward *Camulodunum.* Little awareness of that human avalanche had reached the colony; nevertheless, word spread quickly that *"Boudica's Reprisal was Beginning!"* Along the northern track-ways every Romanized villa and farmstead was being destroyed and any Roman settler or sympathizer was being decapitated. As the tribal mass approached unprotected towns, urgent cries for help were signaled toward Londinium and on to Suetonius who was still far away in Cymruia. I was unable to offer any help other than my 200 guardsmen the *Procuator* had left behind who'd be of little value against thousands of tribesmen now bearing down on Camulodunum.

Since *Catus Decianus* had slipped away with all the *gold* he could carry, command fell to me of his double century, whom I told, "Be ready to cross the river and move west if the Iceni and Trinovanti armies head our way." An hour later, a dispatch rider reported, "Lindum's 9th Legion had marched south, responding to Suetonius' order to protect the colony. Soon it had met an overpowering force beyond the fens and was savagely beaten; its survivors withdrew toward the *Metaris Æstuar* (the Wash). Some are back are Lindum."

As my legionaries urged Londinium's tradesmen to flee upriver toward *Pontes* (Staines) or downriver toward *Vagniacis* or *Durobrivae* (Springhead or Rochester), others loaded trade goods to flee south toward *Noviomagus* (Chichester). Many remained, expecting a rescue from *Glevum* (Glouster, 210 miles west) or *Deva* (Chester, 250 miles northwest)——at least seven days away.

Since I was now commanding only 180 remaining troops in what one scurrying tradesman called *"a madhouse of indecision, awaiting unlikely rescue,"* I sent Antón back among the Trinovontes to learn if the Iceni queen might attack Londinium, or if her movements were just a showy bluff because Suetonius was far away. While waiting for Antón's report, we heard, "Something really bad had occurred to ignite the queen's wrath and cause her to become an *Avenging Spirit* to throw the Romans out of Britannia." Other reports called her a *"Phantom Fury, who'll strike suddenly and hard."* One old tribesman from *Canonium* (Kevelton) said, *"She'll make a quick strike to rid us of hundreds of aging legionaries who've settled amongst us."*

Antón hurried back from his *Chesterford*-through-*Chelmsford* circuit to report, "*Camulodunum's* attack is imminent! I saw dozens of clans massing near *Combretovium* (Baytham House). By now they're likely marching toward huddled colonials who must surely be aware of their deadly peril." He also told me of his most alarming discovery,

What may have kicked off this massive drive was a terrible act performed by six retirees led by a tribune who violated the queen's daughters. It sounds as if *Sabatini,* may've precipitated this tragedy we're facing. Although many stories sounded exaggerated, they're being repeated, saying, "An elderly tribune raped Boudica's daughters while his drunken legionaries restrained her." I also heard, they'd carried the naked queen outside and flogged her, claiming, *"We own this property now and all of its household slaves!"*

I soon heard this rape tale was being repeated across the entire Iceni domain, turning the queen into a mighty foe. A Trinovani woodsman told me, *"Thet lustful tribune 'as lit a flame thet'll burn Britannia ta ashes an'll cost the lives of ever last Romer 'ere."* Another Trinovanti farmer said, *"I'm 'eadin' fer two country villae where I'll plunder enough Romer riches ta never haf'ta work agin."*

Since Suetonius was away in *Cymruia*, I couldn't warn him before losses mounted. We'd sent flag and flare signals along a series of hilltop towers, backed by carrier pigeons, but got no replies. Our horseback messengers would take three to four days to reach him; therefore, I thought, *"I'm on my own to deal with this inflamed situation."* We soon began receiving reports of a catastrophe at *Camulodunum*, told by those few who'd fled across *Blackwater Bay* to *Othona* and *Durobrivae* (Birdwell and Rochester). Some escapees had headed east to *Durovernum* (Canterbury) while others came to *Londinium* expecting relief from the legions. Those moving along Milo's roads in the Southeast were dismayed on meeting runaways from Londinium. Unfortunate news came from *Petilius Cerialis* (*Legio VIIII's* commander) who'd tried to rescue beleaguered veterans, reporting, "We were ambushed short of Camulodunum, making us ineffective against Boudica's army."

To my amazement, Governor Suetonius arrived in Londinium with two staff members and ten legionary guards. When I met him, I asked, "How near are your legions?" He didn't answer, but asked, "How soon will we be attacked?" My uncertainty displeased him, but he answered my querry about his legions, saying, "They're mostly in Cymruia; I've come to determine if we can save this city." When I told him of Antón's findings, he mused,

It's too late to save Canulodunum or Londinium. Therefore, I'll sacrifice both to save Britannia as a Roman province. I want you to move north on *Watling Way* with your double-century and as many veterans as you can impress, and collect all the weapons and horses you can find. *Legio II* failed to join me; therefore, I'm left with *Legio XIIII, Legio XX*, and some *auxiliary* vexillations––perhaps 10,000 fighters. As soon as I return to my legions, I'll march them all toward *Viroconium* and *Pennocrucium* (Wroxeter and Water Newton). From the latter, I'll move down the Watling Street 'til I find a favored site to face Boudica's army that we'll meet soon.

At a quick lunch I asked, "May I inquire, Sir, how'd you get here so fast? He smiled, rubbing his backside, whispering,

We calculated the best route, knowing a straight line to *Londinium* (210 miles) would kill an old *eflatus* like me. We plotted the straightest four-day ride here; Unfortunately, I must reverse that painful trip immediately!

CHAPTER 28

CAMULODUNUM

Just as Governor Suetonius and I were preparing to leave Londinium in different directions, 17 escapees from the overwhelmed colony entered our city, sobbing out tales of horror. These stragglers had been on the south edge of the town and fled from what one described as "a screaming horde of thousands that flooded across our town where only a few hundred armed veterans faced them." Another breathless witness told us,

> From a mile away, I saw smoke rising from the center of town. Agonizing screams were followed by a period of silence, and then by a roar of cheers. We knew our colony had been overrun, but we also knew hundreds of our people had barricaded themselves in the half-finished temple that afforded the only protection from pitchfork and club-armed raiders. Meanwhile, hundreds of wealth-seekers focused on a fanatic search for loot before carrying out what must now be the mass murder of all remaining inhabitants.

One more pushed forward to tell the departing governor,

> I saw smoke and heard thousands chanting tribal war cries. As we raced toward *Mersea Isle*, we heard the rumbling of thousands heading your way. As we reached Merseaside, a single veteran helped us to the island as we clung to his *coracle*, which he paddled back and forth to save many of his friends. From there, ten of us rode an empty

tradesman's craft here to the *Walbrook Dock* where we loaded his boat for our passage to Gallia, hoping to leave on the outbound tide before the raiders could reach us.

From similar reports, I estimated Boudica's army would reach this city in 24 hours. Therefore, my soldiers rushed to tell a thousand remaining residents, "Get away as fast as you can! Boudica's on the march toward us and expects to meet Suetonius up north in a battle to free Britannia. She'll arrive soon to kill everyone here before she heads up Watling Street."

After spreading those warnings, I said farewell to Suetonius and headed toward *Verulamium* to tell those Roman settlers that Boudica's horde would reach their city within four days. On the way we saw hundreds of *Catuvellauni* tribesmen who'd been pushed aside by and now cluttered our northbound roadway. Again, we heard tales of the colony's destruction, including one from a retiree who was *fleeing with his Catu friends.* He recalled,

Two years ago, I took a land grant near *Caesaromagu*s (Chelmsford) on the border between our tribes where the *Catus* treated me better than the *Trints.* Unfortunately, my land was too far from the colony, but was among the best *Trinovanti* holdings; I obtained it with underclass tribesfolk and slaves. We joined a tribal aristocracy, but our leaders bungled that effort, after which the tribe's priesthood rejected our attempts to improve their region.

Such tales illuminated the pent-up feelings against Roman *heavy-handedness* magnified under Emperor Nero and Governor Suetonius. As we reached *Verulamium,* I learned the city and had gained Boudica's attention as a third target on her road to destiny. We hadn't been there long when Antón brought an eyewitness who described the destruction of the temple in Camulodunum. He told us, "As a legionarie who'd married a *Trint* woman many years ago, I'd helped build the white-marble Temple, but last night I witnessed it being used as the holdout for our vastly outnumbered retirees." He continued,

The Iceni and Trinovanti rebels crushed most resistance in one mighty rush. A second wave focused on our 150 remaining veterans who'd barricaded themselves in the temple. It took two days of *gladiatorial* fighting (with dead raiders stacked in piles) as our valiant defenders were slowly exterminated. At the end of their 50-hour resistance, their women were violated and left where they fell, or impaled on the Roman pikes that had pierced hundreds of tribesmen. As I watched from a rooftop that hadn't been torched, I saw thousands of looters dashing about collecting gold and silver items. I saw others digging for lead pipes or hidden coins. I also watched grave robbers wallowing in the rain-soaked cemetery, digging for lead coffins and entombed adornments––throwing skeletons about, gloating on finds, and dancing in looters' frenzies.

In the midst of his gruesome tale, I shouted, *"Enough! All is lost at the colony! Boudica will enter Londinium with her looters and repeat her violence in Sulloniacis* (Brockley Hill) *and Verulamium."* I continued, *"After she destroys these towns, she'll march up Watling Street through Durocobrius* (Dunstable), *Bannaventa* (Whiton Lodge), *Tripontium* (Caves Inn) *Venonis* (High Cross), *and Manduessedum* (Mancetter). *She'll likely meet Suetonius before she reaches additional towns."* I then parked my two centuries ten miles ahead of her slow-moving army, telling my troops,

> We'll move in increments with hers and send riders to the legions to determine where Suetonius plans to make his stand, perhaps where the *Fosse Way* crosses *Watling Street*. Tonight, we'll camp at *Durocobrius* where the *Icknield Way* transects our path. We'll search east of this north-south roadway to see if any Iceni clans are marching from the fens to join her trundling masses that are already north of *Verulamium*.

That evening, I dispatched three cavalrymen to reach *Suet's* distant legions. My chosen riders were carrying fresh accounts of the destruction of Londinium plus details of my position and of Boudica's northward march. Nevertheless, I offered information of her cart-paced train that was slowing her army's movement to fewer than ten miles a day toward Suetonius' rendezvous point short of Cartimunda's Brigantian Midlands.

When my riders returned, I learned Suetonius had rejoined his legions, selected a hillside near *Manduessedum* (Mancetter), and told his legionaries, "Prepare for a battle that may kill us all or make us heroes who saved our Britannic province." His dispatches ordered, "Maintain a watchful position and make an accurate count of *warriors, cavalrymen, chariots, support wagons, and camp followers*; relay that estimate to me as quickly as possible."

During the next two nights, we approached Boudica's camps to count her numbers. Many wheel tracks led us to overestimate her numbers as paths stretched far to both sides of the broad trackway— meandering through fields and farms—where tribesmen had foraged for food to support the supersized army that needed constant resupply.

After we passed *Lactodorum* (Towcester) and swam in the *Nene*, we raced back to the *Ouse* where we saw many of Boudica's army and camp followers swimming nude or dancing around campfires. That view gave us a better count of the rebel army (perhaps 70,000, plus 80,000 followers), which I dispatched to Suetonius that night. I also estimated about six days remained until he'd face Boudica.

CHAPTER 29

BOUDICA'S BATTLE

On April 15th, I led my 180 riders to Suetonius' headquarters where my odd-squad of legionaries, retirees, and Germanic recruits were allowed to remain together as auxiliaries assigned to Marcus' *four hundred hardy horsemen.* At officers' call, Suetonius introduced me saying, "This officer met Boudica a month ago before a former tribune triggered her revenge." He then told of our Londinium meeting, saying,

> When we met, he told me of Boudica's growing army, forcing me to conclude I couldn't defend Londinium, which I left just before she attacked. I've since learned they'd killed everyone in Londinium and Verulamium. While both towns were smoldering, I was riding back here where *Legios XIV* and *XX* were already preparing for a lopsided battle. Unfortunately, *Legio II* hasn't joined us and *Legio IX* is recovering from heavy losses incurred when rushing to save Camulodunum.

Later that day, Marcus told me,

> While Suetonius was with you in Londinium, his scouts located this steep-sloped *coombe* (dale) backed by a dense forest that'll force attackers to race uphill on an exhausting charge. When Suetonius saw this site, he told us (his staff officers), *"The terrain will protect our flanks and its forest will block rear approaches."* He'd approved, shouting, *"This layout will prevent*

Boudica from bringing her thousands to bear on us. This beautiful up-slope will make ambushes difficult, despite her numbers."

Since Suetonius' army had arrived at the prospective battle site before him, he ordered a large-scale practice, placing his legionaries in anticipated battle order, with light auxiliaries on the flanks and heavy and light cavalry on the wings. From a commanding view, he watched one legion and a cavalry squadron make an uphill dash toward the defending legion's compact line. Although his *chargers* stopped short, we all recognized the climb had winded men and horses, diminishing their fighting stamina.

Over the next 36 hours, our army stood by, polishing weapons and shields, eating roasted beef and fresh loaves of coarse bread baked in rock-domed field ovens, and resting as Boudica's army trundled ever nearer, followed by hundreds of loot-filled supply carts. Then, on May 18th, an observer high in a pine-log tower above the field *principia*, shouted down, "Look Sirs! Far beyond those southern hillocks—I see dust clouds rising from an army of ants swarming toward us."

All movement halted a mile away, after which three riders raced forward to a spot where they sat looking at us before planting red, yellow, and green banners as assembly points for parts of the Queen's mighty force. Then as twilight crept over us, her vast army inched into assigned positions. Quickly, 100 chariots advanced toward the center flag and withdrew for the night. Suddenly, their vast campsite became a racous mixture of feeding, drinking, shouting, singing, and finally—snoring.

A few hours later, most of us rose to hear an early morning chant being sung to intimidate our troops; however, our legions took turns singing melodic anthems of their units, which were soon smothered by a hundred-thousand-voice tribal chorus. Meanwhile, their chariot horses were harnessed for a morning charge, while plaid-clad and shirtless foot soldiers applied fresh coatings of woad. At the same time, our legionaries began moving to designated positions where they were served beef, biscuits, and boiled water to assure maximum fighting strength. Since Marcus stood a hundred feet from me, I heard him shout,

Look there! In the midst of those chariots! That's Queen Boudica on the central one addressing her troops. You may soon see her moving among her armies whose commanders are motivating their soldiers to kill us.

Suddenly, a lone Iceni messenger rode forward relaying Boudica's remarks, which he read aloud, *"Governor Gaius Suetonius Paulinus, if you weigh the strength of both armies and the causes of this war, you'll know you must conquer us or die. If any of your men survive, they'll be my slaves."*

Although her gigantic force stood defiantly echoing her bravado, we knew her army was poorly equipped after its strength had been impaired by a four-year disarmament effort that had preceded this rebellion. An important weakness Suetonius recognized was the scores of wagons and carts that cluttered the far end of her field where family members and loot collectors watched, expecting an overwhelming victory. At that point, Suetonius addressed his legionaries, saying,

> Ignore these bloody savages! There are more women in their ranks than men. We've beaten 'em before and when they feel your steel and face your fighting skills, they'll crack. Throw your javelins; knock 'em down with your shields, and finish them with your shining swords. Forget plunder! Just win this battle and you can have everything!

Suetonius's speech was blunt, but when Boudica's man rode back to repeat the speech to her, she signaled her army to charge into the narrowing field in a massive frontal attack. Her nearest warriors swarmed around her as she sent a wave of the first 40 chariots racing uphill, each carrying two swordsmen in a confident attempt to crack our solid line. Near the front, their tiring horses became easy targets. On signal, our crossbowmen effortlessly dispatched the leading charioteers, horses, and chariot riders. Soon our untouched front was littered with dead and wounded men and horses, and wrecked wicker chariots.

On hearing our *Cornicen's* piercing trumpet blast, my west-flank counterpart and I each led 180 riders downhill, racing along both enemy flanks to channel their surging body into a tighter mass. We then swept on to the far arc of wagons to slaughter oxen, draft hoses, and mules, freezing hundreds of support vehicles as an immovable barricade.

On hearing another brassy tone, Marcus and his opposite-flank commander pressed their heavy-horse troopers directly onto the fray, executing swaths of enemy soldiers within easy reach of their long *spathae.* Just ahead of their 80-yard-wide cavalry charge, a second volley of legionary *pila* staggered the enemy's advance as jointed javelins bent when hitting tribal shields, making those heavy spears impossible to remove. After such impacts, each unfortunate soldier was so burdened that he had to discard his shield and fight unprotected.

With Boudicas' tribesmen struggling in knots of compressed confusion, Suetonius ordered his legionaries to advance in secure *testudo-shell* wedges. Because of superior Roman discipline, armor, and weapons, we held a decisive advantage in close-quarter fighting against thousands of tightly packed enemy swordsmen. I then saw Marcus plunge deeper into the fray, sweeping hundreds of opponents aside with his heavy-horse *ala* (wing), trampling scores of Iceni *farmer-soldiers* under their broad-hoofed horses.

As Boudica's losses mounted, her dismayed warriors tried to retreat, but their flight was blocked by the unmovable arc of wagons we'd disabled; hence, many runners were executed as they tried to vault out of our trap. Both squadrons of our light cavalry continued to attack from the outside as the penetrating legionaries kept striking at the heart of their struggling masses, gradually killing most tribal warriors, terrified camp followers, and the disabled pack animals. It was later rumored 80,000 of Boudica'a people fell while fewer than 1,000 Romans were lost. Despite that wild claim, I'd seen many of the vast retinue of Iceni family members fleeing in all directions, purposely ignored by our long-serving, wifeless legionaries.

At the peak of fighting (while each Roman was focused on his nearest opponents) a protective band of Boudica's cavalry led her away, dashing northward toward Queen Cartimandua's Brigantian territory. Although two of my men attempted to follow her, Boudica's rescuers outdistanced our battle-fatigued horses whose riders were unable to catch the fleeing queen.

Because the slaughter on Watling's bloody battleground had passed its peak, Suetonius and his staff overlooked some of the escapees fleeing from the fringes of the intense struggle. Slowly, after six hours of mortal combat, the sound of clashing swords diminished until all fell quiet except for the moans and screams of wounded and dying people and animals. At last, each fighting element sounded recall to reassemble residues of its former ranks and stand prepared to re-engage, as needed.

Since Boudica's remains were not found among piles of bodies on the crimson field of death (even after our troops had stacked mountains of corpses), I ventured to Suetonius' high-ground *principia* to report that two of my troopers had pursued some mounted northbound escapees. He immediately berated me for not telling him sooner, but ordered, "I want you to go Cartimandura's fortress to find Boudica." He added,

> Tribune Marcus told me you helped *Old Scap* find *Caratacus* who was with that Brigantian *canicula* (bitch). He also told me she'd invited you to return. Therefore, I want you to ride to her fortress and ask your regal friend to give me *Boudica* so I can end this bloody rebellion. If the Iceni queen remains a heroic figure, we'll have a hard time keeping relationships with other kings and may loose this whole bloody province.

I then asked, "May I take Marcus and 20 protectors," which Suetonius approved. We then rode 3½ days to *Mamcumium* (Manchester) from where six of us were led to *Cartimandua's* tribal center at *Isurium* (Aldborough) where I'd been before. On our arrival, the stately queen welcomed me in her humorous style, shouting,

> It is a pleasure to see you again my pretty German horse thief. Did you come back to visit me or to kiss my pretty daughters who've spoken often of you? Bring your handsome friend and these fine young soldiers and we'll dine with *Vellocatus,* my new Consort. You may've heard that Prince-Consort *Venutius* is no longer with me after he rebelled against my rule.

After dinner, I broached the subject of Boudica's defeat in our Watling Street battle, which she acknowledged, but denied that the one she'd called "My distant cousin" had come to *Brigantum* for sanctuary from Suetonius. When she asked, "What would my tribes gain by giving you the runaway Iceni queen?" I answered,

> My dear queen, with Suetonius' approval, I'm authorized to assure extended non-involvement in your political affairs, as well as increased access to empire trade, and greater purchases of your tribe's cattle, sheep, goats, swine, and legumes to feed our armies.

To my surprise, she agreed and replied,

Tomorrow *Vellocatus* will lead you to Boudica's hideout, but I'm certain she'll not surrender to you nor the whole Roman army. I've been told she intends to raise a larger army from all 30 tribes with the help of *Venutius* who's protecting her now. Apparently, she expects to become another "Valiant Warrior" like *Caractacus*.

The next morning, we traveled back to *Mamcumium* from where we continued to a protected country estate. *King Venutius* remembered me from my visit 3½ years ago, but was less diplomatic than Queen Cartimandua (whom he'd divorced), saying bluntly, "State your business and leave; we no longer welcome Romans in my part of Brigantia." Since his tone was rigid, I asked, "May I meet your important visitor, Queen Boudica?" To which he responded, "Of course! Come with me to the horse barns." Greatly surprised by his co-operative response, Marcus and I followed him to a large stone building where three sealed caskets stood on stanchions ready for burial or shipment to some secret place for future rallying. As I recovered from my initial shock of his showy display, I turned to disbelief, asking, "Even though these plain coffins are clearly marked, how can I be certain Boudica and her daughters lie within? Even more important, how did each of them die?"

Venutius replied, "They perished by her self-induced poison as they drank with us. As she was slipping away, she requested this form of entombment and a *secret burial place of honor* for a future, grander, multi-tribe rebellion against Rome." Of course I asked, "May we have her coffin opened to verify her presence?" To which he replied, "I cannot honor your request because she wished to sustain the mystery of her possible survival and to protect mid-Britannia from further Roman expansion into my region.

CHAPTER 30

AFTERMATH

When we returned to the battle site, I was surprised to see the grounds had been cleared of most bodies and wreckage. Great piles of bone debris and charcoal remained on which pine logs had been burnt to relieve the gaging smell of death. In addition, wagonloads of loot the raiders had collected at the destroyed cities had been split with half designated for Nero's "Golden-House" and half for the warriors who'd fought so valiantly. It was an impressive collection of gold, silver, and art items, now guarded in large leather tents next to Suetonius' *principia*.

When Marcus and I reported to the governor's tent, I expected to hear a tirade from our leader whose reputation was buoyed, calling Suetonius Paulinus, *"the most successful battle master since Julius Caesar."* Instead of anger, he sat calmly as I told him of Boudica's likely death or her secret escape. He responded casually, saying,

> So be it lads; we'll see what comes of her reputation. Right now, I've other concerns. You may've heard our simpleton emperor is recalling me without honors. I think he's afraid I'll displace him. After tomorrow's award ceremony, I want each of you to lead 500-man *equiti ala* into Iceni territory to pursue those who've escaped our effort to wipe 'em all out.

Marcus asked, "May we know your plan, Sir?" Suetonius replied,

Of course! I've dispatched legionary vexalltions down *Watling Street* to regain control of *Verulamium* and *Londinium* where they'll impress *Catuvellauni* tribesmen into restoring those destroyed cities. I've also sent the 20th legion back to Cymruia to continue my conquest there. I want you and your *angusticlavius* (Ivano) to recapture *Camulodunum* and *Venta Icenorum* while I lead the 14th legion back to my headquarters at *Glevum* until we can get the remaining problems cleared up in *Cymruia* (that some now call *Cambria*). I'll meet you two in *Londinium* before I go back to Rome.

As promised, Suetonius awarded *ornamenta triumphalia* to his victorious commanders and large *phalerae* to thousands of our battle-proven soldiers. He also issued new *paludamentae* (cloaks) to distinguish combat officers from *sagae* worn by wounded soldiers. Although Marcus and I each commanded *quingenariae*, Suetonius designated Marcus *Praefectus equitatus* (commander of our *vexillatio*) and me *Duplicari tribunus angusticlavius* (his vice commander). Suetonius also told us,

You can keep your battle-honored *primus pilae* (*first-Javelin* centurions), your *duplicarii* (seconds-in-command), your long-serving *beneficiarii* (special-duty soldiers), and heavily armed *cataphracti* (cavalry). Since you've accumulated *evocati* (veterans beyond 20 years'), *pabulatori* (foragers), and *tubicini* (signal trumpeters), you'll have 500-man bodies of troops for your assignments to reestablish control in southeast Britannia. I'll also be requesting legionary assistance from Gallia and Germania to restore peace in all Iceni lands.

The next morning, we began broad sweeps on overland trackways, seeking clusters of Iceni and Trinovanti runaways hiding in woods and bracken patches, and living off the land on their slow southeastern treks homeward. Although we'd been ordered to kill everyone and confiscate all hidden booty, Marcus instructed his men to look for frightened widows with farmlands beyond the fenlands as potential concubines.

My *quingenaria's* 20-mile-wide sweep began at the *Fosse Way* between *Ratae* and *Venonae* (Leicester and High Cross) from where we proceeded east below *Durobrivae* (Caster) to the *Ouse* River between the *Metaris* tidal flats and the large *Eel Island* where we found scores of unaccompanied women, attempting to hide from my troops.

On finding so many women and children without menfolk there, I decided to establish a marching camp to sort out fleeing widows from permanent residents and collect gold torcs and rich booty hidden beneath long-sleeved garments. Because I knew of reed-shrouded islets in the waterlogged fens, I paid a merchant one *denarius* to lead me on a wide circuit to reed-shack hideouts where Fensmen rarely left their hidden homes. On a familiar-looking isle, I encountered my former host and his pretty nieces——one pregnant who called me "Uncle."

Following Marcus' lead, I'd chosen not to kill innocent people who feared their gloomy prospects. Since I'd found little cause to exterminate these desperate ones, we moved beyond the black-soiled fenlands, passing scores of chalk-pits where I witnessed the remnants of an ancient industry that one busy flint-knapper told me, *"Our flintin' work 'as been 'ere fer many a yeer. Would ya like ta see me clunch pit, Sire?"*

We descended 30 feet on a shaky ladder where we encountered two chalk-white diggers using worn hirsh antlers used to wrest black nodules from a thick chest-high stratum of hard stones and bigger boulders from a stratum below our feet. In an abandoned, dead-end diggings, I glimpsed three tear-stained women clutching small children. When I surfaced, I saw evidence of centuries of work the skilled old knapper described as, "Our trade-good arrow flints fer furaway fightin' folks." I thought, these older chalk pits are likely hiding scores of hungry widows with poor pospects.

Finally, we arrived at the *Peddars Way*, where we found hundreds more of the exhausted escapees huddled in rain-soaked garments, expecting execution or enslavement. While we were collecting booty, Antón found a thatch-roofed farmstead with big horse barns where we sheltered and fed many of that miserable lot before we turned northward to *Brandodunum* (Brancaster) on the *Mare Germanicus Littus* (the North-Sea Shore). From there we moved toward *Gariannonum* then down to *Venta Icenorum* (Boudica's second homesite), where I established a headquarters in the ransacked villa and set up barracks in her horse barns from where I could govern some of the scattered Iceni tribesfolk until proper Roman rule could be established.

Immediately, I sent forager squads out to confiscate foodstocks for the returnees' immediate needs. I also dispatched riders to find Marcus to compare governing actions and learn if a new governor had been appointed. I needed to know where his headquarters would be, since Camulodunum and Londinium had been obliterated. I also called a meeting with the few remaining tribal elders in a first attempt to rebuild a sense of unity under my temporary rule.

Acting Chieftains

After three weeks of dealing with hundreds of farm widows, I'd become trusted enough to allow the storing of basic foods. Meanwhile, nine petty Roman officials arrived to confiscate the best farmlands, destabilizing my efforts to regain normalcy. Since similar acts had caused turmoil at the two central cities where young tribunes now ruled, the governor ordered his commanders to meet him on a trireme docked in burned-out Londinium to prepare for transferring military rule to dozens of Roman officials arriving from Gallia, Germania, and Rome. Because a new governor had not yet arrived, Suetonius said, "Continue to rule your clans as if you were their chiefs and don't let those opportunists from Rome make a mess of things."

After the meeting, Marcus and I slept next door on a leaky transport that served as a dormer and an ale house where we encountered *Luki* again. He'd just returned from *Regnum* (Chichester), gloating, "I saved my inventory by moving it before Londinium's destruction." In our discussion, I asked, "Do you know the location of your tricky partner now?" He replied,

> As I said before, that headstrong fool went to see Boudica at *Venta* before the blowup. From what I know of him, he probably ignited the revolt. If he's alive, he's likely hiding on my boat near *Gariannonum* after traveling up the *Gariennus Fluss Aestuar* (Yare River Estuary) to meet her. If he's not there, he's at *Caistor* or across the *Oceanus Germanicus* in *Belgica*, or on the *Rhein* in *Batavorum*.

When I reached *Gariannonum*, I sent Antón to search for Sabatini while I dealt with opportunists who'd claimed Iceni lands. Later Antón reported, "Sabatini had been seen on a boat near the *Gariennus* mouth before the rebellion began. I was told he'd put out to sea toward

Germania. At sea, he could've turned south toward the Britannic port of *Rutupae* (Richborough).

When I moaned, *I've lost him again*, Antón asked, "May I pursue him?" I answered,

> Go ask Luki if Sabatini may be returning through *Durovernium* (Canterbury). If he's not there, we'll go to Germania to look for him. He always leaves a destructive trail wherever he goes. Since I'll soon be finished here, I'll request permission to pursue that poisonous rascal wherever he may choose to hide. You're welcome to join me, Antón.

Anticipating recall, Suetonius reinforced his army with troops from Germania to conduct another punitive raid against troublesome pockets of resistance. Most of his efforts proved counterproductive, alarming other tribes. *Gaius Alpinus Classicianus* (a new *procurator*) had told Nero, "Suetonius' brutal actions are causing sympathetic hostilities." An inquiry conducted by *Polyclitius* claimed, "Suetonius' ship losses can be used as a cause to relieve him of his command." Instead, Nero offered the tough general a consulsnip. We then heard, *"Suet's* brutal reputation is being disputed in Rome." Many senators have equivocated saying, "Although he's unnecessarily harsh, he's won our most important battle in 50 years."

With only *Polyclitius'* weak claims, the general staff cashiered Suetonius, forcing him to transfer his army to *Petronius Turpilianus* (a wealthy politician recently named consul). Because of Suet's sullied reputation, *Governor Turp* veiled his inactions in the name of "Neronian Peace," announcing, "I'll forgive all tribal kings who repent."

I noticed six tribunes had come with him to take command of the Britannic legions and our cavalry *alae*. Like most of Seutonius' combat leaders, we anticipated reassignments to Hispania, Germania, or Judaea, or less-desirable staff positions in Rome. While awaiting reassignment, I introduced my successor, *Decius Macrinus*, to my 500 cavalrymen to provide a smooth transition for the young officer and allay troop resentments, knowing their new tribune had no combat experience, especially after all 432 of my surviving troops had just fought in the greatest battle since the AD 9 *Teutoberger Forest* defeat where 12,000 legionaries had been slaughtered.

Decius Macrinus repeatedly asked my advice, requesting a month's delay of my transfer. That delay allowed me to obtain permission to proceed to Germania to search for Sabatini who'd reportedly ignited the rebellion. Fortunately, Governor *Turp* authorized my pursuit of Sabatini, allowing me to take *Antón, Vibi,* and *Barbatus* on my mission.

CHAPTER 31

LOWLANDS

After a month showing *Macrinus* most of the Iceni region from the fens to the *Mare Germanicus*, I set out with my henchmen to find Sabatini. First we dashed to *Londinium* to learn if he'd contacted Luki, who told me,

> Because you've been to *Venta*, he's avoided appearances in Britannia for fear of being recognized as the one who assaulted the royal Iceni maidens. He knows you might send him back to the dismal mine near *Aquae Sulis*.

We then embarked on a slow transport from *Londinium* across the *Oceanus Germanicus* to *Lugdunum Batavorium* (near Katwijk) where we made inquiries about Sabatini. With no satisfaction, we continued along the Rhein to Roman camps at *Traiectum* (Utrecht) and *Castellum Fectio* (Vechtum), and the big legionary *castra* at *Novimagus Batavorum* (Nijmegen) that held 4,800 legionaries and 1,000 auxiliaries. Four years earlier, I'd passed through those camps to and from *Colonia Agrippina*. *Novimagus* had become the most important lower-Rhein settlement where troops were building watchtowers and encampments to protect this Romanized region from attacks by northern tribes. I found eight outlying camps that were being constructed to hold 300 soldiers each.

When we stopped to eat Batavian bread and cheese, Vibi added his historical understanding of the region, saying,

When Caesar entered *Gallia* a century ago, he claimed this area as part of the expanding Roman Republic from where he'd reach deeper into *Germania Magna*. Fifty years later, Augustus sent General Drusus to bring the lowland tribes under Roman rule. Recently a border wall (called the *Limes*) was begun along the lower Rhein, making this river Rome's newly acclaimed border. As more Romans arrived (expanding Claudius' *Rhenic* provinces northeastward to the Elbe), tribal problems caused most new Roman settlers to withdraw to the Rhein's defendable border as forts and vexillations were built along its banks.

Since I'd been here before, I added,

Earlier when I'd served upstream at *Colonia Agrippina,* I'd dealt with five headstrong chiefs in this region. Because the Rhein flowed by *Albaniana* (Alphen aan de Rijn), *Traiechtum* (Utrecht), *Ulpia Trajana* (Xanten), and *Lugdunum Batavorum* (Katwijk), I'd already known those older *Frisii* and *Batavi* chiefs because we shared language, culture, and religion. Some of our haughty commanders who'd come from Rome called their tribes "most uncivilized." With the northward advance of Roman traders, their first contacts brought the *Frisii* into a vigorus commercial relationship until two tribes revolted, destroying *Felvum* (Velzen), after which they remained beyond the *Limes* in what the *Frisii* called "Free Germania."

When I introduced myself to *Legatus Amulius Virius Carantus* to tell him of our search for Sabatini, he said, "I recognize you as a former commander upriver at *Colonia Agrippina.*" He'd been told of my mission and offered me ten guards and a signalman. He also invited us to dine with his officers where I told them of *Boudica's War* and of our efforts to restore peace.

Next morning *Carantus* signaled his dispersed centurions at ten outposts (*Flevum, Lugdunum Batavorum, Praetorium Agrippinae, Matilo, Albaniana, Laurium, Traiechtum, Fectio, Levefanum,* and *Carvo*), telling them to watch for a runaway tribune being sought for treason. I then led my search party north to visit *Frisii* and *Chamavi* chiefs whom I'd met in their *Nederlandish* regions north of the Rhein where Sabatini might be hiding.

Over the next four days, we passed through *Chamavi* lands without success and reached the Frisian fens before turning south through other clans next to the Rhein—again without word of our escapee. When we arrived at *Traiechtum*, I read a signal from *Carantus*, saying, "A former Roman officer had been seen moving from *Gesoriacum* (Boulogne) through *Menapii* territory with three legionary retirees."

As a result, we hurried past *Batavi* lands south of *Fectio* into the *Tungri* forests above *Atuatuca* (Tongres), moving as fast as possible on the road between *Gesoriacum* and *Colonia Agrippina*. As we camped among friendly *Tungeri*, I ask them to alert the *Frisiabomi* and *Texuandi* tribes of a possible southward move by the one we were seeking. Because Sabatini may have learned we'd come to find him, he'd begun moving in diverse directions.

We hired *Stane Flooren* (a *Tungeri* clansman known for his keen tracking-dogs) who claimed, "My hounds can follow any man or beast." I asked, "*Sind Ihre Hunde Laconi, Vertragi, oder Agassi?* (Are your dogs Lacons, Vertrags or Agassians?) He responded in lowland *platt, Ich weiss nicht. Meine Hunde kann alle critters finden, aber Agate ist am besten fur manntrackin. Er kann den kleinest whiffs aus der luft finden und folgen.* (I know not; but my hounds can find all critters. Agate is the best for tracking men. He can sniff out the smallest oders to follow).

I asked, "How much *geld* to work him?" He looked at my shoes then replied, "*Zwo Denari pro Tag und ein goldenes Aureus wenn ich den Mann finde.*" (Two denarius a day and one golden Aureus when I find the man). I agreed and asked, "When shall we start? He replied, "*Nach Ontbijt!* (after breakfast). *Hast du der Mann's odor mit?*" (Do you have the man's odor with you"). "No!" I answered. "But he'll smell like the old boat on which he crossed the *fretum*."

The Chase

Immediately after a breakfast of gruel and strong duck eggs, my six companions and ten *Noviomagus* guards headed north through *Texuandri* farmlands. *Stane* and his skinny son *Mundus* handled two tracker dogs each, including younger ones they'd been training. Without an odor for *Agate* to sniff, we carried the dogs on horseback 'til we reached a recent campsite where *Agate* roamed about testing smells where four people had lain.

Suddenly *Old Agate* bugled confidently, announcing he was ready for pursuit. Before *Stane* released him, he allowed the young dogs to sample four different bedding sites and told me, "*Montieren Sie Auf Ritter*, wir *die*

Hunde folgen!" (Mount up Sir Knight! We follow the hounds). After a half-hour's chase with the dogs running far ahead, *Stane* blew his battered old horn, which brought the young dogs back, but *Agate* sat on a nearby rise to watch as we rested our horses and the other dogs.

Thirty minutes later, we started at a slower pace until we came to a place where the dogs sniffed about until *Agate* was ready to cross the river where two dogs wanted to head upstream, but Aggie turned downstream. When we caught up, we followed him into the *Frisiaboni* region and farther west into the *Cananeflati* fens. Since the muddy marshlands had become too difficult for our horses to wallow onward, Stane told me,

> *Lass die Bewacher und Pferde auf dieser kleinen Insel. Fünf von uns können Agate folgen und uns zu ihrem versteckten Mann bringen. Jetzt ist er müde vom schuften durch diese endlosen fenen Länder. Wir werden ihn bald finden. Kanst du nicht hören, Aggie's Hundmusik ist stärker?* (Leave the guards and horses on this island. Five of us can follow Agate to where your man is hiding. He is tired from struggling through these boggy fens; we'll find him soon. Can't you hear Agate's dog music is stronger).

As we approached another island, we kept the dogs from attacking the one who'd climbed onto low branches of a burled ancient oak. As *Stane* whistled, the dogs quieted, allowing us to approach near enough to identify Sabatini who appeared ghostly after a long foodless run. When he recognized me, he croaked, "Greetings, my *inimicus*; at last we're together again. As you can see, I can run no more. I only ask you'll not take me back to that terrible mine."

We then rejoined *Mundus* whose dogs had found the others. After a well-deserved rest, we took all four to the island where our troopers had established a small marching camp and had prepared a big wildfowl, eel, and marsh-garden meal, on which we feasted. While we'd been gone, two soldiers had located a marsh brewer from whom they'd purchased a bladder of ale that added a lively aspect to our soggy celebration where I paid *Stane* a handful of *denari* and one golden *aureus* as promised for finding Sabatini.

Over the next three days, we wandered back to *Noviomagus* where I thanked *Legate Carantus* for his support and asked him for an upriver boat to deliver Sabatini to King Geron for final judgment. Almost immediately, *Carantus* argued, "He must be returned to Rome because he ignited Boudica's revolt in Britannia. I countered,

> Sabatini's already been condemned by the Senate. He's been exiled, imprisoned, and sentenced to *castratus*. I'd even witnessed his *raptus*-murder of my royal-family cousin, who could've become our tribe's king and made life easier for our legions east of the Rhein. In addition, I've sworn to Uncle Geron and my angry cousins that I'd capture Fulko's murderer, or stand in disgrace before my tribe.

Since *Legate Carantus* had *Batavic* ancestry, he insisted, "Sabatini's fate should belong to the governor or the emperor." I tried to refute his view because I'd face endless delays and meaningless travel. Nevertheless, *Carantus* said, "I'll accompany you to my governor's *Germania Inferior Principia* where we'll let him choose." To avoid an argument, I yielded, thinking, *"What a dumb way to operate as a legate. The governor will resent pushing this decision to him."*

CHAPTER 32

DELIVERING SABATINI

Next morning, I learned from a staff officer that *Carantus* had already briefed his governor, who'd responded as I'd expected, shouting,

> Begone, you gutless weasel! You should've left that *Cinaedus* (deviant) out in the fens for the buzzards. Why waste my time on this matter? I remember when the Senate farted around with Sabatini's case years ago and then left that swine off too easily. Come back tomorrow and bring me a manly decision!

When I told *Governor Turpilianus* of my decision to take Sabatini east of the Rhein to face Chattian justice, he smiled saying, "Good Choice, Ivo! What will you do to him?" I replied, "The final choice will belong to the murdered boy's father——King Geron. No doubt, it will involve a painful death. I'll report to you, Sir, when I pass back through here."

Accompanied by my faithful companions, we departed *Colonia* moving upriver to *Confluentes* (Koblenz) where we entered the *Logana Fluss* (the Lahn) with Sabatini tied on the 12-oar boat's deck. Throughout the afternoon we meandered through endless switchback riverbends to the rapids beyond the sharp west turn above Marburg. Since Sabatini appeared in a state of trauma, we made camp at the *Ohm-River* intersection from where I went onward to tell Uncle Geron we held his son's murderer downriver near his former oppidium before their AD 59 *Hermunduri -Chatti* battle.

The next day, I returned with Geron and three cousins where we drank *dunkelbrau* and ate roasted venison while arguing what punishment should apply to Sabatini. The cousins suggested burning, boiling, burial (alive), and brutal methods of execution, but none could agree on a proper end of one so depraved as Sabatini. Since such cruel ideas were unacceptable to Geron, he agreed to allow Sabatini to live somewhat longer if he'd explain his depravity and account for all the people he'd assaulted or killed in his lifetime. To our surprise, the aging tribune (after drinking three flagons of dark beer) told of his predatory life and his hunt for unwilling boys and girls. The more he drank, the stranger his tales became, confessing,

> There's little satisfaction in *raptus*. For me it's power. I'm a coward who never faced combat, but shrunk from danger. Each time I dominated someone, I felt superior until I faced my own inadequacy and had to find another child to dominate. You'll find these practices common among efete men who've never faced hazards like those of you who were trained to die for others. Unfortunately, Sir, your son was opportune that morning for me to demonstrate my tribunal power to my six young legionaries whom I desired.

As the inquiry continued, Sabatini used a rare word to explain himself,

> When you look at my hawkish visage, you'll see I'm no beauty—one who's never been loved! The term *exoletus* usually means one who's worn out with age, usually applying to those who've passed beyond being an object of desire; they're called *exoleti!* No such person can expect any reciprocity of affection. Since I was odious from adolescence, my objects of sensuality were prostitutes who catered to deviants. The term "Exoleti" also distinguishes effeminate males—*"catamiti."*

At that point, Antón who'd been silent said,

> In his teachings, *Apostle Paul* who taught Jesus' gospel admonished us all in his *First Epistle to the Corinthi*, writing, "People who do wrong *will not inherit the kingdom of God.*" He also emphasized, *"People of immoral*

lives—idolaters, adulterers, catamites, sodomites, thieves, drunkards, usurers,
slanderers, and swindlers will never inherit God's kingdom."

Geron asked, "Who're the *catamites* you named? Some enemy tribe?"
Sabatini answered, "*Catamites* are pederasts named after a boy called
Ganymede who became the intimate companion of an effete young man
in Greece. It's now a bitter insult when directed toward a man." As
I was translating this strange discussion to Geron and my inebriated
cousins who seemed bewildered about Sabatini's admissions, Geron also
asked, "What happens to those you called *idolaters, adulterers, catamites,* and
sodomites." Marcus, who'd drunk little, replied,

We Romans base our afterlife views on Greek concepts of heaven and
hell. We believe our souls are assigned as a result of good or bad deeds
when living. Hell is for those who've committed serious sins and need
harsh punishments. That judgment usually results in endless pain and
suffering. We've been told our departing souls cross the *River Styx*,
where our deeds and misdeeds are evaluated by *Minos, Rhadamanthus,*
and *Aecus* who decide where our souls will reside. All warriors fly
to *paradiso*; honest citizens go to the *Plain of Asphodel*; those who've
offended the gods descend to *Tartarus*.

Geron asked, "*Wohin geht Sabatini?* (Where will Sabatini go?) From
Greek and Roman literary sources, Marcus answered,

He'll descend to *Tartarus* where the very worst sinners are sent. In his
long epic poem *The Aeneid, Publius Vergilius Maro* (Virgil) called it, "The
farthest place surrounded by the flaming *Phlegethon River* and triple walls
to prevent sinners from escaping. Its solid *adamantine* columns are so
hard nothing can cut them. *Tisiphone* (revenge) guards a pit that extends
twice as far into the earth as the distance from here to *Mount Olympus*."
The Greek poet Hesiod added, "A bronze anvil would fall nine days
from heaven before it reached the earth and would fall nine more days
to *Tartarus*." In his epic story, *The Iliad*, the Graecian poet. *Homerus*,
wrote, "*Tartarus* is as far beneath Hades as heaven is above the earth."
At the bottom of this deep pit, sinners agonize in everlasting torment.

Antón suddenly announced, I've been told, *"All souls are redeemable!"* Having viewed *the crucifiction* of the one he called *"Our Redeemer,"* Antón seemed embodied with an *enlightened sprit,* telling us that one he called *Paul of Tarsus* had emphasized, "One's faith in *Jesus* assures us we can share in *His* spiritual salvation." He added,

> Paul had claimed, *"Jesus' death benefited all believers, dying for all sins to be forgiven. His resurrection was of ultimate importance, bringing a promise of salvation to all believers."* He taught, *"When Christ returns, those who died believing in Him (as the Savior of Mankind) would come to life and meet the Lord."* Paul had told us, *"God's Son was crucified for the sins of all humanity. Those believing in Him will live with Him forever."*

Antón continued, "Christ's followers urge us all to live by sanctified standards. Then our *God of Peace* will sanctify us. I pray that our spirits, souls, and bodies will remain blameless unto the coming of our Lord."

Christians are redeemed from sin by the death and resurrection of Jesus, making peace between God and man. By grace through faith, you can gain victory over death. Each believer experiences a renewed reconciliation with God through that sacrificial death, which provides forgiveness in which you can share.

After a long silence considering Antón's spiritual message, we turned to other religions, allowing me to mention an eastern mystery, about which I told of Mithras' unending war of good against evil, his identity as a good spirit, an attendant to the *Lord of Life,* and an agent of the Sun. Although it was acceptable to many Roman soldiers, others said it was too ceremonial. Some Mithratic ideas were also found in Antón's religion: *Salvation, baptism, and the symbolism of the cross and feasts.* To which Sabatini said, "I too was a Mithratic initiate, but the *Couriers* rejected me because of my excesses."

The discussion then shifted to religions that came from the east as slave and migrant populations swelled from conquests and soldiers returned from afar. Some cults seemed influential and distinct from the traditional Roman beliefs. These cults included *Isis* (from Egypt), *Great Mother Cybele* (from Anatolia), *Eleusis, Demeter, Persephone,* and *Dionysus* (from Graecia) and dozens more, which seemed too ceremonial. Even Cicero recognized their value to the masses, writing, "Athens made outstanding contributions to human life——but no gift from heaven was greater than the mysteries. *We've gained a way of living in happiness and dying with a better hope.*"

When religious tolerance and restraint was mentioned, Marcus acknowledged there'd been Augustan periods of suppression, notably against Cybele's orgiastic rites and disorderly *Bacchan* conduct, to which Sabatini responded, "I'd favored all of those lively and noisy festivities, especially when drinking too much wine."

The discussion continued about a bewildering variety of religious edifices that one could visit in Rome. In addition to temples of Jupiter, Mars, and Venus, there were altars to *Silvanus* spirits and too many *Nymphs.* In addition, there are underground *Mithrathian Taurobolia* that excluded women. Finally, at the temple of *Isis,* there was a regal hierarchy of priests under whom initiates experienced so-called *spiritual rebirth,* about which Marcus remembered this passage from *Publius Ovidius Naso's* (Ovid's) *Metamorphosen,*

> *Holy goddess, everlasting Savior of mankind, ever generous in your help to mortals, you protect men by land and sea. You lull life's storms and stretch your hand to rescue mortals. You unravel the tangled web of Fate. I shall always guard your holy divinity in the sacred places of my heart.*

Central to some *Eastern Mysteries* was the concept that one's soul inhabits different bodies. Marcus spoke of Graecian philosophies,

> The mathematician *Pythagoras* taught, *"The soul is immortal and can own another body after death." Plato* claimed, *"The soul can be reborn many times before earning heavenly bliss."* Others preached, "All beings are restored through cycles of purification regulated by the *Law of Karma* governing successive lives with one's soul traveling through different bodies through time." One's soul develops a history of all the good and bad he or she has done on that soul's lifetime pathways. That soul provides a continuing assessment of all decisions made in each life and carries a burden into the next life, affecting actions that should provide new meanings and guide actions toward spiritual purification.

The next day, we moved to another camp where a sober discussion led Geron to demand, *"Tell me more of salvation and what may become of one so evil as Sabatini!"* Marcus responded,

> Karmic actions aren't linked to moral criteria. Instead, every good action allows a person to grow spiritually or cause improvements in others. A good person scores "positive karma," while a bad one adds "negative karma." Favorable debts are repaid in later lives, while negative scores are repaid in painful situations from which lessons must be learned. These cumulative accounts must be settled to expiate obligations from bad actions. Such beliefs hold *"a continuing consciousness incarnates new bodies when each life is no longer useful."* Recorporation is required to pay debts acquired in past lives with one often needing more lives to become free. *Palingenesia* means rebirth—Socrates and Plato both believed in it. Buddhists say we must face the consequences of past lives. The Druids defend it; the Egyptians believe death is just a step toward another life.

After hours of discussion, Sabatini exclaimed, I'm ready to accept Antón's belief in his *Redeemer*. What must I do to gain Christ's promise of salvation, and how will I know if it is true?" Antón answered, "According to *Apostle John*, 'You must wash away your sins and proclaim Christ as your Redeemer. You'll join others who've discovered *His* true path and sin no more. Thereafter, you'll lead others to that Path."

Sabatini countered, "It sounds too simple! You're claiming all I must do is say, *"I believe"* and I'm free of all my bad karma and can join your shining angels to live untarnished by all my former actions, no matter how evil? How may I know if your promise will work?" Antón replied, *"By faith alone, Jesus promised.* Baptism of the Spirit is an experience different from salvation. It'll give you spiritual power and the ability to live a victorious life."

Sabatini's Baptism

The next morning before we moved on, we arose early to watch Antón baptize Sabatini in the *Logona's* cold waters. As they moved to midriver with Sabatini's hands tied, we watched from a nearby bank, expecting a simple immersion ceremony, during which Antón announced,

Hear the Father's ancient promise! Listen, thirsty, weary one!
"I will pour My Holy Spirit; On thy chosen seed, O Son."
Promise to the Lord's Anointed, Gift of God to Him for thee!
Now, by covenant appointed, All thy springs in Him shall be.
Springs of peace, when conflict heightens, Thine uplifted eye shall see;
Peace that strengthens, calms and brightens, Peace, itself a victory.
Springs of comfort, strangely springing, Through the bitter wells of woe;
Fonts of hidden gladness, bringing, Joy that earth can ne'er bestow.
Now arise! His Word possessing, Claim the promise of the Lord;
Plead through Christ for showers of blessing,
'Til the Spirit be outpoured! (Havergal)

As Sabtini arose, Geron shouted, *"Bist du ein neuen Mann?"* (Are you a new man?) Sabatini replied indifferently, "Just wet and cold, Old Man!" Before anyone could restrain him, Cousin Ansgar rushed midstream, forcing Sabatini into the current and holding him under as they were swept beyond our reach. When we finally caught them many paces downstream, Sabatini seemed lifeless and Ansgar looked triumphant, shouting, "Now this *putrescent putzmann* can fall to *Tartarus* where he belongs. While Marcus was trying to revive Sabatini, Geron excoriated Ansgar, shouting, *"Sheistkopf!* You may now share your victim's karmic destiny."

After minutes of resuscitation efforts, Sabatini coughed, taking short desperate breaths and speaking in barely audible tones while recovering from his near-death experience. Later Geron asked, *"Hast du die anderen Seit sehen?"* (Did you see the other side?) Antón also inquired, "Was there a bright light leading to heaven, or a yawning gate to the *pit of everlasting torment?"*

Sabatini answered, "I was in a whirlpool, descending in circles into darkness. My only hope of escape from the *Fiery Acheronic Pit of No Return* was Antón's *Holy-Spirit* and *Redemption* words."

As we moved onward toward Geron's new citadel, I could see Sabatini was in a *pneumonicus* condition vulnerable to cold-weather illnesses, needing care through the hard months ahead. Because of his coughing fits, it appeared the aging tribune might not recover.

Since I'd fulfilled my promise to Geron to capture his son's murderer and delivered Sabatini for Chattian justice, I ask Uncle Geron, "What have you decided to do with Sabatini?" He replied,

I'm uncertain what to do with him now that I've heard of redemption and karmic obligations. I'll keep him alive for a while, but I'd like to borrow Antón to teach us about his gentle religion. Despite Sabatini's dissolute past, it appears an execution might burden me with Sabatini's karmic overload. Because your man believes all beings are redeemable, I'll give the evil one a month to see if his baptism will have had any true effect. If not, I'll let Ansgar dunk him in the *Logona* for a permanent baptism.

I then told Geron, "Marcus and I must return to *Londinium* before proceeding to Rome to rejoin our families." Geron smiled, imploring,

Before you go, Ivo, please remain with us a few days so I can redeem you for delivering Fulko's killer to me. While you're visiting, you can tell our warriors about Rome's mighty legions and our women of beautiful *Aurelia*, whom they call *"Das Lorelei Mädchen."* Yes, indeed, you must return to her and your handsome sons Marco and Vespan very soon.

CHAPTER 33

HOME

As we rode into our tribe's new oppidium, Geron told me why he'd moved to this upland location. He began,

> I'd not been king long when our rivals, the *Hermunduri,* challenged me for control of the salt-producing area by the river that flowed between us. Both tribes believed this river was the place where our prayers got priority from *Tiu* and *Wotan* to whom we'd vowed that if either tribe were defeated, we'd yield lands, and possessions to the winner. In AD 59 we lost the battle, forcing me to move ten of our riverside clans to this upland region where life is hard. When we regain our fighting strength, I shall challenge the *Hermenduri* again for those sweet riverside lands. I hope you'll bring your Roman fighting skills to help us defeat our old rivals.

When we reached Geron's citadel, Marcus and I were greeted with suspicion, since many tribesmen from neighboring clans knew little of us and much about the tribune who'd murdered Fulko many years before. Because Sabatini was recognized as the King's prisoner, the crowd's attention shifted to *Ansgar* who rode triumphantly beside Sabatini, as if he'd been the one who'd captured the fabled enemy.

During the two days we spent with relatives, older tribesfolk welcomed us and asked many questions about Aurelia and Sabina, and our children. We circulated freely (despite my Romanization) as I regained friendships with all but Ansgar who'd become the clan's war chief and claimed the right to execute Sabatini when King Geron tired of him.

In late October Marcus and I rode back to the waiting rivercraft for an easy float down the *Logona* and the *Rhenus* with stops at *Colonia* and *Noviomagus* where I reported to senior authorities before continuing on to *Londinium* for reassignment orders to Rome. At each stop, commanders were surprised to learn that Geron had allowed Sabatini to live and that I'd left Antón behind to deal with religious matters.

Because of nearing winter, Marcus and I planned to take the overland route across Gallia to the *Mare Nostrum* because *Mare Atlanticus* travel was deemed too risky. We expected to go east to *Portus Dubris* (Dover) for the shortest crossing to *Gessoriacum* (Boulogne) from where we'd make a ten-day, 300-mile, horseback ride to *Cabilomum* (Chalon) and an easy 200-mile float down the *Rhodanus* to *Arelate* (Arles). As we discussed our overland ride across Gallia, Governor *Petronius* suggested an easier route he'd traveled,

> Why not ride on two big Gallian rivers? If I were going south now, I'd head down to *Regnum* (Chichester) and cross to Gallia's *Sequana Aestuar* then proceed up the Siene past *Rotomagus* (Rouen), *Parisi* (Paris), *Agedincum* (Sens), and then hire horses for a 90-mile ride to the *Rhodanus*, saving a cold week on horseback. When you reach the *Sinus Gallicus* you can sleep on a coast-hugging bireme to Rome––or if the weather's good, you could strike straight to Corsica and on to Rome.

Marcus agreed saying, "Good advice, Sir! We'll need fresh horses for the ride to *Regnum*. These fine Lusitanis we've ridden for weeks need a long rest. They can trail along as spares. Both Marcus and I will also need a good rest so we can face our wives after these hard years in *Britannia*." Petronius suggested, "Sell me your fine horses; I'd be proud to ride them and will assure the best of care. We reluctantly agreed, realizing the difficulty of moving them across rough seas in late autumn.

The Trip

We departed *Londinium* on November 3rd accompanied by three *Regni* guards, camping the first night on a high ridge of the *Silva Anderida* (the Weald) soaked by rain. The second night, we slept warmly in the regal *Bignar Villa* 15 miles north of *Noviomagus Reginorum* (Chichester) where we enjoyed the hospitality of a retired Roman officer. At *Regnun*, we sent our guards and borrowed horses back to Londinium and waited two days to cross the *Oceanus Britannicus* toward *Juliobona* (Lillebonne in Gallia).

During the transit, we pitched about, taking an extra day to reach *Rotomagus* (Rouen) where we transferred to a river barge on which we headed up the *Sequana Fluss* (the Seine) with overnight stops at *Parisi* and *Agedimcum* (Paris and Sens). Ten miles further, we rode to the the *Liger Fluss* (the Loire) where we continued upsteam through *Deceta* (Decize) and on to *Forum Segusavorum* (Feurs), crossing to *Lugunum* (Lyon), boarding a downriver craft on the *Rhodanus* that promised a restful downstream glide past *Arelate* (Arles) to *Massalia* (Marseille). After two days of enjoying delicious seafood and the region's best wines we embarked on a bireme toward Corsica.

Midway between *Marseille* and Corsica's *sacrum promontorium* (Cap Corse, the Holy Promontory), we were hailed by a westbound trireme that stopped to warn us of rising seas south of *Genua* (Genoa) caused by a storm descending from the Maritime Alps. The sea-wise *trierarchus* recommended we turn south to skirt hazardous storm conditions he'd avoided. That familiar captain was our friend, *Capitáno Gilhardo*, who'd transported us from Hispania to Britannia three years before. As the two ships lurched side by side, he shouted, "*Marco y Ivano*, happily we meet again! Goes it well with you after the great battles in Britannia? *Buena suerte y buenos viaje, mis amigos.*" (Good luck and good travels, my friends).

After that brief interlude, our new Hispanic *trierarchus* ordered his *centurion, nautum,* and *celeusta,* (commander, pilot, and navigator), "*Ala derecha, hombres; vamanos entre Córcega y Sardina.*" (To the right men; we go south between Corsica and Sardina). By the time we neared the narrow *Fretum Gallicum*, the *Mare Sardoum* was rolling too heavily, alarming the crew by the wave height and crabbed angle needed to counter the heavy crosswind. I noticed the excited officers were arguing to alter course past the *Gorditanum Promontory* and to proceed 150 miles south past the *Plumbaria Islands* and the *Chersonesus Promontory* at the bottom of Sardina.

The more the rowers fought gale-force wind and waves, the more we realized we were entering conditions from which we could neither round the northwestern promontory, nor pass safely through the narrow *fretum*. Since the storm's force was increasing, Marcus cynically noted, "We're in greater peril here than when we fought the Iceni."

Moments later, the *nautum* struggled to where we were seated to tie us to flotation bladders while the storm wrenched the ship about and the crew attempted to keep us afloat during the worst pitching and rolling I'd ever seen. Because of a continuous downpour, we'd lost sight of the shore and all sense of direction. Therefore, the *trierarchus* ordered his crew, "Keep the ship aimed into the headwind to maintain this position as long as possible." After wallowing about for more than six hours, it got dark, leaving the entire crew exhausted and the ship filling with water. Since the junior officers had also manned the two pumps, Marcus and I took our turns. By morning, the waves slackened, but the enfeebled crew members kept the bow pointed into the rolling waves while four of the strongest men desperately manned the creaking pumps.

We heard a cheer from the *celeusta* when he spotted his first view of the sun through weakening clouds, providing him with a regained sense of east, but no awareness of the nearest shore. As the storm continued to slacken, some exhausted rowers collapsed in place and were allowed to sleep 20 minutes each, given bits of dried fruit and wine, and forced back to their oars. I then noted fleeting views of the sun directly overhead and saw every rower slide into sleep, allowing the ship to rotate lazily in the slow-rolling waves. I then ask the navigator, "Where is land?" He answered,

> When we turned southward to pass the west side of this great island, I'd intended to proceed northwest of *Isola Asmara*. Despite the crews' best efforts, we remained east of that big western island to become locked within the *Golfo dell'Asmara*. We are now drifting southwest toward *Capo del Falcone* or *Porto Torres*. When this rain subsides and the visibility improves, you'll likely see land just west of here.

As we came to rest, I could see the ship was riding too low in the water. Because of numerous leaks, most rowers had taken turns as pumpers or bucketers pitching water overboard. Then suddenly, as the storm conditions cleared, the *proreta* shouted, *"Mira Hombres! La*

Tierra!" (Look men! Land!). Marcus grinned, saying to me, "It looks like we may be taking an unwanted vacation on a *Sardoumic* island." The *remiges* suddenly found new energy to row the last mile, allowing the *celeusta* to bellow,

> We shall enter that narrow strait between *Isola Asmara* and *Capo del Falcone!* We must land on the gentle strand of that flat island between the northern *Isola* and the opposite rocky *capo*. There we'll drain the hull and make repairs before continuing to *Porto Torres* for provisions.

I saw that the experienced navigator had chosen a smooth landing spot on the southernmost beachhead of the tiny island. He knew the ship was far too heavy for the entire crew to boost onto the shore, even when helped by successive waves. After inch-by-inch of onshore gains, the *trierarchus* ordered. "Drill keelside drain holes––after repairs we shall feast at *Porto Torres!*" As predicted, we were soon afloat to enjoy a brief visit at that sunny Roman port city. From there the *trierarchus* chose a return course through the *Fretum Gallicun* from where he aimed directly east to *Ostia*, arriving at noon 2½ days later.

CHAPTER 34

FAMILY

On arrival at *Ostia*, we hired a four-wheeled *Rheda* for a two-hour, ten-mile dash on the *Via Ostiensis* to Rome and a 2½-hour, 12-mile uphill pull on the *Via Latina* near Tusculum to Sabina's father's *Villa Sciarra latifundium* where the autumn's harvests had just been completed. Halfway between the gate and the villa, we were hailed by the *agrimeister* who told Marcus of abundant produce locked in granaries and cellars, and of Consul *Maximus Carpentius'* lease of Nero's adjacent land (formerly owned by Senator *Aquilus* and willed to us, but seized by *Agrippina*). Encouraged by the prospect of recovering our lands (after *Agrippina* died), we hurried on to the *Villa's* great house where our wives and children had been living during the past months.

Since our *Rheda* could be seen from the elevated villa grounds, I could see from our ascending position that a toga-dressed group had apparently gathered to greet us. As we arrived, I could see each of our dear ones there with the children jumping in eager anticipation.

As we leapt from the carriage, we were greeted with hugs and kisses, followed by a hundred questions we attempted to answer. I was amazed to see how much 12-and-ten-year-old *Marco* and *Vespan* had grown, and saw Marcus' pretty little nine-year-old twins, *Marcella* and *Helena,* both radiating Sabina's beauty and her 13-year-old adoptee daughter, *Flavia,* who revealed adolescent appeal. After I held Aurelia (ending her flood of tears from our long separation), I hugged Sabina and greeted her father and brother with firm handshakes. Remaining aside, *Flavia's* brother *Trupo* asked, "Why comes not *Tio Antón?*" I explained,

"We left him in Germania to teach his religion. You shall see him in springtime. Why do you ask *Trupo?*" He muttered, "Antón is more father than any man; we spent many days together crossing Hispania."

We all moved into the sunny atrium where we enjoyed a special luncheon, told stories of our adventures, and learned of each person's experiences. *Freedmam Solon* (the Greek instructor) joined us to tell of each child's academic, lingual, and mathematical skills. Next, we all took *hora sextas* (*siestas*) before Maximus led us on a tour of both *latifundia* ending in *Villa Sciarra's* tiled *balineum* where we enjoyed a warm soak before a special supper, and finally, a night's seclusion with our wives.

At the Senate

Two days later, Consul *Maximus* proposed that Senator-Initiate *Marcus* be invited to speak before the Roman Senate of his recent battle experiences in Britannia. There was so much interest among the 600 members (including 400 who rarely attended) that only 300 could be seated in the *Curia Julia* (built between 44 and 29 BC to honor Julius Caesar). Because of seating limitations, Consul Maximus granted 200 seats to the frequent attendees and 100 more to members whose names were drawn from a basket. Another 40 were allotted for those who'd stand in odd corners.

The consuls allowed me to accompany Marcus where I would stand beside the *Altar of Victory* that had been placed in the *Curia* by Emperor Augustus to celebrate his 31 BC *Actium* victory. Since we'd arrived early, I tried to remain close to the winged statue, but I was too apparent in my legionary uniform and became engaged in conversations with former legates and elderly heroes. After opening formalities, Consul Maximus introduced both Marcus and me, extolling our roles in two Britannic battles, and welcoming Marcus' return to the Senate. Before Maximus finished introductions, *Emperor Nero* entered to claim his imperial seat before the altar. In response, most senators stood as the 25-year old *Princeps* (first citizen) passed, allowing him time to shake hands with Marcus and occupy his *sella curulis* (bronze chair) that Marcus had vacated.

Unaided by *manus* or *lectus* (script or lectern), Marcus stood before the most important men of the Empire, looked each senator in the eye, and moved smoothly up and down the bright marble room. Confidently, he strode before his attentive listeners, telling a masterful tale of Seutonius' vital victory against Queen Boudica's warriors, and how our blitzing cavalry thrusts had choked an uphill wave of screaming tribesmen, deflecting their onslaught into a deadly slugfest against Rome's mighty legionaries and non-Roman auxiliaries. After his detailed account of our wild contact warfare, he suddenly concluded,

> Great men of Rome, it is my wish to share my moment of recognition with *Praefectus Equitanus Chatti Ivano*, with whom I've served. It was he, more than any other, who has dealt peacefully with Germanic and Britannic tribal chiefs. Please recognize his part in these honors you've granted me today.

When Marcus' brilliant account ended, accolades of *bravissimo* resounded through the *Curia Julia*. Immediately, he was surrounded by senators and former *Legati*—some in ill-fitting uniforms. Just as Marcus pulled me into his senatorial circle, Emperor Nero strode forward to grab attention, lauding speaker Marcus, saying, "Well spoken, *Legatus Marcus Aquilus!* Welcome home from your Britannic wars." Continuing, he added,

> I might have prevented that catastrophe if we'd executed *Tribunus Hosidius Sabatinus*. I've been told that the malevolent *tribune* was judged, exiled, and imprisoned, but when freed, he reportedly raped Queen Boudica's daughters, sparking the uprising. I was also told your brother-in-law captured him, but yielded him to the Chatti king for execution. I've also been told, *"Sabatini lives!"* I must ask, Legatus Marcus Aquilus—*Why?*

At that most embarrassing point to Marcus, I stepped forward, saying,

> Emperor Nero! May I say that Tribune Sabatini remains a prisoner of Chatti King Geron who's trying to understand how a senior Roman officer can be so perverted? Twenty years ago, I witnessed Sabatini

sexually dismember the king's son, *called Fulko,* and saw my ten-year-old cousin bleed to death. That very day, I swore an oath to kill or capture my cousin's killer. Since Roman justice favored Sabatini, I chose tribal justice to deal with Sabatini's perversion.

Without acknowledging my explanation, he said to me, "I'd like you and Senator Marcus to join me at the palace to discuss other matters," then quickly turned to speak to former *proconsuls* and *legati.* Aside, Marcus whispered, "Be careful, Ivo; many of these old legati got rich by confiscating large shares of the army's booty after successful campaigns and making commanding positions so lucrative that consuls still vie for those enriching opportunities."

Before Marcus could continue, the famous *Titus Flavius Vespasianus* (under whom we'd both served during the Britannic invasion 19 years ago) stepped up to greet us, bemoaning his deflated career,

> After doing nothing for eight years, I became a consul. Before Claudius' death, his *praepositus ab epistulis* (in charge of imperial correspondence and military postings) had conspired with *Valeria Messalina* (Claudius' 3rd wife) to manipulate the emperor. After his misdeeds were exposed, *Narcissus* committed suicide, after which I got no command appointments. Now, however, I may become *Proconsul of Africa Nova;* do you wish to join me?

Marcus quickly responded,

> Perhaps next year, Sir! We've just returned from three years in Britannia, Hispania, and Germania. We need to stay home with our families for at least a year and work to regain our lands. Thank you for your consideration, Sir; we both look forward to serving you again!

Before we departed, our now famous former Governor *Suetonius Paulinus* (whom others called *Old Suet*) hailed Marcus, saying, "Thanks *Marcus Aquilus* for praising my strategy that won our great *Watling Street Battle* against Boudica." After recalling his years of Britannic authority, Suetonius added remorsefully,

It's surprising how quickly one can become an *extraneus* (outsider). Because of accusations of excessive brutality in our spectacular battle, I wasn't awarded a triumph nor given a much-deserved follow-on post. Now, I have very few friends in court. Beware, my good lads! Your days of glory can be brief among these purple-striped toga wearers.

CHAPTER 35

VILLA ANTIGUA

Back at *Villa Sciarra* we enjoyed leisurely evenings with our families where we told tales to Marco, Vespan, Flavia, Marcella, Helena, and Trupo, and bounced Dexter and Linkus on our knees. In addition, we spent nights with our wives and mornings riding our best horses.

Early on Monday, I rode down to Rome with Consul Maximus and Marcus who were attending a senatorial session in the *Curia Julia*. We planned to spend four nights in Marcus' townhouse on the *Collis Esquilinus* (the Esquiline Hill). Consul Maximus explained,

> After Senator *Aquilus* died, it took me two months to identify all of his holdings. I found he had three *villae* here on *Collis Esquilinus* and three lesser ones on *Collis Caelius* (the Caelian Hill). Since our *Kingdom Era*, these hills have been the most fashionable districts where the wealthiest Romans live.

When we arrived, *Marcipor* (the elderly caretaker) met us with his wife *Matidia* (the housekeeper). I stood gaping at the magnificence of the lavish villa, complete with colorful murals and tessellated-tile floor mosaics. Maximus then described details of these two special hills to me,

> This Esquiline Hill has three prominent spurs: the *Cispius*, the *Oppius*, and the *Fagutalis*. This one where we're standing is the best because it's nearest the Senate and other important buildings. This hill was favored 700 years ago by *Servius Tullus* (Rome's sixth king) who moved here. The

Maecenas Gardens were sited here long ago among terraces, libraries, and great villas.

I asked *Marcipor,* "Do you live here year around?" He answered,

> Yes. most honorable *Ivonicus*; there are two categories of residents. Half are *inquilini* (living here full time). Others are *exquilini,* (who have country *villae,* like Senators Marcus and Consul Maximus). I am fortunate to live beneath this magnificent structure where I see people from across the Roman world flow by each day.

When Marcus and Maximus left for the Senate, I spent the day being guided through central Rome by *Marcipor* who knew the city well. When I asked him of the origin of his name, he explained,

> I was born in *Thracia* and became a soldier at *Byzantium* where I was serving when the Romans turned my city-state into *Romana Provincia Thracia.* I became an auxiliary infantryman and served 20 years to earn Roman citizenship. Senator Aquilis appointed me caretaker of this *villa* on *Collis Esquilinus* that gave *Mati* and me a good life serving him. Since most household servants are former slaves, the term *por* (boy) is added to a master's praenomen. Mine was *Publitor* under Senator *Publius Aquilus* and is now *Marcipor* under *Senator Marcus Aquilus.*

Since I'd never traveled east, I asked of his homeland. He replied,

> The eastern provinces have a long history of war. After the 3rd *Macedonian War* and our subjugation to Rome, *Thracia* lost its independence and became a Roman tributary. About 70 years ago, Thrace lost its client status after which my country was split into two Roman provinces: *"Provincia Thracia"* and *"Moesia Inferior."*

When Maximus and Marcus returned, they showed me a palace invitation to a "business luncheon" with the emperor and his advisors. Because the word "business" was included, Marcus speculated "military assignments." Maximus interceded, saying, "Such appointments wouldn't include me, unless he's offering me a *proconsulship.*" He then told us,

I've heard Nero plans to build an impressive new palace on an elevated site on *Collis Caelius* where Marcus owns three more properties. If so, we must be careful because Nero has the power to confiscate personal properties by rationalizing his actions as, *"The most good for the most people."*

The Neronian Proposal

As specified in the invitation, we arrived at the palace at the exact time, met by the Commandant of the *Germani corpus custodi* who said to me in lowland platt, *"Willcommen zurück, Herr Valburga, Ick glaube du hast unter dem Kommandant Cornelius Sabinus gedient, nicht wahr?* (Welcome back Valburga, I believe you'd served under *Commandant Cornelius Sabinus,* Is that not true?). I confirmed my former role as he led us to a atrium where we met a staff member in charge of the agenda.

Moments later Emperor Nero arrived—again complementing Marcus on his speech before the Senate. He then looked over the food presentation, pointing to ten items that were delivered to our table in oversized dishes. After gorging himself on rare delicacies and quoting one of his new poems, he said to Marcus,

I've been told you inherited *Villa Antigua* formerly owned by Senator *Publius Aquilus,* but seized by my mother who claimed adjacent lands owned by my father where *Aquilus* built a villa for your sister. I've also learned *Consul Carpentius* won a senatorial judgement to restore the property to you, which I've ignored. Still in question are farmlands, which my agents leased to Consul Carpentius. I've learned you've taken possession of six city *villae* on the *Esquilinus* and *Caelius Hills.* Is this information true, my heroic friend?

Marcus looked to Consul Maximus (who nodded agreement), then replied,

Yes, indeed, My Emperor! Although I came to Senator Aquilus' funeral at the same time as your mother's, I'm now catching up on these matters. Only yesterday did I learn of the five city *villae.* Consul Maximus told me he'd show me each of them today.

Nero responded, "Before you do that, I have a proposal for you."

> I'm no farmer and rarely go into the countryside. Instead, as a poet and artist, I love this city's appreciative audiences. Therefore, I shall propose a simple trade of your six *villae* for clean titles of my Mother's lands and forgiveness of taxation on all of your lands during my lifetime.

Consul Maximus asked, "Sir, does this request bear on a plan for a new palace to be sited on those hills?" Nero answered, "Yes indeed, Consul Maximus! My golden house will outshine any structure in Rome! However, I'll require some of your villa sites before next year, as well as your part of the broad valley before them so my engineers can begin foundational works. To which Maximus responded carefully,

> We wish to retain one special villa on the *Fagutalis Spur* nearest the Senate because those *Esquiline* sites are not in the master plan your architect revealed to senior senators who also live on that hill. I'd like for Marcus to retain his *Esquiline villae* because of our senatorial requirements. In addition, Sire, assured value increases will surely follow your development.

Nero looked gloomy and sat analyzing the counter proposal. After a side discussion (in which confiscation was surely being considered), Nero smiled, saying, "You may keep the *Esquiline villa*; however, I reserve my imperial rights to purchase or trade for it should my Golden House require more land. Do you accept my proposal, Senator?"

Marcus replied, "*Yes, My Emperor!* Consul Maximus and I shall deliver a written copy of our agreement for the signatures of all now present. Is that satisfactory Sir?" Nero frowned at Marcus, but agreed, saying,

> Enjoy your ancient *latifundium* and your *Esquiline villa*, Senator. Since you and your brother-in-law are wealthy Roman officers now, I won't post you far from Rome for at least a year. Go tell your wives of this agreement and make your farmlands increasingly productive to feed my hungry population.

As we departed, Marcus told me of Senator Aquilus' final written instructions that said,

> Remember this timeless piece of wisdom my son: *Farmland is the truest beneficium from which all real wealth comes.* Hold onto your land through the hardest of times and feed your people well because they make the land productive. My land gift to you will benefit thousands through the ages. Protect it, improve it, and do not sell or divide it.

CHAPTER 36

ANTÓN

Ten weeks after we'd left Germania, Antón arrived at Villa Sciarra to find that we'd moved into our restored villa on the adjacent farmland. After welcoming him, we proceeded with our housewarming feast with neighbors and Senator Aquilus' closest friends attending. Throughout, we noted that *Trupo* followed Antón everywhere. After the special dinner (when discussing Antón's time with King Geron), Trupo remained nearby, appearing happier than I'd ever seen him. Marcus also noticed their apparent bonding (likely formed in Hispania) and of their reversions into Galician conversations about their long horseback ride across Iberia, sealing their close relationship.

Still later, Antón told us, "Sabatini remained alive, but in poor health, listening to my daily lessons about Jesus and his Apostles." Antón added, "Since my language skills didn't include German, Sabatini attempted to translate my tales for King Geron and his holy men, who asked many questions I couldn't answer. Nevertheless, my greatest success was with Geron, who asked if I'd tell him more about the ones I'd called Apostles?"

I then told him of my years as a young soldier in Judaea during the time of Jesus' crucifixion, and of my viewing the dieing prophet nailed to the crossbar that I'd seen him carry through Jerusalem. I also told his listeners, "The one called *'The Redeemer'* forgave his executioners, saying, *'Father, forgive them, for they know not what they do,'* followed by:

188

'*Today you will be with me in paradise,*' and '*It is finished. Father, into your hands I commit my spirit.*' As I spoke, Sabatini interrupted, pleading, 'I wish to die on a cross to pay my karmic debts!'

Antón told us how his ideas about *Salvation and Reunion with God* had profoundly affected Geron and his tribesman, asking for more information.

I told them 'At least five religions believe in resurrection' while most philosophers considered *return-from-death ideas* preposterous. Despite denials, *resurrection* became the central issue, split between *resurrection of souls* and *resurrection of all believers* (*Eschaton*). Nevertheless, I said, "Some Graecians still study what they called *Soteriology* (the salvation doctrines) that have special significance in many religions.

Antón told us, "Geron accepted the idea of a ghostly spirit," explaining,

Some religions believe the soul is the only part that can be resurrected. Plato claimed the soul would leave an inferior body to inhabit another. Meanwhile, the idea that Jesus was resurrected *spiritually* gained popularity, but the *Apostle Luke* reported Jesus had implored, "*Behold my hands and feet. Handle me and see, a spirit does not have flesh and bones as you see I have.*" I told my doubters that many argue, "*Only His spiritual body was resurrected.*" Others claimed, "*His material body was resurrected on earth.*" Now 32 years after *His* death, most Christians believe a *physical resurrection took place.*

Antón then talked about *Judgment-Day beliefs* and of *miracles* done by Jesus and his prophets to distinguish between *resumption-of-life* and *beginning-of-immortal-life* arguments, quoting Apostle Paul who'd said,

Christian faith hinges on Jesus' resurrection and human hopes for a life after death. Jesus commissioned 12 apostles to raise the dead, but most Christians claim those miracles were different from *His final one that would abolish death once and for all.*

Antón summed up his Chattian missionary efforts, concluding, "I convinced Geron, Sabatini, and some older ones that Christianity offers a better path than competing religious philosophies across the Empire." When I ask Antón how my cousins had responded, he replied, "Ansgar's hardened warriors preferred the old Germanic religions."

I then asked, "Who was the one you call *Tiago*?" He answered, "My introduction to Christianity was by his recruiting efforts in Hispania seven years after Jesus' crucifixion." He added,

> I'd been discharged from the Roman cavalry after sustaining broken legs from a horse fall. While regaining my strength, I attended religious orations by the one who claimed to have been closest to Jesus. Strongly affected by having witnessed crucifixions, I was eager to learn of *Tiago's* elevated views, which hastened my recovery, enabling me to join you in Iberia 14 years ago.

After recalling details of our first meeting on that horse drive, Antón told of the Apostle *Tiago,* whom others called *Iacobus*—the first of *Jesus'* 12 apostles and one who'd witnessed *His Holy Transfiguration.* Antón continued,

> Following Christ's ascension, the one also called *Iago* spread the Gospel across Israel and other Roman provinces—traveling to Iberia where his name became *Tiego.* At *Caesaraugusta* in AD 40, the Virgin Mary appeared to him, after which he returned to Judaea, where *King Herod Agrippa* had him beheaded. After Tiego's martyrdom, disciples carried his body to *Capori concello Padrón* on the Galician coast, and inland to San Tiego's gravesite (a place later called *Santiago de Compostela*).

Antón concluded with a prayer to his teacher,"*O glorious Apostle Santiago, chosen by Jesus to witness his transfiguration on Mount Tabor—obtain for us strength and consolation so we may be victorious in life and deserve a victor's crown in heaven.*"

Conclusion: November AD 63

The following morning, Marcus and I discussed what might lie ahead. We agreed we'd likely be at or near Rome during AD 64, followed by two more years of legionary service, perhaps under *Vespasianus,* who'd hinted of his possible generalship in *Africa Nova* where we might earn key commands or senior staff postings, with Marcus serving as a legate, and me as a diplomat.

Antón joined us at breakfast, mumbling another prayer and looking sadder than before. When I asked, "What's troubling you, Antón?" He explained, "Excluding those eight painful years recovering from smashed legs, I've completed 25 years of auxiliary service with the Roman Army and will soon receive my bronze citizenship diploma and a land warrant. Because of the army's no-marriage law, I've no family, and see little need to return to my homeland. As a result, I'd like to know of any reason for me to remain here with you." Anticipating such an eventuality, I responded,

> Antón, you've been through good and bad times as my problem solver and eyes-and-ears in troubled provinces. Hence, I've given some thought to this occasion. Although I can't give you land, Aurelia and I can provide you a permanent home here. Would you like to establish a top-breed horse farm and a Hispano-Roman riding school adjacent to Villa Antigua?

He replied, "What a wonderful idea, Sir! I'd stock such a place with dozens of Lusitani colts from the horse-and-land-rich *Estremaúran Vettoni Magnificus* (Grandee) from whom I'd bought beautiful mares and stallions like those you've given as diplomatic tokens." He continued, admitting,

> I was born in AD 11 and am now 52 years old. Since most soldiers die before 70 because of hard lives, I have few prospects for marriage unless I return to Britannia to find a widow or pick a good slave woman here.

At that juncture, Marcus interjected,

> Antón, I've noticed you and Trupo are best friends. Sabina and I talked about Trupo's change when you returned. Since we have five other children, we're willing to transfer him to you if you both agree, and if you'll allow him to continue his education here under Solon and Vibi.

Antón smiled broadly, shouting, "The Lord's blessing upon you my wonderful friends. When shall I fetch the foals and colts, and where shall we build the big stone barns? I must tell Trupo now. What else must I do?" Surprising us, he knelt, looking up to thank his God for answered prayers,

> *King Eternal and Immortal——We, the children of an hour,*
> *Rise in raptured admiration——At the whisper of Thy power.*
> *All Thy glories are eternal——None shall ever pass away;*
> *Truth and mercy all victorious——Shine with everlasting ray;*
> *Thou art God from everlasting——And Thy years shall have no end;*
> *Changeless nature, changeless name——Ever Father, God, and Friend.* (Havergal)

That evening Marcus received a letter from Emperor Nero commanding him to attend a property-holders' meeting at the *Curiae Veteres* on the Palatine Hill.

End of *Ad Britannia* Part II
Part III follows——AD 63 to AD 80.
Note: *Rome burns in 64; Nero dies in 68.*

APPENDIX I

FOUR PROVINCIAL REGIONS

Britannia

Because of ancient sea trade, Phoenicians, Carthaginians, and Greeks knew of the far Britannic Isles as early as the 4th century BC. The Greeks called the region *Cassiterides* (tin islands) where Carthaginian sailors had visited a century earlier. *Britannia* became the Latinized name of those islands inhabited by Iron-Age Celts. That name originated from *Prettanike* after the *Pretani* tribesmen who lived there. The Romans called that region *Insulae Britannicae* which included *Albion*, *Hibernia* and *Thule* (England, Ireland and the Orkneys). Caesar's 55 and 54 BC invasions failed, but a century later Claudius' success led to the establishment of a Roman province called *Britannia* that lasted 400 years. After Caesar's earlier attempts, Emperor Augustus planned, but cancelled invasions in 34, 27, and 25 BC. Emperor Caligula also cancelled an AD 40 effort. Three years later, Emperor Claudius succeeded and organized what became *Provincia Britannia*. By AD 47, his legions held the southern half of the island, but tribal resistance delayed control over *Cymruia* (Wales). In AD 61 a tribal rebellion nearly ended Roman rule. Instead, a Romano-Britannic culture emerged of people who came from many parts of the empire with legionaries and foreign auxiliaries garrisoned across the province to halt insurrections and control further invasions. Following the AD 61 Boudican rebellion, *"Britannia"* became personified as a female deity wrapped in a white robe bearing spear and shield.

Germania

Ancient languages provide a basis for understanding Rome's enemies. Germanic languages originated in southwestern Russia and spread west by tribal migrations early in the 3rd millennium BC. A thousand years later, Greek and Italic speakers dominated Mediterranean regions, while Celts claimed central Europe until overrun by Germanic speakers during the 1st century BC. Germania was first described by Julius Caesar in 55 BC. In his Gallic campaigns, he extended the Roman Republic to the Rhein, subduing German tribes on that river's west bank. More than 60 years later, Emperor Augustus' legions vanquish tribes as far east as the Elbe River. His planned conquest collapsed after he lost three legions in 9 AD. Although Emperor Tiberius campaigned eastward, two Roman provinces remained west of the Rhein (*Germania Inferior* and *Germania Superior* centered on *Colonia Agrippina*). Teutonic Germans were a northern linguistic group called "less civilized than Gallic Celts." Caesar used the term *German* to identify tribes beyond his area of control. He noted cultural differences in "the wild eastern region requiring military vigilance." He also told of western tribes who called themselves *Germani* to avoid being associated with "Gallic indolence." He described some *Belgic* tribes as *Germanic* because they used non-celt languages and left place names showing their earlier presence. The word *Germani* is said to combine *ger+mani* (near+men) like Old Irish *"gair"* meaning neighbor. Five German divisions were noted—(1) Western dialects on the Oder and Vistula Rivers, (2) Eastern *Istvaeoni* dialects on the lower Rhein, (3) *Irminoni* dialects on the Elbe, (4) *Ingvaeoni* dialects on Jutland, and (5) Northern dialects that became diverse Germanic languages. In the 1st-century AD, Tacitus, Pliny, and Strabo named 40 tribes along the Elbe, Rhein, Danube, and Vistula Rivers; Ptolemy named 69. Diverse *Germanic* languages are spoken by Norwegians, Swedes, Danes, English, Icelanders, Faroens, Austrians, Aleman-Swiss, Dutch, Liechtensteiners, Luxembourgers, Flems, Afrikaners, and Frisians whose languages were derived from ancestral German dialects.

Mauretania

Mauretania had existed as a Kingdom of Moors from the 3rd century BC, who'd lived near Mediterranean harbors to trade with Interior Berber tribes. The area became a Roman client kingdom that Emperor Claudius annexed in 33 BC as a Roman province ruled by an imperial governor. Claudius divided the province with the western *Tingitana* half, extending south to *Sala Colonia* and *Volubilis*, and east to the *Oued Laou* River. Its southern military camps at *Tocolosida* and *Ain Chkour* regulated movements of nomads and transients in occupied areas. *Volubilis* had about 20,000 inhabitants of whom 15 per cent were Iberians. The Romans had previously claimed all of *Mauretania* north of the *Atlas Mountains* as part of Augustus' expansion. Legionaries patrolled the province to *Exploratio Ad Mercurios* (the southernmost Roman settlement). Roman holdings reached *Anfa* (Casablanca) founded on *Azama*, a Phoenician port. During Claudius' reign, the road system followed the Atlantic coast through *Iulia Constania, Zilil, Lixus,* and *Sala Colonia,* and later to *Casablanca;* an eastern branch ended in *Tocolosida.* Three Atlas ranges reach 1,500 miles across central Mauretania, separating fertile regions from the desert. The highest ten peaks over 13,000 feet are in the southern range. In the 5th century BC, the Carthaginians visited the *Iles Pupuraires* far down the Mauritanian coast. In the 1st century AD, a factory processed *murex* and *purpura shells* for a rare dye that colored the purple stripe in senatorial togas.

Hispania

Hispania was the Latin name of the Iberian Peninsula. Indo-European migrants came there in the 1st millennium BC, followed by *Tartesi* and Celtic speakers who settled along the coasts with Greek colonizers. Latin was the official language throughout 600 Roman years. By the Western Empire's end in AD 476, all original languages had become extinct except Basque. *Old Vetus Latina* was the basis of most Romance languages. After Rome's 1st conquest of Carthage, merchants established commercial ports leading to the Roman invasion of Hispania in 218 BC, followed by much of the *2nd Punic War* being fought on the Iberian Peninsula against Carthage and its Iberian allies who supported Hannibal's transalpine invasion of Italy. After its 2nd defeat, Carthage relinquished its commercial empire to Rome where Iberian silver deposits founded a thriving economy based on metals, olives, oil, salted fish, and wines that were traded throughout the growing Roman Empire. Gold mining became the most important activity in Iberia's far northwest. In 197 BC, Rome divided the peninsula into *Hispania Citerior* (near) *and Hispania Ulterior* (far). In 27 BC, *General Marcus Agrippa* further divided the *Ulterior Region* into *Baetica* and *Lusitania,* after which Romanization proceeded rapidly. Certain Iberians were admitted into the Roman aristocracy, participating in the governance of Hispania. Native aristocrats ruled regional tribes from centers on Iberian land systems. *Olissipo* (Lisbon), *Tarraco* (Tarragona), *Caesaraugusta* (Zaragoza), *Augusta Emerita* (Merida), and *Valentia* (Valencia) became principal cities as the economy expanded, providing gold, tin, silver, lead, wool, wheat, olive oil, wine, and fish sauce that was transported from improved harbors. For the next 500 years, the three Hispanic provinces were bound to Rome by law, language, and a road system that brought newcomers from many parts of the Empire. Emperors *Trajan, Hadrian,* and *Marcus Aurelius* were born in Hispania in the 1st century AD and became dominant in the 2nd century. Rome dominated Iberia until invading tribes arrived in AD 409, after which the Visigoths defeated the Alans and Vandals in 418. Roman rule that had survived in the East was restored over Iberia until the Suevi captured the capital city in 439. Germanic Visigoths from southwest Gallia took over Tarragona, the last Roman-held province in 472 and confined the remaining Suevi in Galicia and Lusitania. In AD 476 the western half of the Roman Empire collapsed, leaving Hispanic provinces to local self-rule.

APPENDIX II

ANCIENT TRANSPORTATION

Although Mediterranean trade arose much earlier, large-scale oceanic commerce began during the early days of Carthage. The Greeks had developed the three-bank oared *trireme* in 480 BC, making single-row oared warships obsolete. *Triremes* were up to 120 feet long with oarsmen occupying 90-foot mid-ship sections with paid free men (rather than slaves) rowing those ships. From 264 to 146 BC, Carthage and Rome fought three Punic Wars. During the 1st Punic War (264-241 BC), the Carthaginians had reached their peak as the primary Mediterranean Mercantile Power. As inheritors of Phoenician technology, Carthage began delivering cargoes to all parts of the Mediterranean. Rome developed and excellent road system and forged strong commercial and political bonds between Italian cities and beyond. During the 2nd Punic War, the Romans began building big fleets of fast warships and transports repelled by banks of oarsmen on crowded *triremes* and *quinquiremes*. Overland invasion forces were dependent upon logistic-support vessels. During these wars, Rome began linking its empire using a growing merchant fleet, while expanding its military road system to far parts of the Empire. It became necessary to govern conquered provinces and send legions (needing material support) to outposts where invasions might threaten security. As ancient ships grew larger to move heavier cargoes, sails propelled them that depended on prevailing winds to reach far destinations. Merchant ships carried wheat, lumber, exotic animals, glassware, pottery, wine, and olive oil. Most liquids were transported in sealed *amphorae* with pointed bottoms that made it easy to stand them in wooden racks. One of the busiest trade routes lay between Alexandria, Egypt and Rome's port of Ostia. As the Empire grew, locally grown grain was insufficient to feed Rome's expanding population. Year after year, empire ships traveled from Egypt carrying grain to Rome and cargoes on which the Empire depended. The importance of North African grain was not lost on generals or governors who might wish to usurp the throne by threatening the arrival of the grain fleet. The prospect of mass starvation in Rome could bring a general to the rescue or end an emperor's reign.

APPENDIX III

ROMAN SEX ATTITUDES

Modern writings often characterize ancient society as depraved. Despite those views, shame, modesty, and legal strictures regulated most transgressions. Officials called censors determined social rank and could remove citizens from equestrian orders for proven misconduct. Roman society was patriarchal and masculine with citizens obligated to govern themselves sexually. A proper male had to keep his masculinity intact because a lack of *vir* could harm his status. Virtue (*vir*) was the manly ideal, while chastity (*castitus*) was the feminine ideal. Because female sexuality was a basis for order, female citizens were honored for integrity and fecundity. Women were held to a stricter code with *castitas* and *pudicus* (chastity and purity) describing a moral person. As a result, upper-class women had to sustain high standings. Although men strayed, women could not because husbands demanded certainty his children were not a lover's. It was a point of pride for a woman to be married only once, but divorce held no stigma. Remarriage was expected after a ten-month wait to assure a child's paternity was not questioned. After a marriage ended, women arranged subsequent marriages because children enhanced social standings. Augustus' adultery laws passed in 18 BC codified *Lex Julia de adulteriis* to punish women for extramarital affairs. Married women were expected to ignore a husband's philandering, since there were endless opportunities for men to find widely available low-class women. Excesses could make men disreputable, but censure was rarely aimed at one's use of inferior-status partners. Homosexuality was widely scorned, but Romans discriminated between "Penetrator and penetrated." Virility denoted masculinity. While effeminacy was denounced as a violation of military discipline, subject to execution. A soldier's masculinity was maintained by preventing his body from physical compulsion. Mastery of one's body was an important aspect of *libertas*—lacking self-control indicated he was incapable of governing others. Men who submitted to penetration were reviled. The worst insult for a man was to be called "girlish." *Lex Scantinia* laws restricted same-sex activities among freeborn males. Roman soldiers were required to maintain self-discipline. Strict commanders banned prostitutes from the *castrae* (camps), but accepted their nearby presence. Soldier marriage was banned to discourage families from impairing mobility. As legions settled into permanent forts, attachments with tribeswomen grew into *conubium* that rights gave family members citizenship at its soldier's retirement. The rape of a freeborn male became a capital crime after the *Lex Julia de vi publica* defined forced sex, making the rapist subject to execution, a rare penalty in Roman law. Rape of a boy was called 'The worst of crimes—along with raping female virgins or robbing a temple." Laws punished wickedness, but didn't blame the forced person. Freeborn children wore a purple-bordered *toga praetexta*, marking their inviolable status. It was impermissible to use obscene language near *praetexta* wearers. Freeborn boys wore a bulla as a visible warning they were off limits. Laws protected children from predators, with rape of freeborn boys a capital crime. Such protections applied to freeborn children, but not to slaves or captives. Slaves could be used for sex; one could use his own, but couldn't compel those of others. Slaves couldn't marry, but could live as *contubernales* with children added to an owner's wealth. *Lex Peotelia Papiria* laws established a Roman citizen's body was fundamental to *libertas*. Such protections extended to household slaves. The *materfamilias* could be judged by her slaves' behavior. Male slaves were not to be groomed effeminately or used sexually, because a slave's dignity should not be debased. Legal agreements on selling slaves could include *ne serva prostituatur* covenants that prohibited their use as prostitutes. Sex with one's slaves was not considered adulterous because slaves were bound by ownership and household loyalty. A family often lived under the same roof with its slaves and could share a bed; hence, some slave children were born as biological half-members. Roman *Infamia* status could not be escaped; freeborn persons could lose legal standing if convicted of misconduct. The *infamia* category included prostitutes, pimps, actors, dancers, and gladiators—all liable to corporal punishments. A citizen's liberty was defined as "freedom from physical coercion or punishment." Those who performed for pleasure were excluded from protections. Male actors were *infame* because they imitated women—males who accepted penetration were called *cinaedae* (sea-fish). Emperor Augustus mandated public decency and discouraged lewd behavior during his conservative reign. Roman men delighted in their manly *vir* with women obliged to *castitas* and *pudicus*. As a result of his moralistic views, Augustan *modesty and legal strictures* regulated transgressions throughout much of the Augusto-Claudian Era.

APPENDIX IV

MORALITY REFORMS

Augustus (Emperor from 27 BC to AD 14) accomplished far more than most of his successors during his 41 years on the throne. Unlike his successor who died early, Augustus lived into old age and wrote when near his end, *"I found a city built of sun-dried brick; I leave her clothed in marble."* Many believe his success was his ability to make needed changes, like morality. Most important among his concerns was the need to restore Rome from its moral decay. Many people believed *"the Republic's decline had resulted from an erosion of morals and leadership."* Roman citizens believed their virtues had decayed by *"civil war and selfishness of politics."* Augustus realized he had to (1) restore faith and values, (2) revive customs and traditions, and (3) return to" old-fashioned conservatism" by focusing on the private and public lives of Rome's upper classes. With powers granted by the Senate, he had the authority to do so, but found some laws were hard to enforce, making rigorously framed laws ineffective because of open revolt, obliging him to amend penalties. The emperor also sought to renew the practice of worship, appointing himself *pontifex maximus*, the secular head of the Roman Empire and its religious leader

APPENDIX V

LATIN GLOSSARY

Aerarium	Roman Treasury
Ala	Cavalry wing
Auxilia	Auxiliary units
Beneficiarii	Privileged soldiers
Calagae	Boots/hobnailed boots
Centuria	Unit of 100 men (later 80)
Centurio	Commander of a century
Cingilum	Dagger or Sword Belt
Civitas	Administrative subdivision
Clipeus/Scutum	Shield
Cohors	Basic subunit of a legion
Comes/Comites	Companion title of various offices
Contubrium	Eight-man subunit of a century
Curia	Place of assembly
Decuio	Commander of a turma
Dolabra	Trenching tool
Duplicarus	Second in command of a turma
Eques	Member of the Roman Equestrian order
Fiscus	Emperor's treasury where money was stored in baskets
Gladius	Primary sword of Roman foot soldiers
Hispana	One who served in Iberia
Lancea	Light spear
Legatus	Commander of a legion

Legio	Main fighting unit
Lorica	Body armor
Miles	Soldier
Mille Passus	Roman Miles-one thousand paces
Optio	Second-in-command of a century
Pereginus	Non-citizen of Rome
Phalera	Military disc award
Pia fidelis	Loyal and true soldier
Pilum	Javelin
Praefectus Castrorum	Third-in-command of a legion
Praetor	Magistrate ranking below consul
Praetor Pereginus	Administrator of justice among foreigners
Praetor urbanus	Presided in civil cases between citizens
Prefectus	High administrative official or chief officer
Propraetor	Praetor sent out to govern a province
Prorogatio	Extension of imperium beyond one's magistracy.
Quaestor	Lowest ranking regular magistrate
Sesterce	One-quarter of a denarius
Spatha	Longer cavalry sword
Tribunus	Mid-rank officer
Turma	Basic subunit of a cavalry ala
Vexillatio	Detachment of soldiers
Vitis	Centurion's twisted "swagger stick"

APPENDIX VI

TOWNS OF FIVE ROMAN PROVINCES

Britannia

Roman Name	Modern Name	Modern County Name
Aqua Sulis	Bath	Somerset
Brandunum	Brancaster	Norfolk
Caleva Atrebatum	Silchester	Hampshire
Camulodunum	Colchester	Essex
Deva	Chester	Cheshire
Dubris	Dover	Kent
Durolipons	Cambridge	Cambridgeshire
Durovernum Catiacorum	Canterbury	Kent
Durorivae	Water Newton	Huntington
Durovigutum	Godmanchester	Huntington
Durnovaria	Dorchester	Dorset
Gariannonum	Burgh Castle	Suffolk
Glevum	Gloucester	Gloucestershire
Isca	Caerleon	Monmouth, Wales
Lactodorum	Towcester	Northampton
Lindum	Lincoln	Lincolnshire
Londinium	London	Greater London
Manduessedum	Mancetter	Warwickshire
Mona Island	Anglesey	Anglesey, Wales

Noviomagus	Chichester	Sussex
Segontium	Caemarvon	Caemarvonshire, Wales
Trimontium	Newstead	Northumberland
Venta	Caister	Norfolk
Venta Belgarium	Winchester	Hampshire
Venta Silurum	Caewent	Monmouth, Wales
Veralamium	St. Albans	Hertfordshire
Viroconium Cornoviorum	Wroxeter	Shropshire

Germania and Gallia

Roman Name	Modern Name	Modern Province/State
Asciburgium	Asberg	Niederrhein, Netherlands
Argentoratum	Strasbourg	Grand Est Alsace, France
Aqunicum	Budapest	Central Hungary
Arelate	Arles	Alpes Cote d'Azur, France
Atuatuca Tungrotum	Tongreren	Limburg, Belgium
Augusta Trevorum	Trier	Rhineland-Palatinate, Germany
Augusta Vindelicorum	Augsburg	Swabia, Germany
Bonna	Bonn	North Rhine-Westphalia, Germany
Burgdigala	Bordeaux	Gironde, France
Castra Regina	Regensburg	Bavaria, Germany
Colonia Agrippina	Cologne	North Rhine-Westphalia, Germany
Confluentes	Koblenz	Rhineland-Palatinate, Germany
Gesoriacum	Boulogne	Pas-de-Calais, France
Lugdunum	Katwijk	South Holland, Netherlands
Massila	Marseilles	Bouches-du-Rhone-Alpes, France
Mogontiacum	Mainz	Rhineland-Palatinate-Germany
Narbo	Narbonne	Occitanie Province, France
Nicaea	Nice	Alpes-Maritimes, France
Novaesium	Neuss	North Rhine-Westphalia, Germany
Noviomagus	Nijnegen	Gelderland, Netherlands
Traiectum ad Mosam	Massticht	Limburg, Netherlands

Vindobona	Vienna	Vienna, Austria
Praetorium Agrippinae	Valkenburg	Limburg, Netherlands

Iberia and Mauretania

Roman Name	Modern Name	Modern Government
Bracara Augusta	Braga	Braga, Portugal
Brigantium	La Coruna	Galicia, Spain
Caesaraugusta	Zaragoza	Zaragoza and Aragon, Spain
Calpe	Calp	Alicante, Spain
Cartago Nova	Cartagena	Murcia, Spain
Gades	Cadiz	Andalucia, Spain
Hispalia	Seville	Andalucia, Spain
Legio	Leon	Castile and Leon, Spain
Lixus	Laranche	Larache, Morocco
Olisipo	Lisbon	Lisbon, Portugal
Palma	Mallorca	Balearic Islands, Spain
Pollentia	Pollens	Balearic Islands, Spain
Pompelo	Pamplona	Foral de Navarra, Spain
Portus Cale	Oporto	Porto, Portugal
Sala Colonia	Chellah	Rabat, Morocco
Salamatica	Salamanca	Salamanca, Spain
Tarraco	Tarago	Tarragon and Catalonia, Spain
Tingi	Tangiers	Tanger-Al Hoceima, Morocco
Walili or *Volubilis*	Meknès	Meknès, Morocco

BIBLIOGRAPHY

Ancient History Atlas, 1700 BC-AD 565, London, Weidenfield & Nicholson, Ltd., 1978.

Anthony, Hid, *Roman City of Veralamium*, St. Albans Council, English Life Pubs, Ltd., 1978.

Beddoe, John, *Races of Britain*, London, Hutchinson & Co., Ltd., 1885.

Baddeley, St. Clair & Linda Duff Gordon, *Rome, Its Story*, London, J.M. Dent and Co., 1904.

Bord, Janet & Colin Bord, *Guide to Ancient Sites in Britain*, London, Granada Pubs, 1979.

Birley, Anthony, *People of Roman Britain*, London, Batsford, Ltd., 1979.

Birley, Robin, *Civilians on the Roman Frontier*, Newcastle, Frank Graham, 1979.

Bunson, Matthew, *Encyclopedia of the Roman Empire*, New York, Facts on File, 1994.

Capes, W.W., *Roman History: Early Empire*, New York, Armstrong & Co. Undated.

Cassell's Latin Dictionary, Marchant, and Charles, Eds, New York, Funk & Wagnells, 1959.

Clayton, Peter, *Companion to Roman Britain*, Ware, Phaidon Press, 1980.

Treasures of Ancient Rome, London, Bison Books Ltd. 1986.

Comont, Franz, *Mysteries of Mithra*, New York, Dover Pubs, Inc., 1956.

Collingwood, R.G., *Roman Britain*, London, Oxford University. Press, 1924.

Collins, A.E. and E.C. Price, *Beginnings of Chesterford*, Chesterford Archaeology Group, 1980.

Connolly, Peter, *Roman Army*, Edinburgh, Mcdonald Educational, Ltd., 1975.

Greece and Rome at War, London. MacDonald Phoebus, Ltd., 1981.

Correll, Tim and John Matthews, Atlas of the Roman World, Oxford. Phaidon Press, Ltd., 1982.

Cowan, Ross, *Roman Legionary: 58BC-AD 69*, Botley, Oxford Osprey, 2001.

Creighton, Mandell, *History of Rome*, London, Macmillan and Co., Ltd., 1957.

Cunliffe, Barry, *Greeks, Romans and the Barbarians,* London, Guild, 1988.

Diereke *Schulatlas fur Hohere Lehran Stalten*, Georg Westerman, Ed, Braunschweig, 1929.

Dunnett, Rosalind, *Trinovantes*, London, Duckworth, Ltd., 1975.

Fanfani and Ruspantini, *Highlights of Rome*, Florence, Ramelby & Co., 1957

Fields, Nic, *Boudicca's Rebellion AD 60-61*, Botley, Oxford. Osprey Publishing, 2011.

Fowler, W.W. *Religious Experience of Roman People*, London, Macmillan Ltd., 1911.

Frere, Sheppard, *Britannia: History of Roman Britain,* London, Book Club Associates, 1974.

Gibbon, Edward, *Barbarism & Fall of Rome*, Toronto, Collier-Macmillan, Ltd., 1966.

Gibbon's *Decline and Fall of the Roman Empire*, London, Bison Books, Ltd., 1979.

Gold, Alan, *Warrior Queen, Story of Boudica.* London, Penguin Books, Ltd., 2005

Grant, Michael, Ancient *History Atlas, 1700 BC to AD 65.* London, Weidenfeld and Nicolson., 1981.

World of Rome, New York, New American Library, 1960.

Roman Emperors: Biographical Guide to Rulers of Imperial Rome, M. Grant, Ltd, 1985.

Sick Caesars: Madness & Malady in Imperial Rome, Barnes & Noble, 2000.

Twelve Caesars, New York, Barnes and Noble Books, 1996.

Grosser Historischer Weltatlas, München, Kartograpiche Gesamt, Heinz Hieshmann, 1978.

Harney, L.A., *Roman Engineers*, Cambridge, Cambridge University Press, 1981.

Havargal, Frances Ridley, *Poems,* New York, E.P. Dutton & Co., 1881.

Haywood, John, *Atlas of Celtic World*, London, Thames and Hudson, Ltd., 2001.

Hooper, Finley, *Roman Realities*, Detroit, Wayne State University, 1979.

Hogg, A.H.A., *Guide to Hill-Forts of Britain*, London, Granada Pubs, 1975.

James, P. and N. Thorpe, *Ancient Inventions*, New York, Ballantine Books, 1994.

Jimenez, Ramon, *Caesar Against the Celts*, Edison, NJ, Castle Books, 1996.

Johnston, David, *Roman Villas,* Aylesbury, Shire Publications, Ltd., 1979.

Kiepert, *Atlas Antiquus Zwölfte Berichtigte Ausgabe*, Berlin, Dietrich Reimer, 1900.

Kindersley, Dorling, *World Reference Atlas.* New York, Dorling Kindersley Publishing, Inc., 1994.

Knightly, Charles, *Folk Heroes of Britain*, London, Thames & Hudson, Ltd., 1957.

Kohout, Natalie, Boudica: *What Do We Really Know?* BoudiccasWrath@gmail.com, 2005.

Laing, Lloyd, *Celtic Britain: Before the Conquest,* London, Granada, 1979.

Lendering, Jona & Arjen Bosman, *Edge of Empire.* Rotterdam, Karwansaray BV, 2012.

Littelton, Margaret and Forman, *Romans, Their Gods, and Beliefs,* London, Orbis, Ltd., 1984.

Livius, Titus, *History of Rome I & II,* New York, Arthur Hinds Co. Undated.

Luttwak, Edward, *Grand Strategy of the Roman Empire*, London, Johns Hopkins Univ, 1979.

Mason, Francis & Marty Windrow, *Know Britain*, London, George Philip Pubs., 1974.

Massie, Alan, *Augustus: A Novel,* London, Sceptre Books, 1987.

Matyszak, *Legionary: Solider's Unofficial Manual,* London, Thames & Hudson, 2009.

Mazzolani, Lidia, *Empire Without End*, New York, Harcourt Brace, Inc., 1976.

McCollough, *First Man in Rome*, New York, Avon Books, 1990

McEvedy, Colin, *Penguin Atlas of Ancient History*, Harmsworth, Penguin, Ltd., 1967.

McNally, Michael, *Teutoburg Forest 9 AD*, Oxford, Osprey, Ltd. 2011.

McWhir, Alan, *Roman Glouchester,* Glouchester, Alan Sutton, Ltd., 1981.

Mead, CRS, *Mysteries of Mithras,* Holmes Publishing Group, Edwards WA., 2000.

Mommsen, Theo, *Provinces of the Roman Empire*, New York, Barnes & Noble, 1996.

Muller-Alfred, Theodor, *Deutschland*, Bayreuth, Gondrom Verlag Bayreuth, 1977.

Murray's Small Classical Atlas, G. Grundy, Editor, New York, Oxford Univ. Press, 1904.

Murry, Dave and Barry Murry, *Ancient Art of War at Sea*, Broderbund, 1987

208

Myers, P.V.N., *Ancient History*, Boston, Ginn & Company, 1896.

National Trust Boards (Richard Quick, Ed.), *Discover Roman Britain*, Fairwater, Cardiff, McLay & Co., 1977.

Ordnance Survey, *Ancient Britain Maps*, Maybush, Historical Maps, 1964.

Londinium, Descriptive Map and Guide to Roman London. Southampton, OS, 1981.

Peddie, John, *Invasion: Roman Conquest of Britain*, London, Guild Pubs, 1987.

Piggott, Stuart, *Approach to Archaeology*, London, Adam Black, Ltd., 1965.

Portable Roman Reader, Bash Davenport, Editor, New York, Penguin, 1959.

Potter, T.W., *Roman Italy*, London, Guild Publishing, 1987.

Priestly, H.E., *Britain Under Romans*, London, Frederick Ware & Co., Ltd., 1967.

Radice, Betty, *Who's Who in the Ancient World*, New York, Penguin Reference., 1984.

Ramm, Herman, *Parisi*, London, Duckworth & Co., Ltd., 1978.

Reece & James, *Identifying Roman Coins*, London, Sealby, Ltd., 1986.

Rees, Sian, *Ancient Agricultural Implements*, Shire Archaeology Series, Ltd., 1981.

Reinhadt, Kurt R., *Germany: 2,000 Years*, New York, Ungar Press, 1950.

Regni, London, Dockworth & Co., Ltd., 1973.

Rivet, A.L.F. and Colin Smith, *Place Names of Roman Britain*, London, Batsford, Ltd., 1981.

Robinson, H. and K. Wilson, *Myths & Legends of All Nations*, Littlefield, Adam & Co., 1978.

Rodewald, Cosmo, *Money in the Age of Tiberius*, Manchester Univ. Press, 1976.

Roman Britain: 55BC-AD409, London, Robert Fowler Publisher, 1979.

Roman Britain: Full Color Wall Chart, London, Sunday Times, 1983.

Roman Roads of Europe, London, Cassell. Ltd., 1981.

Ross, Anne, *Everyday Life of the Pagan Celts*, London, Batsford, Ltd., 1970.

Scarre, Chris. *Smithsonian Timeline of the Ancient World*, London, Dorling fKinderley, 1993.

Sear, Frank, *Roman Architecture*, London, Batsford, Ltd., 1982.

Siegmeri, Otto, *Deutschland*, München, Verlag Ludwig Simon, Undated.

Simkins, Michael, *Warriors of Rome*, London, Blanford Press, 1988.

Sheppherd, William R., *Historical Atlas*, New York, Henry Holt and Co. 1929.

Shutz, Herbert, *Romans in Central Europe*, New Haven, Yale Univ. Press, 1985.

Prehistory of Germanic Europe, New Haven, Yale Univ. Press, 1983.

Sitwell, N.H.H., *World the Romans Knew*, London, Hamish Hamilton, 1984.

Starr, Chester, *Rise and Fall of the Ancient World*, USA, Rand McNally, 1960.

Stobart. J.C., *Grandeur that Was Rome*, London, Book Club Associates, 1971.

Suetonius, Gaius Tranquillus, *Twelve Caesars*, Middlesex, Penguin, Ltd., 1979.

Sutcliff, Rosemary, *Eagle of the Ninth*, Oxford, Oxford Univ. Press, 1954.

Mark of the Horse Lord, New York, Henery Walck Inc., 1965.

Song for a Dark Queen, London, Knights Books., 1980.

Silver Branch, Harmondsworth, Penguin, Ltd., 1980.

Lantern Bearers, Harmondsworth, Penguin, Ltd., 1981.

Sunday Times. (Cunliffe Consultant) *Roman Britain Full-Scale Wall Chart, Map and Guide*, undated.

Todd, Malcolm, *Northern Barbarians: 100BC-AD300*, London, Hutchinson Co., 1975.

Van Ness-Myers, Philip, *Rome, Its Rise and Fall*, Boston, Gian & Company, 1900.

Van Sickle, C.E, *Political History of the Ancient World*, Westport, Greenwood, 1947.

Wacher, John, *Roman Britain*, London, J.M. Dent Sons, Ltd., 1980.

Coming of Rome, New York, Charles Scribribner's Sons, 1979

Walker, Arthur Tappan, *Caesar's Gallic War*, Chicago, Foresman & Co., 1907.

Waltari, Mika, *The Romans*, New York, G.P. Putnam's Sons, 1966.

Warry, John, *Warfare in the Classical World*, London, Salamander Books, 1980.

Webster, Graham, *Boudica, The British Revolt Against Rome AD 60*. London. Batsford, 1978.

Roman Invasion of Britain, London, Batsford, Ltd., 1980.

Rome Against Caratacus, London, Batsford, Ltd., 1981

Roman Britain, Observer Maps, Undated.

Roman Conquest of Britain, London, Batsford, Ltd., 1973.

Wellesley, Kenneth, *Long Year AD 69*, Bedminister, Paul Elek, Ltd., 1975.

Wheelock, Frederic M., *Latin,* New York, Barnes & Noble, Inc., 1960.

Who's Who in the Ancient World, Betty Radice (Editor), Bungay, Penguin, Ltd., 1973.

Wikipedia Free Online Encyclopedia, 2016.

Wilcox, Peter, *Rome's Enemies: Germanics & Dacians*, London, Osprey, Ltd., 1982.

Wilder, Thoroton, *Ides of March*, London, Longmans, Green & Co., 1948.

MAPS OF THE ROMAN WORLD

Gaul on the eve of the Gallic Wars. Source: courtesy of Wikipedia File "Gaul"

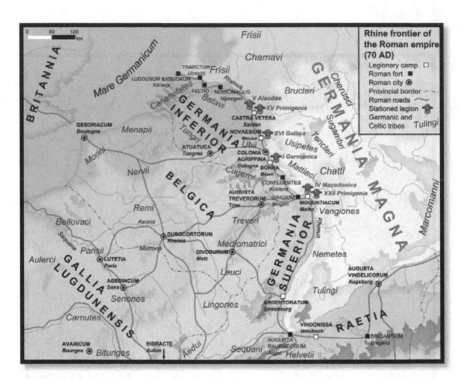

The Rhine Frontier of the Roman Empire around 70 AD. Source: Wikipedia, the Free Enclopedia.

Map of Hispania and Mauretania. Source: Wikipedia, the Free Enclopedia.
File: Imperium Romanum

Map of Ancient Italia. Source: Wikipedia, the Free Enclopedia. File: Imperium Romanum.

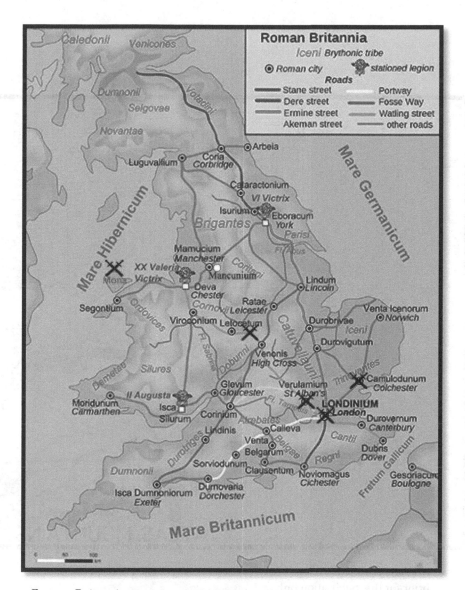

Roman Britannia. Based on <u>Wikipedia</u> content that has been reviewed, edited, and republished. <u>Original image</u> by Andrei nacu. Uploaded by <u>Jan van der Crabben</u>, published on 26 April 2012 under the following license: <u>Public Domain</u>. This item is in the public domain, and can be used, copied, and modified without any restrictions.

Roman Mauretania. Source: Map created by Sally Walker with permission to print for this publication only.

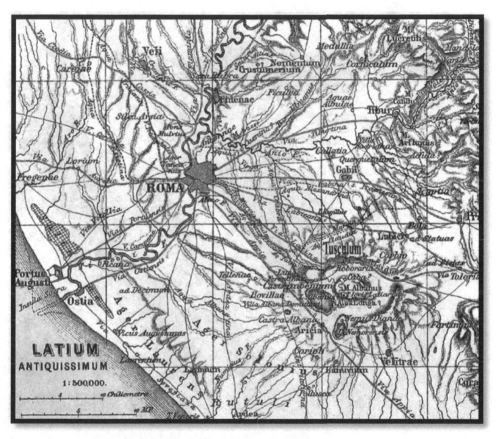

Latium Antiquissimum. Source: From Ostia to Roma, Mons Albunus, and Tusculum, Berlin 1854.

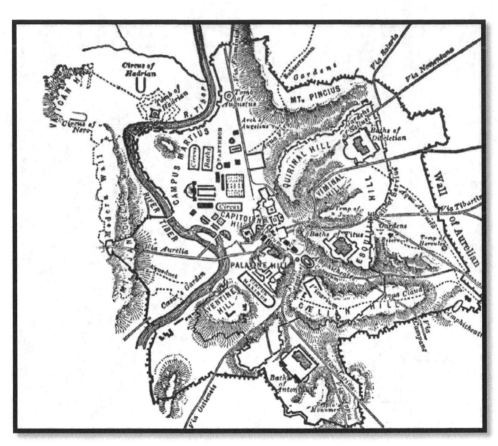

Plan of ancient Rome. Source: NSRW from Wikimedia Commons, the free media repository with edits made by Sally Walker.

OTHER WORKS BY THIS AUTHOR

Hessian John Series: Escaping from his European homeland, a partly trained German surgeon is forced to start a new life in the American South where he learns of love, loss, war, and intrigue. This five-book series takes readers from rural Germany to the great Mississippi River plantations and on to Wyoming, California, and many other places. He served in two American wars and one in Europe, living through some of the most turbulent times of the 19th-century.

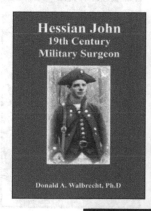
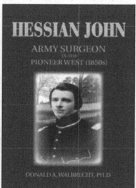
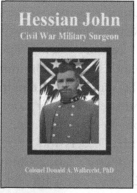

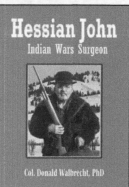

On Silent Wings: Four U.S. military astronauts undertake a yearlong space mission to avert a worldwide catastrophe as a massive asteroid approaches Earth. Scientists and politicians argue for and against a plan to capture the onrushing body into an Earth-Moon orbit, so its valuable nickel-iron mass could be harvested for use in space. Written in iambic tetrameter, this epic poem tells of a struggle to prevail over the grave celestial threat. A Cambridge University Astronomer said, *"This epic poem is better than Lord Byron's. It's a refreshing return to classical poetry—A brilliant tour d'force of a near-future, deep-space mission."*

Ad Britannia I: This historical novel is about a Germanic horseman who served as a Roman auxiliary cavalryman during the early 1st century when Emperor Claudius' powerful legions invade Britannia. Driven to revenge the murder of a childhood friend, Chatti Ivo pursues a corrupt Roman tribune across much of Western Europe, to become favored by tribal leaders and Roman aristocrats, including Emperor Claudius himself. During these first 29 years of his life, Ivo sees much of the good and bad of the young Roman Empire and finds

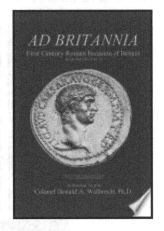

love with Aurelia (the beautiful daughter of Mainz's legionary commander) whom he rescues from the Rhine during his tribe's retaliatory raid against the arrogant tribune.

ABOUT THE AUTHOR

Colonel Don Walbrecht (the 11th Operational SR-71 pilot) served 30 years as a U.S Air force officer, participating in advanced–development projects, leading Pentagon operational planning & budgeting actions, and holding transpacific and transatlantic staff and command positions. In five years of U.K.-based service, he was the Chief USAF Negotiator, dealing with Ministry of Defence and Royal Air Force officials, and serving as Vice Commander of the former 26,000-person *Third Air Force*. He earned history and literature master degrees from the George Washington University and the Cambridge University, and a Diplomatic-History PH.D. from the University of East Anglia. He has published six historical novels and a scientific-fiction *romaunt*, with *Ad Britannia III* in the works.

Printed in the United States
By Bookmasters